SLAY LESS
TYLOR PAIGE

SLAY LESS

FINAL GIRLS
BOOK TWO

TYLOR PAIGE

This book is for all the Whorror Babies who prefer their masked men silent, yet demanding. Michael Myers is a hottie, who knew? You knew.

This book is also dedicated to a reader turned genuine friend, Lee-Anna Mullins. Thank you for being here from the beginning.

THIS BOOK IS RATED R

Slay Less is a horror romance novel with topics that can be upsetting, uncomfortable, and for some, triggering. I encourage you to consider this list to know exactly what you are going to see while reading this book. This story features murder, grooming, dubcon, forced breeding, spiders, death by suicide, choking, breath play, callous discussion of sexuality, bondage, gaslighting, incest, stabbing, knife play, primal play, darkness, electro-shock therapy, kidnapping, callous discussion of mental health, noncon, blood, violence, spanking.

The Soundtrack

Like music with your books? Here's the playlist I made to go with it. In no particular order:

https://open.spotify.com/playlist/3VmcADgKV8R3NTy QrlVO5x?si=b788b4f601124392

- Degrade Me- TX2
- Build God, Then We'll talk- Panic! At The Disco
- Love is Dead and We Killed Her- Doll Skin
- Voodoo Doll- The Funeral Portrait
- Heaven Was Full- Tx2
- Killer Queen- Mad Tsai
- If You Like It Or Not- The Brobecks
- Most Beautiful Plague- Say Anything
- The Nobodies- Marilyn Manson
- I Wanna- The All-American Rejects
- You're Gonna Go Far, Kid- The Offspring

- Surrender- Billy Talent
- Gorgeous Nightmare- Escape the Fate
- Better- Guns N' Roses
- MORE- The Warning
- Messiah- Crawlers
- <maybe> it's my fault- WILLOW
- THE MASTER- Witchz
- Cut Me Open- Of Virtue
- Monster- Gabbie Hanna
- August 28th 3:30 a.m.- Automatic Loveletter
- A Choice- TX2
- Bedroom Talk- The Starting Line
- Die Romantic- Aiden
- I Want to Be Buried in Your Backyard- Nightmare Of You
- Warm Me Up- The Audition
- Shake It Out- Manchester Orchestra
- Vitamin R- Chevelle
- We're All To Blame- Sum 41
- The Rapture- Scene Queen, MOTHICA
- One Word- Kelly Osbourne
- Insomnia- Marmozets
- Monster- Meg & Dia
- Captivate You- Marmozets

THE RULES TO SURVIVING A SLASHER

Hey! So, first off, I hope you enjoy Slay Less. Please consider leaving an honest review wherever you do reviews when you're finished. If you do, tell us what rule was your favorite. I'm partial to Rule 52 myself... Now, to cover some bases.

Spoiler alerts!

This book is *meant* to be fast paced, absurd, and well, a horror story. Not just with the Michael Myers mask. That was purely for the Whorror Babies. No, I'm talking about it all. The classic, group of strangers in a new place. The confusion over who is alive and who is not, and the rules not making any sense. The weird secondary plots that kind of just comes in and comes right back out, the quick kills and cheap thrills, and how we move fast to avoid thinking about how stuff doesn't make sense. (Why doesn't she just run the other way?) No, this was meant to be fun, spicy, and overall, a solid slasher story. Keep that in mind while reading, and I think you'll enjoy the book for what it is, a horror porno.

Four years ago.

"Jeez, Delaney. How many Candygrams did you get?" April, my best friend and neighbor gaped as I stepped out of school, my arms full of valentines.

"A few." I grinned devilishly. Most girls were lucky to get even one heart-shaped sucker. I'd gotten thirteen.

"What else did you get?" she asked as we started our trek home, our boots crunching through fresh snow. I tucked my other valentines inside my coat.

"Hold on. Priest should be coming," I said, pausing at the gates.

April rolled her eyes. "I don't see why your mom makes you walk with him. I walk by myself when you're not here. It's barely a mile."

"We've had this argument. My parents worry about creeps, so Priest has to come with me basically everywhere." Even though I was fifteen now, practically an adult, I was still treated every bit like a child, and Priest was my babysitter.

"It sucks that you guys are related." April swooned as he

exited the school; late again. "He's the hottest guy in eleventh grade."

"Stop." I pretended to gag. Priest and I had grown up together since we were toddlers when our parents met in a widow's support group. Despite there being no blood ties, he was still my brother in every sense of the word. I glared at April as Priest sauntered over. "I won't let you come over anymore if you keep drooling."

"Fine, but I want to know who you got valentines from."

"Fine."

"What's fine?" Priest joined us, flicking his long hair out of his face, revealing his bright green eyes.

"Nothing." I shot April a cautious look and started walking. "Let's go."

"Okay, now tell me. Did Deshawn send you one? I heard he did." April hurried after me.

I glanced back at Priest, who had his ear buds in and phone out. He didn't want to hear my girl talk any more than I wanted to share my conversations with him.

"Which Deshawn? Mason or Lewis? Because yes." I said, and we both erupted into giggles.

"You little slut!" she squealed. "I hate you so much right now. Both? Who else?"

Smugly, I rattled off the names of the boys who gave me candygrams this year. We went through the merits of each one and whether I should date any of them or not.

"Who are you going to take to the dance?" April asked.

"I don't know. I'm not sure if I want to date guys my age." Heat warmed my face as I glanced back at Priest, making sure he wasn't listening.

"Delaney Duvall!" She waved her mittened finger at me. "Who? I knew someone special gave you that big Valentine. Show me!"

"I actually got two special ones. But the big one?" I

wiggled my shoulders, hinting at what was just inside my coat. "That came from Marco Brandis."

"Marco Brandis! From the house at the end of the street? Delaney...he's like—old."

"Twenty-five," I admitted and pushed her forward.

"Your parents are gonna murder you!"

"Only if they find out." I glared at her. "And they won't."

"You can't possibly be thinking about this. When did you even start talking to him?" We turned on our block.

"We met at the hot dog place in the mall when Priest took me Christmas shopping."

"I can't believe this. My best friend is dating an older man!" She sighed. "How romantic."

"Not yet. We're just talking. He knows people won't like it, so we're just getting to know each other. But I'm going to meet him this Friday for an official date." I left a swooning April at her door, swearing her to secrecy, and joined Priest.

"Heard you were popular today?" He snickered at home as we peeled off our winter gear.

"Jealous?" Priest was every bit the annoying, asshole big brother. He loved to dull my shine, but I refused to let him today. I rushed to my room to admire my valentines. I tossed all the candy and notes and cards on my bed. And then screamed!

Was I the most popular girl in ninth grade now? Maybe because I was nicer than the other girls. Or that my mom finally let me wear lipstick to school. I spent the afternoon going through each love note, deciding to write thank you notes back. I took my time, saving the best ones for last.

When I got to my locker between History and English, a pink envelope dangled out of the little slit, with my name on it. It was a beautiful pink card, laced with red roses. Opening it, I found a small note, which broke my heart for whoever had the courage to write it.

"I've spent months trying to figure out how to say it to you, but I'm not ready yet, so enjoy the card, Laney Duvall."

The only one who called me Laney was Priest.

I wished they'd left a name, so I could tell them thank you, but it wasn't signed.

A knock around dinnertime interrupted my thoughts, and Priest swung open the door, leaning against the doorframe. "You coming to dinner? Marta made Italian chicken."

Marta was our housekeeper. Our parents were so busy, and my mother wasn't exactly housewife material.

Priest's eyes settled on the array of gifts. I tried to scoop them up, but it was too late. He quickly grabbed Marco's card.

"Hallmark?" He snickered, turning the oversized heart-shaped card. "How inspiring. Which loser spent their allowance on this?"

Priest enjoyed being mean to me. Making fun of my clothes, my friends, whenever I did something different with my hair or makeup. It hadn't always been this way, but over the last year, he'd become a real jerk.

I stood and snatched the card back from him.

"If you must know, I got them from an older boy, a man. Because he sees how much I've matured this year."

Priest's dimpled smile slid off, and his eyes darkened. "Laney, you're in ninth grade. How old is this guy?"

"It doesn't matter. What matters is that he loves me and wants to take me on dates and go to dances and you're just jealous because you've never had a girlfriend."

"Who is it, Laney?" He stepped closer, looming over me. I'd never seen Priest like this before. Eyes blazing, jaw tight, fists clenched. He was shaking with rage.

"No one," I lied.

"Tell me."

"Marco Brandis," I confessed. "But you can't tell Mom and Dad!"

"Marco Brandis?" There was a sudden shift in the air, and Priest turned to leave. "I'm going to go eat."

The tension in the dining room was deafening. Priest was fuming and ate quickly. He was finished before I could get even halfway through my plate.

"Priest!" I stood when he did. He was halfway to the stairs when he turned. The Michael Myers mask he'd worn for Halloween this year sat abandoned on the side table. He snatched it up as if noticing it for the first time in months.

"What?" His gaze pierced my heart. He'd never looked at me like that before.

My body and soul screamed for me to ask the question that had been weighing on me since I got the handmade card with my nickname on it, but I couldn't. The answer, regardless of what it was, would change our relationship forever. I chose the coward's way out instead.

"Don't tell Mom and Dad, please," I begged. "about Marco."

"Fine." He stormed up and slammed his bedroom door shut.

That night, I was restless. Marco didn't message me, which was unusual. I cried, praying my brother didn't share my secret with our parents.

The next morning, sirens woke me up.

What's going on?

"Hello?" Groggily, I called April.

"Oh my god, Delaney, Marco Brandis was murdered last night."

The Uber driver unloaded my suitcases and left before I could thank him. As I stood before my childhood house, unchanged for four years, my phone rang. Removing a pink glove, I answered, "Go for Delaney."

"Oh god, you're still doing that?" Summer laughed from the other side. "Please, girlie. Anyways, did you make it home?"

I found the key hidden under a plaster robin and entered the dark house.

"I just got here." Shutting the door quickly to get out of the cold, I shivered and flicked the lights on. The living room lit up. "Holy shit. Nothing's changed."

"That's kind of creepy," Summer said.

"My parents have always traveled a lot, even before they shipped me off to Shelley Vale," I said. "I bet Marta spends more time here than they do."

"That's so weird, dude. It's like a staged dollhouse."

As I traveled the ghostly house, I laughed at her comparison. It was apt. Outside, we'd been the perfect family. Inside, not so much. Well, not that I could remember, anyway. I'd always had a hard time remembering things.

Reaching the first floor, I was surprised to find my school pictures had continued to be updated every year. All the way up to grade twelve. Priest's stopped at eleventh grade.

That was the year I'd been sent away.

I shook the dark memories away and continued to the second floor.

"Did your parents know you were coming? Where even are they?" Summer asked, pulling me from my thoughts.

"Madrid, I think. I'm not sure. Ron's originally from Spain, so they go every winter. Mom always sends me the cutest clothes."

"Makes sense, since she rubs elbows with all the fashion moguls."

Before I was born, Mom had been a model in Europe. She retired when my dad died, and then she met Ron and decided never to return to modeling, but instead worked behind the scenes as a photographer, and lucky for her, she met a man who wanted to help.

"Do you want to see my old room?" I switched to video call. At the end of the hallway, I found my room locked. "Oh, that's weird."

"What?" she asked. "I can't see anything."

"Hold on." I pulled out an old membership card from my wallet and slid it between the door, then pushed.

The smell of Luv's Baby Soft perfume hit my nostrils, bringing a smile to my face as I reached for the light and turned it on. Grabbing my phone and bags, I waved the camera around.

"Wow, it looks like a princess threw up in here."

"I know, right? I love it."

"How big is that bed?"

"Queen. Perfect for sleepovers." I beamed, touching the familiar comforter.

"Did they let you take anything when you left?"

"Just my clothes, art stuff, and oh! My V.C. Andrews books. I was obsessed with them at the time and threw a kicking and screaming fit when my mom tried to make me leave them." I smiled, recalling how truly immature I was.

"You were spoiled rotten!"

I fell backward onto my bed. "I was. Well, okay, I still am. They are paying for the retreat. Although they don't know it yet."

"And what else?"

"What do you mean?" I switched off the video.

"Oh, come on, Delaney. Everyone knows you're loaded."

"My parents are loaded. I have an allowance."

"An allowance!" She screeched. "Adults don't have allowances, Delaney!"

"They are funding me until I can get published," I whined and sat up. "They understand that writing a good book and getting an agent takes time. Anyways, I'm starving. I'm gonna go eat and then get some rest before the flight tomorrow."

"Oh yes. Moth will be there, waiting for you," Summer teased.

"He will be. He just doesn't know it yet. What time will you get there?"

"As long as the weather lets up, I should be heading to the airport tonight and get to the hotel hella early in the morning. My mom's paranoid. She thinks they're gonna cancel my flight."

"Don't say that. You're going to make it. My parents will kill me if I have to pay for that suite by myself."

"I know, I know. Good vibes only. Everything's going to be fine. All right, lock the doors, eat your food, and I'll see you tomorrow."

I turned to my suitcase with a sigh. Soon, I'd be at The Vincent, flirting with Moth, my celebrity crush, at the bar, and eventually getting his hotel key.

As I checked my bags, I realized I'd only packed for the retreat, not my layover tonight. I opened my dresser drawer and found an old nightgown. It was a slight struggle with the holes, but I tugged it on and examined myself in the mirror. I almost wondered if I should bring it along to the retreat. It was giving Nymphet vibes. Would Moth like that? I hoped so, considering the other clothes I'd packed.

I bounced down the stairs, imagining for the millionth time my first interaction with Moth, the famous author known for touring with rockstars and writing about his experiences. He was the whole reason I signed up for the writing retreat in the first place. I wasn't a published author yet, and haunted hotels weren't exactly my vibe, but giving my virginity to Moth and then writing the hottest love story ever told about it absolutely was.

I'd just popped a pepperoni pizza in the oven and was dancing to Marina's Electric Heart album, when I was startled by the front door jiggling open.

A tall man in a large winter coat entered, freezing too upon seeing me. He removed his hood, trailing his gaze over my body slowly, until our eyes met, and the recognition hit.

"Priest?"

Blood pounded in my ears as I stared. The house was lit, music blared, and the smell of garlic wafted from the kitchen. But it was the woman standing frozen, staring back at me, in the middle of the living room, dressed like a baby doll, who captured my attention.

"Laney?"

Her chest heaved. Her large, doe eyes were bright and surprised. She was even more beautiful now than she'd been before. It had been four years, and not a day had gone by that I didn't fucking miss her.

Laney was short, her long mousy brown hair, heart-shaped face, and full pink lips were as I remembered. But she had still changed a bit; if her curves were anything to go by. In that tiny, frilly dress, I saw everything. Her full breasts, wider hips...

Jesus fucking Christ. Laney was hot.

"Hi." She waved, turning down the music and adjusting her dress. "I didn't realize you were going to be here."

That's because no one knows I'm here.

Had she forgotten everything? Or had our parents not told her what happened after she left?

"I've been staying here on and off. Are you moving back?"

She shook her head. "Just for tonight. My flight was delayed. It was kind of a last-minute decision. I hope I'm not intruding."

I took my coat off and hung it up. "It's great to see you, Laney." When I opened my arms hesitantly, she rushed into them, pressing her soft breasts against my hardened muscles.

"I know! I missed you so much! How've you been?"

She missed me? She really must not know then.

"Good." I laughed and I placed my chin atop her thick hair, inhaling deeply. My body stirred with the memories. "Are you still using that same baby powder perfume?"

"My room still reeks of that perfume. I low-key love it." She lifted a piece of her dress and sniffed.

Me too.

"Are you cooking something?"

"Yes. I found a pizza in the freezer from Marta. You hungry?"

I was, but not for food. I followed her into the kitchen, watching her ass bounce with every step.

"How old are you now?" I asked, taking my eyes off her panties playing peek-a-boo with the dress.

"Nineteen." She smirked. "You forgot our age difference?"

"I guess. It *really* is great to see you, Laney," I said as we ate.

She didn't seem to be afraid of me at all. How... odd.

"That's shocking, considering the last time I saw you, we fought like cats and dogs," she teased.

"I was a bit of a dick, wasn't I?"

"Ha, a bit? I fucking hated you when we were teens. Did you forget how much you tortured me?"

If only she knew the reason why I treated her like that. "So, what were your plans for tonight?"

Underneath the table, my cock was so fucking hard it

strained against my jeans. I couldn't think about anything other than what it'd feel like to be inside her.

"Uh, nothing exciting. A movie maybe. I'm pretty boring these days."

"A movie? I wanted to catch something. Do Mom and Dad still have their cards attached to everything on the TVs?"

I nodded, trying my hardest to play it cool. On the outside, I was having a casual meal with my step-sister whom I hadn't seen in years. Inside, all I could think about was peeling off her tiny panties and having her sit on my face while she kept the rest of her dress on. Fuck!

"Sure, let me go upstairs and change first." I excused myself, not waiting for her response. Her bedroom door was ajar, and I peered inside. It was just as I remembered it. Back then, they had locked her door and I never had the chance to pick the lock before they sent me away as well. It had been months since I returned, but I'd been too scared to open it. But now, she'd opened it for me herself.

I changed into a pair of flannel pants and pulled off my shirt. I eyed myself in the mirror, overanalyzing everything. Would no shirt come off too obvious? I flexed, admiring the muscles I'd spent long hours lifting weights for. Why not show them off? Besides, it was the hard-on that was my issue; it fucking refused to go away.

I debated a quick jerk before I went back down but thought better of it. If by chance she felt what I felt, pure carnal desire for the one person we couldn't have, I didn't want to spoil things. Instead, I forced my arousal down, thinking of dark places and things I wished I'd never dealt with, and finally, was able to go back downstairs.

When I returned to the ground floor, I smelled her perfume right away and my cock betrayed me. I took a few breaths before entering the living room, where she sat on the couch, crying.

"What's wrong?"

"Summer." She sniffled, wiping tears off her flushed face. "My roommate for the retreat. She just texted me that she's not going. Her mom won't help pay for the plane ticket or the hotel because she's afraid of the snowstorm!"

"Is it that big of a deal?"

"You don't understand." She glared through teary eyes. "Mom and Dad are going to kill me when they see how much I spent on this suite. They'll cut my cards off and then I won't be able to work on my novel and then I'll be stuck working a-and—" Panic gave way to hiccups.

"Laney, everything is going to be fine." I reached for her hands. She flinched away, and my heart did the same. Was that a flicker of her memory? "Where's this retreat?"

"New York," she managed through tears. "For a week."

"Okay, how about I join you? I'll pay for Summer's half. Mom and Dad don't have to know," I blurted out. Was this a good idea? Her and I sharing a room with no one else who knew us around? Could I control myself? Did I want to? This could be my final opportunity to tell her how I'd felt for her for a long time. Was it ridiculous to even consider?

What if she remembered what happened four years ago?

Question after question sped through my brain, vying for attention, but I couldn't decide on any of them. In the end, as I stared at her pink, bee-stung lips, and imagined how they'd feel on mine, I knew I didn't care anymore. I wanted to tempt fate. Surely, if she knew what I did, she'd understand it was all because I loved her.

"You'd do that for me? I thought you hated me."

Oh, Laney darling, you are so far from the fucking truth.

"I could go for a little vacation."

RULE 4 - PRIEST
MAKE SURE SHE'S ASLEEP FIRST.

I sat on my bed, scrolling through the website for the Vincent Hotel. The building had an old, Art Deco design, though it seemed a bit worn down from the outside. I skimmed through the history of the hotel and went to the events page, where Laney's retreat was listed.

"Haunting for words: A writer's retreat."

Tristan Bridges, an unknown author, was leading it. He was a professor for some college in Ohio, but all I saw was a guy who probably fucked his students.

Laney had paid a hefty sum to attend. She'd always liked to read. And I vaguely recalled her having journals. It made sense for her to want to be an author, but this retreat was for established writers. Why would she want to go so badly?

After I agreed to take her friend's spot in her suite, she gushed about it.

"He's been hosting it for the last three years. Everyone who goes raves about it. It's invite-only."

"How did you get one?"

"What? I can't get opportunities because I'm not going to college?" Her body language shifted defensively.

"No, because you're not published, and this is for published authors, right?"

"It is. Tristan made an exception for me because of Summer. He's her professor. I'm probably his diversity pick." She laughed it off. "Hispanic and unpublished. But that's okay because I'm so excited to go. Summer is missing out."

"Apparently," I muttered. "Is there a pool?"

"Indoors." She went on and on about how excited she was to join all these authors for a full week, but my mind was elsewhere. How could she act like she didn't remember?

She'd seen me grab that mask.

She yawned, and we walked upstairs together, but I knew I wouldn't be getting any sleep tonight. After saying our goodnights, we closed our doors. Then I researched the hotel and packed my suitcase with a week's full of clothes. I packed my carry-on with my laptop so that I could work. Considering my profession, Laney and I were truly perfect for each other. I had to show her that this week.

I shut my light off and stopped playing on my phone. Closing my eyes, all I could see was Laney in that skimpy nightgown. It triggered my memories, but it was hazy.

Pictures hung on the walls from Halloween, Christmas, and birthday parties. Family photos with the four of us looking like the perfect family sat on the mantle. When I came back this summer, the only updates had been her school photos.

It almost felt like I'd lived two different lives. One with her in it, and one without. But now, they were colliding, and I was so fucking...

My cock wept for my attention. I'd spent far too much time with my door locked as a teen, wishing I didn't feel the way I did. Step was not a word ever used in our household, despite knowing that there was no blood between us. But I had always seen her as my sister until one day... I didn't.

On her fourteenth birthday, our parents had rented two motel rooms for her and her friends, with an adjoining door, much like we'd be doing this week. I was allowed to invite two of my friends to join our parents in the other room, while Laney had her party on the other side.

Everything was just as it always had been until I went downstairs with Carson and Kaleb, and there she was, in a light pink frilly bikini. It gave me whiplash.

Laney wasn't my sister.

She waved at us and then cannonballed into the hotel pool. I turned and instantly hurried to the bathroom, where I stared at my sixteen-year-old dick, responding to my sister. It was wrong.

But now, we were both adults. Would it be wrong to view her differently? We'd been apart for so long that we were practically different people. It was like strangers meeting for the first time.

My erection refused to give up. I got out of bed for water. It wasn't like me to have restless nights. Although, when I opened my door and saw Laney's ajar, I knew I wasn't thirsty. I'd gotten up to see her.

I stood at her door, listening for a long moment. Slowly, I pushed it open. Tiptoeing, I crept up to her bed and took in her sleeping form.

She was so beautiful. Being the daughter of a Mexican supermodel, how could she not be?

Unable to resist temptation, I reached for her comforter and eased it down her body, inch by inch. She was curled into a fetal position, cuddling one of her stuffed animals.

Hair covered her shoulders, and I brushed them away, exposing her. Her honey-colored skin was flawless. She rolled over, her dress hiking up over her smooth, flat belly. Her breasts bounced with the movement, tempting me further to touch them, to tug one of her beautiful nipples in between my teeth. It would be paradise.

I gave in, reaching for my cock and pulling it out of my pajamas. I slowly stroked myself as she slept. She was everything I'd imagined and more so. Those long eyelashes, those full lips, her tight ass. I worked myself at a torturous pace.

She rolled again, and her eyes fluttered open, sending me into a panic.

She blinked slowly as if in a daze. I waited for her to fall back asleep before darting out of her room and back to the safety of mine. My cock had softened from the scare, but once my door was shut it returned. I slid my pajamas off and stalked to my long mirror. I stroked faster, imagining the look on her face when she saw just how much work I'd put into my body.

All for her.

I knew she'd return to me. Laney was mine the moment our parents met, just neither of us knew it yet. Sending me to that fucking place did nothing. I broke out to find her, and here we were, together again.

I imagined her kneeling down and sucking the life out of me as I whispered how beautiful she was with her lips encircling my length. My eyes settled on the tattoo just above my V-line leading down to my cock.

Laney

And I came.

Rule 5 - Delaney

Get to know the villain.

The blaring alarm jolted me awake, pulling me from my dreams. I sat up and pushed off the blankets, I had to pee. Hurrying to the bathroom, I was surprised to find myself... wet. *It must have been a good dream,* I decided, before hopping into the shower. What had I dreamed about?

I hadn't seen Priest yet this morning. I returned to my room to dress and do my hair and makeup for the flight. When I stepped out of my room, he was coming out from his with his bags in tow and hair still wet from the shower. My brain short-circuited for a moment as I took him in. I hadn't realized until now how good a man looked with a few days of unshaven cheeks. As I stood entranced by Priest's emerald eyes, it hit me.

Priest. I'd dreamed about him.

Despite him being ridiculously hot and overly nice now, he was still my brother. My brain began to ache as a memory was trying to creep in, but a mental wall held it back. What was it?

"You look a little too nice for a plane ride. Kinda

cold, don't you think?" he said, interrupting my thoughts.

I twirled in my pink mini-skirt. "I just want to look my best, always. Ready?"

"Yeah, one thing, before we go."

"What's up?"

"If I go with you, pay half the room, not tell Mom and Dad, I want one favor."

Anxiously, I waited, "Okay?"

"Don't tell anyone how we know each other."

What exactly was his intention?

"You mean that we're..."

He nodded, his gorgeous eyes dipping down my body and then back up to me. "Related?" He smirked. "Yeah. Don't tell anyone."

"Okay." Memories resurfaced from middle school, where he would say the same things. That he didn't know me. He was an only child. I was just some weird girl who came to live with him. My shoulders and mood fell at the realization. He still didn't like me.

As we headed to the airport, I regretted accepting his offer altogether.

"Why are you pouting?"

I crossed my arms and looked out the plane window.

"It's all coming back. How big of an ass you are."

He stiffened beside me.

"I agreed to drop a few grand so you can go write a story at a haunted hotel and I'm the ass?"

"Why don't you want people to know about who we are? Am I not worthy of sharing your last name anymore? And I never asked you to spend the money. You could have said no," I snapped, glaring at him.

He sighed. "I can't say no to you, Laney."

I didn't know what that meant. I turned away and gazed at

the darkness outside. It was snowing quite a bit, but not terribly.

"Is the storm that bad?" Nothing was going to stop me from going to this retreat.

"It will be," Priest said, looking rather bored. "I get why people canceled."

We looked around the plane. Half of the seats were empty due to cancellations. From Michigan to New York, it was only a two-hour flight, and for that, I was grateful. My makeup would stay fresh, and I wouldn't be jet lagged by the time we reached the hotel and I had my meet cute with Moth.

"So, what exactly have you been doing since I saw you last, brother?" I asked, trying to change the subject. We'd spent all morning arguing, I realized, as I stared at his perfect jawline, that I didn't know adult Priest at all.

"It feels weird to hear you say that," he muttered. *"Brother."*

"Why?"

He shook his head and shifted his arm on the armrest, grazing my hand with his pinky. It sent an exciting shiver up my arm at the contact. "It's been four years since I've seen you last. What do you want to know?"

"How was school? After I left?"

"I have no idea." His expression darkened instantly. "I left shortly after you did."

"Where did you go? An alternative school or something?" Our parents wouldn't talk about Priest or anything regarding Marco's murder after I'd been sent away. I'd hardly talked to them at all.

"I'd rather not talk about it."

"What about after school?"

"This and that. I just got back a few months ago. I keep to myself."

"What college did you go to?"

"I didn't. I told you I didn't want to talk about it. You weren't the only one whose life was turned upside down."

"I'm sorry," I said softly. "I wish I hadn't been sent away."

"Do you remember why you were sent away?" His words were like a small electric shock to my system. That was a good question. I squinted and tried to think.

"I'm not sure. Marco Brandis. I had a crush on him." I shook my head as the details grew fuzzy. "I remember being afraid of Mom and Dad finding out and then... he died? Didn't he? Marco?" I looked up at Priest, hoping he remembered more than I did.

"He did. He deserved it. Guy was a fucking pedophile." Priest relaxed in his seat. "That's all you remember?"

I nodded and shifted the conversation. "What do you do now? For work."

He snickered.

"What? Come on, tell me." I nodded toward his bag on the empty seat beside him. "What kind of job do you have?"

"I'm an editor," he replied, gently tracing the top of my hand lightly. It tickled, and I tried to pull away, but he squeezed my hand.

"Like for a newspaper?"

He continued to tease my nerve endings with his feathery movements. "No, for spicy books."

"Spicy as in..."

Priest leaned in so close to my ear, his warm breath and the smell of mint toothpaste invaded my senses. "Does STFU-ATTDLAGG mean anything to you, because it does for me."

My face flushed hot. "Priest!"

He threw his head back and cackled so hard.

"You do not!"

"I do. I've built up quite a business. From the look on your face, you very well may have read one of the books I've worked on. Or are you writing one?"

"Oh my god, I don't know what to say."

"You don't have to say anything. Like I said, STFUA—"

I put my finger up and shot him a look. "Don't you dare!"

"Can you guys tone it down?" the woman in front of us hissed. We looked at each other and burst into laughter. She stood up and glared at us. We hunched down until she turned away again.

"Well, now, I'm curious to see your kindle," he teased.

"Absolutely not."

"What are you into? Vampire mafia?" He elbowed me playfully.

"I'm not telling you."

"Or maybe hot rockstars?"

I ignored him and picked up my water.

"Or is your writing even dirtier than my clients' books?" Priest leaned in, his teeth grazing my ear and sending my heart racing. "Laney, Laney, you dirty girl."

The pilot's voice suddenly interrupted us, startling me so hard I jumped, and Priest laughed even harder.

Oh god, he was too much. Too cruel, too charming, too hot...

"I think this is a bad idea—lying about each other," I said as we stepped off the plane.

Priest leaned down again and his tongue flicked my earlobe again, sending a thrilling shiver through me right down to my core.

"Why? Do you like it when I call you *little sister*? I find it kind of hot, myself."

Me too.

A tall, slim, good-looking man who had obviously gotten cheek implants, stood, holding a placard that said, VINCENT HOTEL. His hair reminded me of every boy band member in the 90s; dark, full, and parted right down the middle. His clothes told me he had money, and he used it to nip and tuck.

Priest and I, after gathering our luggage, made our way to him.

"And you are?" he asked. His English had a hint of a Russian accent.

"I'm Delaney Duvall. Summer Gwinn couldn't come, so I brought another person to bunk with."

The man nodded. "I am waiting for a Juniper and Annie."

Eventually, a stunning woman with a sharp black bob and bright red lips strutted toward us. She wore skin-tight pants and a peacoat. It was giving Snow White fashionista.

"Annie Fernwood."

A beautiful black girl dressed in all black with black lipstick joined us soon. She had a high ponytail that cascaded tight curls down the left side of her face and boots with six-inch heels. "Juniper Park."

The man nodded and together, we followed him to a shuttle van.

"I am Arden Salovei. My family owns the Vincent. Gloriana, my sister, and I maintain it. Is everyone ready?" he asked before taking off. We got onto the snowy road and started toward the hotel.

"So, how do you know Tristan?" Annie leaned over her seat in the back and asked us all. Juniper didn't smile but replied first.

"We've known each other since childhood. I'm the reason he got into paranormal investigations. I come every year."

"What are you?" Annie snickered. "A psychic?"

"Actually, I am. Tristan respects my findings and values what I have to say. Each year, we get more and more readings from the trapped souls of the Vincent, and I publish my findings. Why were you invited?"

"My father helped save his job after that last incident. You know the one, with that girl?" Annie smirked. "He owed us one, and I've been wanting to be invited since he started this."

"I don't believe you." Juniper said.

"You don't have to." Annie replied cooly.

"What do you write? Romance?" Juniper asked, a note of condescension in her voice.

"Better romance than to catch ghosts," Annie retorted. "And no, actually. I have a publishing contract for a four-book psychological thriller series."

"Ooh, a contract? Who did you get on your knees for to get that? Or was it your Daddy?"

Priest and I exchanged a look and let the two very polarizing women go at each other. Eventually, Annie fell back into her seat and kicked my back.

"What about you two? Since when does Tristan invite couples?"

Priest and I shared another look, but before I could reply, he answered her, "He didn't. The girl who was supposed to come bailed because of the storm. I'm just here to enjoy the vacation."

"Does he know this?" Annie raised an eyebrow. "That you brought a date?"

"I'm not her date," Priest said. "I heard there was a pool and she needed a suitemate, so here I am."

"Suite? So you're not sharing a bed." Annie grinned, no longer talking to me, but focusing on Priest. "That's good to know."

Irritation swelled inside me. Why was she so quick to hit on him?

"Ugh! I can't wait!" She slid back and threw her hands up. "This is going to be such good research for my novel. I can't wait for the ghost tour."

"Ghost tour?" My curiosity piqued and I turned.

"Didn't you get the itinerary?" Juniper asked.

"Was it an email? When did he send it out?"

"I got mine in the mail. There's a few classes and then some group brainstorming sessions," Annie explained. "There will be time to do other activities too..." Her gaze raked over Priest again. "What did you say your name was again?"

"Priest."

"Priest. One of our classes is about the human body and how it responds to things. Tristan needs models. Maybe you should do it. I would love to study *your* body."

I took a calming breath. "Arden, you said you guys take care of the hotel?"

The driver nodded.

"Have you seen any real ghosts?"

"I see many things throughout the day. Who is to say they aren't just a guest?"

I rolled my eyes. Was he afraid we'd leap out of the moving vehicle if he answered it straight? Or was this all part of the experience?

"You must see them if you do ghost tours. Or is it just a gimmick?" Annie asked.

"Gloriana is the guide. She will be able to answer any questions you have about the hotel and its previous guests." We got off the freeway and started up a long, one-way road that made me dizzy looking out the windows. My stomach seized and my breathing quickened, as we slid on the ice. Maybe there was reason to panic about the storm.

"Everything is fine," Arden reassured us. "The heavy snow is not here yet. We have plenty of time to get there."

The snow wasn't what I was worried about, I wanted to snap. I was worried about falling off this cliff! Priest reached for my hand. I took it and squeezed. I closed my eyes and focused on my breathing, and eventually, Priest murmured that we were on flat land again.

I opened my eyes. We were off the winding cliff, and I could see the hotel sitting atop a hill over a small forest of trees.

My nerves about falling to my death turned into nerves about Moth. This was it. In less than an hour, I'd be in the same vicinity as my celebrity crush. He wasn't a huge celebrity, but he was big enough that when I told all my friends how I lost my virginity to him at a haunted hotel, they would think I was the coolest. Maybe he'd even write about me in one of his memoirs.

Summer thought it was silly, for me to not have done the deed yet. She and most of our friends lost their virginities ages ago, but not me. I'd dated throughout high school, but I never allowed any of them to get past first base. Those boyfriends were all losers. I didn't want some boy to just give me three pumps and pull out. I'd read too many romance novels to accept that pitiful nonsense. No, I wanted the real deal. Passionate lovemaking in which I was the first to orgasm, not the man. With foreplay and talking and roaring fires and silk sheets. Real men knew how to satisfy women, and I wouldn't settle for anything less.

My last submission to an agent had been returned with painful critique. I'd actually cried.

"It's obvious your sexual life is lacking. To write a good romance, you need to experience the world more. Go, have some affairs, get some years under you, mature, and you are welcome to submit again."

I didn't need years. I just needed Moth.

I came to this retreat to make sure my first time was with someone I knew would be worth my virginity, and I couldn't wait to see what this week had in store. Hopefully, I'd find myself in bed, naked and gasping, sooner rather than later.

Arden drove through the trees and right up to the building steps. He parked and leapt out to open our door. Tristan came out of the hotel with a man who had long blond hair, tattoos everywhere, and the face I'd had saved over and over again in my phone.

Moth.

Laney's eyes widened. What was she looking at? I followed her gaze to a tall, blond guy with tattoos who looked like...

Moth.

I remembered him.

My nerves tightened as we climbed out of the shuttle van and stretched while the driver got our bags from the back. Arden, while young, looked every part of the creepy caretaker of a haunted hotel. I hid in the back, hoping Moth wouldn't see me right away. He was talking to Tristan, who I recognized from the website. He greeted his guests warmly, throwing his arms around the women and kissing their cheeks.

"Annie! Juniper! Delaney! Where's Summer?" He frowned.

"Summer's mom pulled her funding because of the storm," Laney explained. Tristan's brown eyes flicked over to me with a hint of irritation. Laney motioned to me. "This is Priest. He's going to stay in Summer's room."

Tristan's smile waned, but he extended his hand to me. "Tristan Bridges. I'm hosting the writer's retreat."

As I began to introduce myself, I realized why Laney hesitated. We shared the same last name. While they never went through with the legal adoption process, they wanted us all to have the same surname, so hers was changed to mine when our parents got married.

"Priest McMahon." I panicked only a moment before giving him the last name of the quarterback from the 1985 Chicago Bears team, Jim McMahon.

"What do you do?" he asked with a tight smile.

"I'm a freelance fiction editor."

"Oh, you work with Laney?"

I glanced at her. She gave me a quick nod. "Yes," I answered.

Tristan sized me up. I was easily six inches taller than him. My arms were three times the size of his twigs, and if I wanted to chest bump him, I'd send him flying. He was scrawny compared to me, and that felt good. But I wasn't concerned about him. I was more worried about the other man with him.

"Well, welcome. I was so looking forward to seeing Summer produce something wonderful, but now I look forward to seeing what you do." He offered his hand again and when I shook it, this time he squeezed tight. I smiled back, pretending I didn't notice his pathetic attempt at dominance.

Grabbing our suitcases, we started up the stairs of the tall two-story brick hotel. Despite having read about its size on the website the night before, I was still surprised. Even more so now that I knew Tristan, a simple college professor, had rented it completely out for only a few people.

"How many people were invited, Tristan?" Annie asked.

"Eight. Four, including Summer, were unable to make it." The bitterness in his voice was evident.

Giggling from the back of the pack sent the hair on my neck straight up. I turned my head to see Laney beaming up at that stupid blond fuck. He looked mildly interested at best at whatever she was saying. His eyes were more focused on her chest, which was now conveniently on display, having unzipped her winter coat. He still hadn't noticed me.

"Laney, we need to check in," I called back to her. She gave me a side eye and waved me on. I couldn't get my key without her so I stood off to the side, away from everyone. I observed them from a distance. Moth looked like a buff Tony Hawk. I had hoped I'd been mistaken outside, but there was no denying it as I stared.

He saw me watching them and started to tilt his chin when his eyes lit up with recognition.

Fuck.

I strode over and smiled tightly.

"Are you working on a book, Moth?" Laney asked him.

"I was planning on it." Moth was staring at me, his green eyes alight with a wicked interest. "But now that I'm here, I'm thinking of scrapping my original plan. I've got a new focus."

"This place is very inspiring." Laney nodded. "Maybe we can do some plotting together." She put her hand on his forearm, and it caused my eye to twitch, which Moth took in.

"Are you starting fresh this week?" he asked her.

"I am," Laney said. "I've been... saving myself... in case you wanted to work together."

Moth and I shared an identical expression as we realized just exactly what she was saying. She wasn't talking about writing.

Laney was a virgin.

Oh, fuck no.

"So, your name is Moth?" I asked, feigning ignorance, and interrupting them. I was not going to let my little sis give this douchebag her fucking V card.

"My government name is Timothy. I go by Moth. I prefer it," he explained, just like he had when we first met three years ago. That was the dumbest fucking thing I'd ever heard.

"My sister goes by Liz. Her government name is Lizard," I said, just as I had then too.

Moth roared with laughter and reached his arm out, patting my back. I wanted to backhand him, but it was only day one, no need for that just yet.

"It's gonna be a fun week." His words were friendly, but the slap on my back was not.

"It is! I've been looking forward to this week for months now. Even more so after I heard you were invited, Moth. And during Valentine's." Laney sighed.

"Yeah?" He chuckled and peeled her off him. "Nice to know I have fans everywhere." He shot me a look, almost as if we were buddies. I wasn't his fucking buddy. When I looked away from him, he turned and grinned at Laney. "I can't wait to... work with you."

He was baiting me, just as he had back then. Her swoon was almost audible. Laney's cheeks flushed a deep red and her brown eyes glittered.

"Okay!"

"Jesus Christ," I muttered just as we got to the reception table. I put my arms on the counter and motioned with my thumb back at her. "She's got our reservation."

A blonde woman who reminded me of a skeleton with makeup and filler greeted me with a bored look. "Name?" she asked in the same Russian accent as Arden.

I pulled out my wallet.

"Laney," I called out, exasperated. "Will you get up here?"

"Oh, sorry." She giggled and hurried forward. "Delaney Duvall. I have the suite." She reached for her wallet, pulling out her ID and credit card. She looked back at me expectantly.

I handed her mine and she presented it all to the woman.

She looked at my ID and card, read my name, and raised an eyebrow, but said nothing.

"Two keys each. Each bedroom has its own door to the

inside, but you can access the full suite from the door in the middle as well. Call for service. My brother, Arden, will help you. Housekeeping is once a day. Here..." She handed us two key cards. "Enjoy."

I turned and looked for an elevator, finding one across the room. "Come on."

"I'll wait down here with Moth."

Her, alone, with him? Fuck no. My eyes flicked to Moth, who was grinning at me. He knew he had me by the balls. I could almost read his thoughts.

Does she know?

"Go ahead with your boyfriend, Delaney. I'll catch you soon. We can get a drink or something." Moth clicked his tongue and pointed at me.

Laney's face fell, as Moth turned and went down the hall, as if she'd never even existed. To him, a raging narcissist, she probably didn't. Together, we went to the ancient-looking iron gate elevator and got in.

"Is that why you came? To hook up with that guy? To give a total stranger your virginity?"

"Does it matter? You've already ruined my chances." She huffed and once the squeaky elevator made it to our floor, she stormed out and began looking for the doors to suite number 13. I reached the doors as she was fumbling with the key card. Her anger had her hands shaking.

I leaned down and whispered in her ear, "Let's not fight again. Remember what happened last time?"

RULE 8 - PRIEST
WATCH FOR OTHER KINDS OF MONSTERS.

Four years ago

Fuck!

I needed to calm down. This had gone on too far. Two years. I'd been crushing on Laney, my step-sister, for two fucking years, and today, I let my mask slip. I'd almost confessed everything.

I walked into her room, fully prepared to tell her exactly how I felt, only for my plans to be throttled by some pervert down the block. I don't even know what happened. One minute my heart was racing, my palms were clammy and I was struggling to find the words, and the next, my mind was blank. My heart slowed, I was calm, and the only thing on my mind was... murder.

I had dinner, and instead of sharing my feelings, I glared at Laney and shoved my food in so fast I threw it up as soon as I got upstairs. I'd almost ruined everything. If Mom and Dad knew how I felt, they'd kill me. I had to fix things with Laney before everything went to shit. But how?

As I paced my room, I formulated a plan. I'd simply go in

and talk to her. Apologize for getting angry and then take it from there. Her response would help me decide my next steps to smooth everything over.

Mom and Dad didn't have to know a thing.

I reached for my door handle and paused. Could I have a calm conversation right now? I was too pissed about her confession I couldn't concentrate on anything else. Every time I looked at her, all I saw was Marco Brandis, kissing and touching her. He was a grown man who worked at the mall and still lived with his parents, talking to a fifteen-year-old! I couldn't let that happen.

My anger returned, and I paced some more, trying to calm myself. Laney was mine. Not any of those stupid boys who gave her candygrams, not Marco fucking Brandis, mine. I knew it was absurd and disgusting to feel this way. Her dating people was normal. Me dating people was normal. But I didn't like it.

Eventually, I felt calm enough to go talk to her, but when I stepped out of my room, I found her door wide open, and she was gone. I heard the shower turn on. Laney took long showers. I had plenty of time to snoop. I walked inside her all-pink room and decided it was probably better for me to look around rather than confront her directly.

I went to her bed, where the pile of cards and candy lay scattered. I sat at the edge and picked one up. It was one of the school's candygrams. A simple heart with a green, cartoon worm on it, holding a heart. Boring, unoriginal, and she had three of the same one.

Delaney,

You're the prettiest bookworm I've ever met. Will you go out with me?

-Nolan

So cheesy. I rolled my eyes and picked up another one. It read similarly. A compliment, followed by the request. As I kept reading through the stack, I wondered if she'd say yes to any of these boys. What would she have done if I had asked?

I tossed the last candygram note aside and then picked up the large, store-bought card. I opened it and disregarded the cringy poem in favor of the handwritten note on the blank side.

> Delaney,
> I've never felt this way about a girl before. You're so much more mature than all the other girls I've talked to. It's a connection that no one else has. I can't wait for Friday. To see you face-to-face since Christmas. It'll be our first... everything....
> X

My hands shook when I finished the note. Christmas? This had been going on for two months? I tried to think of where she could have seen him and it hit me. I had taken her to the mall to buy presents. I had unknowingly brought her right to him!

The coward didn't even have the balls to sign it. He knew exactly what he was doing and how disgusting it was. I tossed the card down and looked for the last one.

Mine.

When I didn't see it, I began shifting her blankets and then looking under her pillows, but it was nowhere to be found. My blood ran cold. What did she do with it? Did she know it was me who sent it? Was she going to tell Mom and Dad? Or had she just tossed it in the trash in favor of Marco's?

As I was frantically searching for the card to take it back and burn it, I found her cell phone on her dresser. I picked it up and found it locked. Scoffing, I typed in the code she'd been using for years. 5980. Mom's birthday. Sure enough, it opened and I went to her messages.

There was nothing. She was immature, but she wasn't stupid. I started looking at her apps, trying to find where she'd been talking to Marco, and when I accidentally clicked on her Calculator app, it asked me to put up a code. That was odd.

I typed in 5980 and it didn't work; it wanted five numbers. I thought about it and then typed in another code. 61346, her grandpa's birthday. Mom was planning his 75th birthday party and the date had been plastered on our fridge for months.

As it went through, I snickered. I knew Laney more than she knew herself.

The code unlocked page after page of messages with the perv. Looking at the dates each text was sent, I'd been right. They met when I took her shopping. How fucking ironic. I was doing something nice for her, trying to show her that I could be someone she could rely on, and she fell into the arms of someone else. A pedophile.

I heard the shower turn off and I realized I'd been in her room far too long. Panicking, I began pushing buttons and managed to download the entire thread. With a quick click, I sent it to my phone and tossed the device back on her shelf. I scurried back to my room just as I heard the bathroom door open and her soft pats on the floor as she returned to her bedroom, most likely wrapped in a pink towel, to start her nightly routine of creams and lotions.

Taking my phone out, I plopped down on my bed and began scrolling through Laney and Marco's conversation. This was evidence of a crime. It was so painfully obvious that Marco was much older than the girl he was talking to. She was asking him what dress to wear to the father- daughter dance in the spring, while he was complaining that he had to pay his own health insurance because his parents couldn't cover him anymore.

For weeks, this guy had been telling her everything she wanted to hear. How pretty she was, how mature she was. I wasn't going to let Laney just be another conquest for him. I got to the bottom of the file, reading every single message, growing angrier and angrier with each one. By the time I was done, I saw red.

I went to my inbox and typed a shitty message to him, but then backtracked and decided to try something different.

> Me: Hey Marco, you gave me your number at the mall the other day.

> Marco: Hey baby, I remember you. You were the cute one. What's up?

So not only was he flirting with Laney, he was flirting with all the teen girls.

> Me: It's Valentine's Day. I didn't get any candygrams at school.

> Marco: That's just because the boys don't know any better. If I was still in school, I'd send you so many lollipops. Do you like lollipops?

The photo that followed made me drop my phone with disgust. He had no idea who I was and he was sending dick pics? I was done. I leapt up, fully prepared to show Laney the message when I saw something and changed my mind.

My Michael Myer's mask from Halloween.

RULE 9 - DELANEY
DON'T TRUST FUCKBOYS.

"You want a drink?" Moth smiled at me, and I melted. I'd been so shaken up by Priest's words just minutes before, that I fled our room, tossing my bags on the couch and running back downstairs. Memories of his snide and cruel remarks when we were teens flashed in my mind, but his exact wording confused me.

The last time we fought?

I had no idea what he was talking about. All of my worries about Priest and his cryptic words to me disappeared as my attention focused in on the hot guy I'd been dreaming of meeting for months.

"I can't legally drink yet," I admitted.

Moth ran his tongue along his lips. "Alright, we got a youngin', let's go get you some juice and we can chat." I followed Moth to the bar.

"So, Priest, is he your boyfriend?" he asked as soon as we were seated. His eyes dipped, admiring the ample cleavage I had made sure to show off with this outfit. I recalled the deal I'd made with Priest. I couldn't say we were related, but his profession and my aspiring one gave us the perfect alibi.

"He's my editor. I don't want to talk about Priest. What about you? Are you single?"

A man in a tuxedo came from seemingly nowhere and asked us what we wanted to drink.

"Just a cold beer for me. She can't drink." Moth snickered.

The bartender gave me a once-over and nodded. "I shall make her a mocktail."

"To answer your question." Moth shook his head. "No, I am not single. I've been married for about two years now."

My stomach dropped, along with my jaw. "You're not wearing a ring."

He raised his hand. "We don't. It's an open marriage."

The bartender returned, setting a beer in front of Moth, and offering me a pink drink in a martini glass.

"The pink drink, for the pink girl." He nodded to my outfit. I took a tentative sip and found it quite tasty.

"Thanks!"

"Order this during your stay." He left through the door again, leaving Moth and me alone in the bar while low piano music played from speakers overhead.

"An open marriage?" I raised a skeptical eyebrow. Moth took a sip of his beer.

"Gwen and I have been together since we were teenagers. Friends mostly. She's bi and prefers women. We were just a 'when you're in town, look me up' couple, and then she found out she was sick. She needed insurance. So, we went to the courthouse and got her taken care of."

"Do you guys live together?" I was trying to comprehend this news, all while attempting to act older than I was. Moth needed to see that I could handle this.

"I crash at her place when I'm in town. It's not often. It's always been that way. She has her girlfriends." He took a sip of beer and leaned over the bar, reaching for my hand. "And I have mine." My heart sped up. I could be his girlfriend?

"Is she still sick?" I asked.

"Chronic illness. I'd rather not talk about Gwen. Let's talk about you. You're a writer?"

I sipped my drink and tried to relax as Moth kept his hand on mine. I told him that I'd just graduated and was trying to finish my first manuscript.

"Tristan knows I'm not published like the rest of you, but he still invited me. I'm hoping it will lead to some new opportunities."

"Sounds like you'll be doing a lot of firsts this week." Moth grinned wickedly. I thought I was going to explode! Yes!

"There you are! Delaney Duvall, you sneaky fox!" Tristan burst into the room, waving a chastising finger, causing both Moth and I to pull apart. "I've been looking all around for you."

"You have?" I reached for my drink again. The bartender had just refilled it.

"Are you drinking?" His dark brows furrowed. "You're only nineteen."

"It's a mocktail. What's up?"

"The storm caused some of our guests to be unable to attend this week's retreat. I had you all paired up for critique, and your partner is gone, so we need to find you someone to work with."

"I can be Moth's partner!" I looked over quickly.

Tristan shook his head. "No, no, that will not work!" He brought his hand to his mouth and gnawed on his knuckle. "He's partnered with Annie. I planned everything just so. I can't go mixing everyone around. Will your friend, the one you brought, Priest. Would he be your partner?"

I laughed. "Priest? He's not a writer." Tristan's eyes grew so wide I thought he'd explode. I put my hands up. "I'll ask."

He exhaled, ignoring my last statement. "Thank you.

Now, the next crisis. My model is not coming, so you will be taking his place."

"Model?" I smirked and looked at Moth, who was silently observing everything. "I'm not a model."

"Models are bodies to pose, examine. They breathe life into your story. You agreed when I invited you that you would help where needed, so you will be filling in that day. Consider yourself off the hook after that."

"Fine." I rolled my eyes. "Anything else?"

The bartender appeared again and asked Tristan if he'd like a drink. Tristan sat on the stool next to Moth. "A nice white wine, if you can. Moth, how is the new hobby going?"

"Hobby?" I leaned forward to not get thrust out of the conversation. Moth flicked his tongue out appreciatively.

"I'm learning how to tattoo. I've got an apprenticeship starting after the retreat." He turned to Tristan. "I brought my equipment if you want to be a guinea pig."

Slowly, we were joined by Annie and Juniper. Tristan was asking more about his tattoo work and I was left in the dust. I turned to Annie, trying to hide my disappointment.

"It's obvious what your goal is this week but what about your hot friend?" Annie asked.

"Priest?"

I sipped my pink drink.

"Yeah, is he available?" When she grinned, an unusual sense of jealousy flared inside me.

"No, he's my partner."

"Only for writing-related things. I've got Moth, although I wouldn't mind a trade." She gave me a pointed look.

Juniper laughed. "Good luck. Tristan doesn't like changes. If he picked you to be with Moth, then that's who you're staying with."

"Who's your partner?" I asked the sarcastic psychic.

"Tristan. He claimed he couldn't trust anyone to do my writing justice." She rolled her eyes. "I love him, but sometimes he can be a little extra."

"Are you two...?" I pointed from Tristan to her.

She burst into laughter. "Oh sweetie, no. I've had far more female lovers than men. Tristan will never be in my bed. We just go way back. He's basically my brother."

Priest slid back into my mind at the mention of the word, brother. He still hadn't come back down.

"I like that idea," Moth said to Tristan and then turned back around quickly. "Delaney, what do you think?"

"About what?" I hadn't been listening.

"Before your modeling session, you should be nude."

"Me?"

"Yes, what do you say, Delaney? Lay in front of us bare, so we can admire your true beauty, and much like the pages we write, offer critique."

Critique? On my naked body? The room collectively stopped breathing as Tristan launched his newest idea. Moth's attention turned back to me. He put his hand on my knee and began sliding it up my thigh.

"Maybe not, Tristan. I don't think she's ever let anyone see her so vulnerable. I mean, she's not even published yet. She doesn't know what it's like." The double meaning in his words caused my core to pulse. "I'd love to be your first, Delaney."

My heart stuttered. I wanted that too. For years, I held off, watching my friends all go through with it, thinking eventually I'd find the perfect guy. But the longer I held off, the more I realized how silly keeping my virginity was. Losing it to Moth would be a great story to tell.

He pulled his hand back. He smiled and patted my knee like a child.

"Go up, unpack, and start thinking about where you want

your first time to be. And I'll meet you there so we can do it in private." Heat flooded my face as his words settled around the room. He cleared his throat and chuckled, enjoying my utter discomfort. "Writing critiques, that is."

RULE 10 - DELANEY
LEARN HOW TO LIE.

"I've got to hit the head. I'll be back. Don't go too far, Delaney Duvall." Moth took his hand off my thigh and slid off his stool, heading out of the room. The moment he was gone, Annie and Juniper pounced on me.

"You are way too desperate," Annie scolded.

"It is a bit cringy to watch," Juniper admitted.

"I don't know what you're talking about."

"Oh, come on," Annie whined. "The whole innocent little bird thing? Come on, you don't need to lay it on so thick to get into his pants."

I blushed. "You think?"

The two shared a look, and Juniper's eyes turned sympathetic.

"Oh sweetie, come, sit with us." She took my drink, and I followed them to their booth in the corner.

"Is this how you always are? Your move?" Annie asked pointedly.

I shook my head. "My move?"

She flicked her hands toward the bar, where Moth had just returned. He looked around for me and when he saw me, he frowned, but waved and then turned to Tristan beside him.

"You know, to get attention, your flirting style. It works, but I don't think you need to lay it on so thick." Annie shrugged.

My stomach twisted. "I've never really flirted with anyone seriously. Was it bad?"

The two burst into laughter, making me feel even more embarrassed. I looked down at my pink drink, feeling utterly silly.

"Moth had his eyes on you the moment you got out of the van," Juniper said after she stopped laughing. "I bet if you ask for his room key right now, he'd give it to you."

"Although I'm not entirely sure why you'd want his key when you've got that ridiculously hot piece in your room already." Annie snickered.

"Who? Priest?" I laughed. "He's not—" I paused, shook my head, and looked back to Moth. "Priest isn't interested in me."

"I call bull on that. He was practically growling at Moth when we got here. Girl, he's jealous." Juniper laughed.

Jealous?

"No, if anything, he's just protective. I'm not Priest's type." As I said the words, I realized I didn't know if that was true or not. What was Priest's type of woman? Probably someone like Annie; confident, beautiful, and experienced.

"Well, if you're not going to fuck him, I just might." Annie brought her drink to her lips and looked at me over the rim.

"You said you don't flirt, does that mean you're..." Juniper raised her eyebrows at me.

I clicked my tongue bitterly. "I am. That's why I'm trying to..." I tilted my head toward the bar. "If I'm going to write a good romance novel, I should at least know what it's like."

Juniper snickered. "There are tons of people who don't have sex that write romance, good romance."

"Yeah? Well, according to the literary agent who got halfway through my manuscript before tossing it in the trash, I can't. To quote her words, my sex scenes were 'painfully inaccurate', and 'she could tell that the author had never experienced love or romance'. That's why I came this week."

"Well, fuck that agent, for starters." Juniper's face grew angry. "I'd just go indie at that point. Make a shit ton of money and then send her the middle finger."

I opened my mouth, but was interrupted by Annie.

"Even if what that agent said was true, which it's not, you're not going to get love or romance in a week," Annie said, chuckling. "Certainly not from Moth. You're entire plan is ridiculous."

"Sex and love are two totally different things. You're not going to find it here at the Vincent Hotel," Juniper said.

"Well, it's a place to start," I defended. "I just want to lose my virginity. That's all. I kept holding on to it, waiting for the perfect guy to come along and now it's just embarrassing. I just want one hot romp, is that okay?"

"Fair enough." Annie tilted her drink at me. "Let's toast then, to Delaney giving it up to the hottie at the bar!"

Her toast sent us into giggles and we lifted our drinks and turned to the bar, only to see someone had joined the other men.

Priest.

I stopped laughing. Annie saw my reaction and laughed.

"Honestly, I'd let either of them in my pants. Or both. Both could be fun." She and Juniper shared a laugh. I tried to relax, but I was on high alert, fully aware that while Priest may be sitting next to Moth, seemingly engaged in their conversation, he was still watching me.

"You never said how you guys met." Juniper pulled my attention from Priest.

"He's my editor," I lied.

"You have an editor but not an agent?" Annie cocked her head. "Sounds like you're already thinking about going indie."

"I haven't really decided," I said. "We just happened to meet and he's been helping me with my novel."

"I bet," Juniper teased. "The man looks even hotter without the thick coat and winter gear. If he flexes, that shirt is going to pop right off."

Annie swooned. "My kind of man. Hot and someone else's." She glared at me, but it was more playful than mean.

"What do you mean?" I looked between them.

"Well..." Juniper stirred her drink with the little plastic stick. "Whether you think there's something there or not, it's pretty clear that Priest likes you."

That was ridiculous.

"How so?"

"He held your hand the entire ride up here," Annie started. "And he looks at you with big eyes, like he'd do anything for you. His eyes are very expressive."

"You just met him," I pointed out.

"Yes, but I'm a writer. I know what I'm talking about. The man, whether you can admit it or not, has some kind of feeling about you."

"Maybe annoyance." I smirked. "I don't see it."

"You don't have to. You'll feel it pressed against your ass in the morning." Annie laughed and then held up her hands. "Look, I'm just saying, appearance-wise, Priest beats Moth, hands down. Maybe he's not as charming, but I don't think it would be any sort of consolation prize to let Mr. Editor take your virginity over the guy who looks like he puts his dick in anything warm and wet."

I couldn't take it anymore. I slid out of the booth and stood. "I'm going to go try flirting again, thanks for the tips, ladies." I lifted my head high and stormed over to the bar, ordering a fresh pink drink.

I stood between Priest and Moth and greeted them. "Hey! What are you guys talking about?"

"Welcome back, Delaney Duvall." Moth grinned. "Priest and I were just catching up. I knew he looked familiar in the lobby, but it wasn't until a little bit ago I remembered where we'd met."

"Oh?" I turned to look at Priest. "Did you guys go to the same school?"

Priest's eyes grew large and Moth grinned.

"Cunningham County."

"That sounds like a prison."

"It felt like one, right, Priest?" Moth nudged him. Priest didn't respond. Instead, he reached for his beer and took a swig while glaring at Moth.

"I only did about a year over there, but Priest, they called you a lifer, didn't they?" Moth smirked. I looked between them. They were having some sort of silent conversation between them.

"How can you be a lifer at a college?" I asked.

"Didn't I say I don't want to talk about it?" Priest asked sharply.

"Oh, come on, she's just interested in knowing who she's sleeping with." Moth's words held an edge to them that caused a low growl to come from Priest's throat. "In the suite, I mean."

"She knows what you mean," Priest snapped.

"I'm confused," I said, and before I could ask more questions, Priest swung his fist at Moth's jaw.

I was fast, but Moth was faster. He blocked my fist and shoved me back.

He'd been goading me all night, telling me and the others at the bar how much sex he'd be having this week.

"And I thought I'd be spending my Valentine's getting drunk alone and jerking off."

It was then that Laney came up and inserted herself.

"Priest!" she screamed and tugged on my shoulder. I leapt up and glared at Moth, who was giving me a shit-eating grin. He knew he had me by the balls. Again.

"What are you doing?" Laney screeched. I forced myself to calm down, exhaling slowly. "Nothing. I'm going to go up and finish unpacking. I'm tired."

I took the stairs instead of the rickety elevator. It was made of metal and squealed every inch of the way up. I got to our suite and opened my door. The moment I was inside, I screamed.

"Fuck!" I paced the room, shoving stuff off the table.

Moth. The universe had a fucked-up sense of humor. The one chance I got to show Laney that we could be more than brother and sister, and fucking Moth, of all people, was here. I remembered the twisted fuck. He arrived at Cunningham, smug as shit, laughing as they did his intake. It wasn't the laughing that was abnormal. No, most of the people at Cunningham weren't entirely sane. Manic laughing was common at all times of the day there. Moth's laugh wasn't maniacal; it was dry, sarcastic as if he found it amusing he'd been locked up, as if he weren't meant to be there. After meeting him, it was obvious that he was right where he should be.

But, he got out.

I stormed the room, making a mess of it until I calmed down enough to put it all back together. It was almost embarrassing how childish the act was. If Laney saw the room, I'd be mortified.

Once the room was in order again, I set to unpack, putting my clothes in the closet and my toiletries in the shared bathroom. I wondered if Laney would be bothered by having to share space with my few items. She always complained when we were younger. Had she changed much? It certainly didn't feel like it. Once everything was cleaned up and put away, I had nothing to do. I sat on my bed and looked around. What now?

I picked up the brochure they had left on my side table. Room service, gym, pool, hot tub, ghost tour, bar, hedge maze. *I would find something to fill my evening.* The moment I stepped out of the suite, my anger returned, albeit to a lesser extent than before. I'd catch that fucker alone at some point this week and make it known that Laney was mine and no one else's. I just hoped I'd catch him before he managed to get her in his bed.

I roamed the hallways, taking in all the antiques and art on the walls. It was an upscale place. No wonder Laney was panicking about having to pay for it on her own. Mom and

Dad would notice that bill. As I explored, I made sure to note where things were. The kitchen, the offices, parlors, etc. I didn't like the idea of being lost.

Being trapped.

I found the doors to the backyard, and with a gentle push, discovered they were still open. Snow fell heavily, but the wind had paused, hopefully long enough for me to check out the maze. It was almost eerily quiet, except for the crunch of my boots on the snow.

The hedge walls were twice my height and thick. I peered into them and couldn't see to the next side. I shivered, swearing to myself for not wearing my coat. Was it colder in here? Moving carefully, I made note of every turn I made. This maze was impressive and a little haunting. Someone could easily get lost inside.

Trapped.

The very idea of it made me move faster. I was at the very end of the maze when I spotted something sticking up from the snow. I bent down to pick it up. I brushed the snow off and then jerked my hand back.

A Michael Myer's mask.

How? My heart raced as I stared at the white rubber with brown hair glued to it. This was a dream. It had to be a nightmare. I stared at it for a long time before burying it with a swipe of my boot and storming back inside. It was some sick joke of Moth's, I was sure.

Back inside, I followed the directions throughout the hotel, quickly finding the pool. I shed all of my clothes except my boxer briefs and dove into the water. Rising to the surface, I then began a breaststroke. I needed to shake the feeling of being trapped and swimming would do that.

All the twists and turns. Left, right, right again. I repeated the maze in my head, and then again, and one more time for good measure. I'd spent four years, trapped. I wasn't going back.

I reached the end of the pool and paused, lifting myself to my chin and shaking my head like a dog. A figure loomed on the other side of the frosted glass. I couldn't see them clearly, but it was a broad, masculine frame. I paused, watching it for a moment until it disappeared, heading back toward the lobby.

Was it Moth, checking to see what I was doing so he could take Laney up to his room and rob her of her virginity before breaking her heart? My anger returned, and I kicked off the walls of the pool and resumed my laps. My muscles burned and my lungs screamed for oxygen, but I kept going, coming up for air and nothing else.

I swam until I was no longer angry. I collapsed backward on my last lap and floated aimlessly, looking up at the fluorescent lights. I could do a week here. I'd figure out what to do about Moth and then I'd have my time with Laney. I was going to be her first.

I got out of the pool, only to freeze a few steps away when I saw the sickeningly familiar mask sitting neatly atop my clothes pile.

RULE 12 - PRIEST
IT'S NEVER A COINCIDENCE.

I snatched the mask up and looked around.

"Hello?"

"Hello, Priest."

I spun around.

"Carson?" I stood, frozen, in just my wet underwear, watching my old friend from high school step into the room. "I thought—" I swallowed and tried again. "How did you get here?"

"I've always been here. How did you get here?"

"I'm on a mini vacation. Do you work here?" What were the odds that my old friend from Sherwood was now working in the same hotel I was visiting in New York?

"I saw Delaney at the bar. I assume you came together."

"We're sharing a suite." Setting the mask aside, I reached for my clothes and tugged them on, despite being soaking wet. "She's probably still at the bar."

Carson stared off into the distance, so I snapped him back to attention.

"Yes, with Moth." He snickered. "She seems bound and determined to have his cock this week."

A growling noise escaped my throat. I didn't like it at all. Moth was not worthy of being with Laney, as her first or second or at any time.

"Yeah, that's not happening."

"He's helping her work tomorrow. He wants to be the first to co-write with her."

"That'll be the only first he gets."

"And what? You'll take the other?" He turned. "You, Priest Duvall, her brother!"

"Stepbrother. You know that, you fucker."

"I do, but does she?"

"What's that supposed to mean? This is stupid. Why are we talking about this? What about your accident? What happened with that?" I sat on a beach chair and shoved my boots on.

"I'd rather not discuss that." He tightened his fists and tugged on his jacket.

"It wasn't an accident." I had heard about what he'd done, but the local paper must have gotten the last bit wrong. Carson seemed... fine.

"I said I don't want to talk about it!" he snapped, startling me.

"My bad. Okay, we won't talk about it. I just... I was sorry to hear about it."

"So was everyone else. Now, on to you fucking your sister. Did you not figure that shit out while you were gone?"

"You have no idea what you're talking about."

"Fair enough. Laney has grown, hasn't she? I mean, she was cute back then, but now... I don't blame anyone who shoots their shot."

"If you try to hit on her, Carson, I'll—"

He put his hands up with a chuckle. "Don't worry. I'm safe. I saw you exploring the maze. How did you like it?"

I shrugged uncomfortably, remembering the enclosed feeling. "Why are the hedges so tall?"

"So that no one climbs them. You got out just fine."

"Panic is a great motivator." I snatched the mask off the tile. "Did you dig this out of the snow just to fuck with me? Or did you put it there in the first place?" I waved it in his face.

"I did not do either. Although I do recall the visitor who abandoned it there. He'd gotten lost in the maze." There was an uncomfortable silence when he didn't elaborate. I didn't believe him. How else had the mask gotten inside and with my belongings? I sighed and looked toward the door.

"Well, all right. I guess I'll see you around the hotel. Maybe on your off time, we can catch each other for a beer or something." Carson, while looking just as I'd remembered, only slightly older, was different now. I couldn't place it directly, but the hair on my neck stood with alarm. I had no intention of catching him for a drink. In fact, I was going to avoid him as much as I could.

"Sure. And maybe then we can talk about your stint at the psycho ward." He laughed.

I paused with my hand on the knob. "Excuse me?"

"They wanted to send me there, but I didn't want to be associated with people like you."

"Like me?" I turned back. He didn't know shit about me.

"We all heard the stories about you two. Delaney was being hauled off to a nunnery and you were taken to Cunningham's. The nunnery must have worked since she's still playing the innocent little girl. The better question is, did the nuthouse work for you too?"

I closed my eyes. "Stop."

"Why? What are you gonna do? Run me through with an axe?" He laughed, and I launched at him, shoving him straight into the pool. Water exploded all over the room as my childhood friend flailed, trying to catch his balance.

I scooped my stuff back up and stormed out, not bothering to check to make sure he caught his breath. He could fucking drown for all I cared. I was sure he wouldn't mind, considering his little accident just months ago.

I returned to the suite, tossing everything on my bed, and despite myself, I began tugging at my hair and pacing. The nuthouse. The psycho ward. How fucking dare he. Was he going to go around the hotel telling everyone what he thought he knew? Everything he'd been told was just rumors. If he knew so much, he'd know about how I left the fucking place.

Covered in chlorine from the pool, I left my bedroom and found the bathroom. It was huge with a shower and a separate bath. The room was almost the size of the bedrooms. Despite the decor being reminiscent of the Gatsby era, it didn't look aged, but rather well-kept.

Finding soaps and shampoo already inside, I quickly stripped and washed all the chemicals and anger away. I remembered now, just how often he used to get under my skin in school. He knew exactly what buttons to push, but to openly talk about Laney like that? As if he knew how I felt about her? It was a brave guess, at best, and I took the fucking bait.

I stepped out of the bathroom after my shower. Just then, Laney opened the suite door and came in, smiling until she saw me. I smirked, striding through the living room. Her eyes drifted along my muscles. I could feel her raking her gaze over me, and confidence built inside my chest.

"I've worked hard for this body."

"I see that."

"If you don't stop staring, then I'll drop the towel and give you something else to admire."

"Oh god." She flew to the other door, rushing through it. And as I stared after her, it hit me. If she was a virgin, had she ever even seen a dick? By the loud click of her door locking, I'd say no.

Rule 13 - Delaney

It's smart to have a flashlight.

I stayed with my back pressed to the door, holding my racing heart. Holy shit. Priest was... stacked. I shook the image of droplets running down his toned body and the wild smirk dancing on his lips as he caught me staring. Priest was so hot.

Steadying my breathing, I went back out and grabbed my bags, quickly returning to my room. The decor was incredibly beautiful. Everything was pink and gold, much like my bedroom at home and the wardrobe I'd brought. I sighed happily and gasped when I spotted my bed. I tossed my bags down and hurried to it with excitement. A bouquet of paper roses were scattered all across the blanket. I picked one up and examined it. It wasn't just made of paper; they were book pages.

How romantic.

I gathered them up, set them on my worktable, and returned to unpacking. I had packed my best clothes. I planned every outfit with my mission in mind. I was the complete opposite of Moth, and that would draw him to me. Like a moth to a flame. God, maybe I was a terrible writer.

Seeing as I'd be sleeping alone tonight, I chose my most chaste nightgown to sleep in. Summer had taken me shopping for clothes that were sexy yet innocent.

I slipped on a white, ruffled nightgown with pink bows in the center of my chest and on the matching panties. While I planned on not going to sleep quite yet, I did my best writing while feeling confident and sexy, and this nightgown checked both boxes for me.

At the bottom of my suitcase, I came across a box I didn't pack. It had Valentine's Day wrapping paper and a small card, written by Summer.

Happy Galentines!

This is just in case Moth isn't all that you hoped. I wanted to make sure you had a rose on Valentines. You'll thank me later.

Cautiously, I opened the box and lifted out the small, rubber, red rose. What was this exactly? Despite being completely alone, heat rose in my face. Some sort of sex toy. God, I should know this stuff. The longer I looked at it, the more absurd I felt. I was a grown woman. I could own a rose, or whatever this was. Most women had sex toys. I bet Annie and Juniper had them. Even brought them. I shoved it into my bedside drawer. I'd wait to test it out until after I'd slept with Moth. Hopefully, Moth knew how to pleasure a woman and I wouldn't need it. Was it possible to orgasm during your first time?

"Penny for your thoughts?"

I spun around and glared at the open door, where Priest, now clothed, stood leaning against the frame with his arms crossed.

"Nothing. Just figuring out my plans for the rest of the

night. I was going to try some writing. What are you doing?" I folded my arms under my breasts. His eyes dipped instantly, telling me he noticed. I tugged on the bottom of my night-gown, feeling self-conscious.

"What was in the box?"

"How long were you watching me?" Heat flooded my face.

"Just long enough to watch you put it in your nightstand. Based on your face, I have an idea."

"Will you leave me alone? I have needs just like everyone else."

"Then why are you so embarrassed?"

"I-I prefer the real thing," I stated boldly.

He laughed. "How do you know? You haven't had it."

I glared at him. "I'm sorry I respect myself more to—"

"Bullshit!" He rolled his eyes. "You're trying to give it up to a guy who calls himself Moth and is a pathological liar. Respect is not what I saw downstairs."

Tears stung my eyes, and I pointed out the door. "What do you know? You didn't try to call me or message me for four years. You don't get to play big brother now. I can sleep with whoever I want." The look on his face told me otherwise, but he knew I was right. He didn't control me. Maybe when we were younger, he could threaten and blackmail me to get what he wanted, but not now. We stared each other down for a long moment before I continued.

"And what's more, Tristan asked me to be a nude model for one of our class days and I said yes."

"Like hell." Priest stepped forward, and I did the same.

"You can't stop me. I will be sleeping with Moth, I will be posing nude for the class, and you will always be my brother."

I stopped. I didn't know where that last part had come from. My brain began to ache as a memory tried to burst through my fog, but I couldn't quite figure it out. Had I said something to him like that before? When?

Why?

"Laney." Suddenly, Priest's hands were on my cheeks, holding me gently. "Don't do this."

"Why not? It's my body."

"Yes," he agreed. "Respect it enough to not waste your first time on someone like him."

I blinked away the frustrated tears. He wasn't saying anything different from what my friends had said when I told them my plan. There were plenty of good men to pick from, so why a complete stranger who was married?

"I don't want to talk about it anymore." I brushed his hands away. The lights above flickered and panic shot up my spine. Priest gave me an odd look and then a flicker of remembrance flashed on his face. His hands went to my hands, squeezing tightly.

"It's the storm. Just some strong winter wind. It'll be fine."

My stomach tightened as the lights continued to flicker and glass around the room rattled. My heart raced to the point of painful as I feared for—The lights went out completely. I screamed, and Priest instantly pulled me into him, covering my mouth.

"Sssh, it's fine. You're safe. The lights will come on in a second." But they didn't. Priest rubbed my back and continued to try to calm me, but the deep-rooted fear took over my brain and I sobbed. "Laney, you're fine. Here, come sit on the bed."

I let him lead me to the bed. He tried to let go of my hand, but I held tight.

"I'm just going to go see if anyone has candles or flashlights or something. Maybe we have an ETA on when the power will come back on."

I pulled my legs up and fell back onto the bed, curling myself up in a ball.

"Okay, I'll be back in just a second. Stay here."

In the back of my mind, I knew it was a silly fear. An absurd trigger, a childish one. It was just a storm. No electricity? Who cared? But a switch flipped whenever it happened. I reverted back to the child who had no one to protect her from the loud, scary storm. No one but Priest, who hadn't been there.

It was easier, once Priest began saving me from the wind and rain. After that night, he'd refused to leave the house if there was a storm, in case I needed him. But after I'd been taken away, I was forced to handle the darkness alone. Each time, I still ended up a crumpled mess until morning. The windows rattled and the wind howled outside, sending me back to a dark time in my childhood.

"Laney, I'm back." Priest returned and sat at the foot of the bed. "Power is out until morning. I didn't realize you were still like this."

I kept my eyes closed. "You weren't there. You don't understand." I tossed the words at him, knowing they weren't fair. He touched my foot, and I jerked away.

"I know, I should have been there, but I'm here now. Let me help you get through this."

Flashes of the night that started my lifelong fear of storms and the outages poured one right after another through my mind.

Priest slid his hands up my legs, massaging the tight muscles and saying soft, encouraging words to get me to relax. "Ssh, everything's fine. No one's going to get hurt. I'm not at summer camp this time. I'm here, Laney." He tugged my legs loose and sat me up. He pulled me into his lap and began to rock me until I stopped crying.

"See, I'm here. I'll always be here. I'm not going anywhere."

"But you did. You left me!" I clamped my hands over my ears to stop the loud banging coming from the windows. Priest grabbed my wrists and yanked them down.

"I said I'm not fucking leaving," he snarled. "I swear my life on it. I'm not going anywhere ever again. Why do you think I left Cunningham's?"

"What?"

"Never mind," he snapped. A shiver coursed through me, and Priest stood, taking me with him.

"Where are we going?"

"Nowhere. I'm just putting you in bed."

"You said you weren't going anywhere." My voice came out sharp and worried as he laid me down and lifted the blankets for me to climb under.

"I'm not. I would like to not lay in bed with jeans, however. Are you going to let me leave the room to go change into pajamas, or am I getting in bed with just my underwear?"

A belt buckle clinked. "Laney, tell me what you want."

RULE 14 - DELANEY
CHANNEL YOUR FEAR INTO SOMETHING ELSE.

"Stay with me."

My heart raced wildly as Priest removed his clothes to climb into bed. My cheeks itched from the sudden eruption of crying I'd just had. I hated how triggered I was by the dark, and yet, I couldn't fix that part of myself.

Neither could they.

I shook the dark, foggy, flashes of memories out of my head. Priest lifted the blanket and slid under with me, pulling me into his chest. He was warm and his muscles hard. I fought the urge to turn and run my hands down his chest so I could feel each line, and instead, shifted into a fetal position and let him wrap his body around me.

"You're gonna be all right, Laney. I'm here."

"But you weren't." I pouted, my chin beginning to quiver again. "You weren't and I was alone and the nanny—"

Flashes of that night mixed with my memories of the doctors in Shelley Vale. Over and over, they tried to make me forget, but the storms brought everything back. Priest placed a single finger on my lips to quiet me.

"I know. It was horrible. The babysitter abandoned you,

but you survived, and you've survived every storm since. This snow is going to pass over, and tomorrow, everything is going to be fine. You'll laugh."

"How do you know?" Despite my tears, with each inhale of Priest's sensual cologne, I found my heart slowing to a more manageable rate. I snuggled deeper into his embrace, and he tightened his hold around me. "I was supposed to spend all night..."

I didn't want to say. He'd make fun of me. Even now, at my most vulnerable, Priest would take whatever I said to him and use it to hurt me later.

"Playing with your new toy?" he teased.

I was confused for a moment, but then mortification flooded through me as I remembered Summer's gift. In my state of panic, I'd all but forgotten about the small, rose-shaped vibrator in my nightstand.

"No! I told you, I'm not going to use it."

His hands shifted, and my heart raced as his fingers traced down my bare thighs. He had a gentle touch, and my skin prickled at the sensation. What was he doing?

"Do you remember, the first storm after the tornado? When I came to your rescue? You were hiding in your closet and I pulled you out. We cuddled in bed just like this until morning."

I swallowed as his hand found the edge of my nightgown and began tracing my skin.

"Not like this. You had pajamas on," I pointed out. His warm, muscular thighs pressed against my own in a way I'd never felt before. It was... desire.

"And your nightgown wasn't thin and see-through. Back then, I was just a brother, almost as scared as his sister, trying to keep her calm. But now..." His hand dipped between my thighs, and I tensed. He stopped and breathed into my ear. "Things feel different."

"This is wrong, Priest," I murmured, but not with enough conviction. If it was wrong, why did it feel so... exciting? "It's bad." Suddenly, I felt like a child, back in our shared house. If our parents came in, they'd lose it. But we weren't at home, and I didn't have to stop him.

"I like being bad." He grazed the front of my panties with his thumb, and I gasped as my core pulsed. He chuckled and continued playing. "And I bet you do too."

If I'd known this would happen, I wouldn't have allowed him to see me in my nightgown. Or would I? No. I hadn't seen Priest in years. He'd been a complete and utter bully to me in our teen years. He was hurtful every second he got the chance to be. Yet, here he was now, cuddling me because of the storm.

"Tell me, Laney, has any man touched you here before?"

I closed my eyes and shook my head shamefully. Priest, my brother, was the first, and I still hadn't pushed him away. It felt... good.

"You certainly prepared for this week. You're so smooth." Priest slid his hand under my panties and cupped my freshly waxed mound. "He's not worthy."

"And you are?" My breathing hitched as he traced his fingers down the line that parted my lips. I arched my back, and as I pressed my ass against his hips, I felt...

Oh my god.

Priest was...

"This is what you've been doing to me for years, Laney." He ground his body against mine, pressing his huge... length into my behind. "This is why they sent you away. Why we couldn't live together anymore. Because I wanted you." Distracted by the size and his words, I had all but forgotten his hand between my thighs. That was until he slid a finger between my folds, and I gasped. "And you may not have realized it, but deep down you felt the same."

I'd stopped breathing as Priest slowly swirled around in my wetness, my *arousal*. My brother had done this to me. I'd let him touch me, hold me, make me wet, and now, I was about to...

"Oh..."

Priest found my clit. "How does this feel?" He shifted and rolled me onto my back. He loomed over me, his finger still taunting me with surreal pleasure.

"Gooood," I groaned and opened my eyes. It was dark, but now, I wasn't as terrified of the storm as I had been. I was too overwhelmed with feelings to think about what was happening outside.

Priest lifted my nightgown with his other hand and cupped my naked breast.

"You are fucking gorgeous," he gushed and bent down, taking a nipple into his mouth. My mouth parted as his tongue ran over the sensitive tip, bringing it to attention. "God fucking damn it, Laney." He lifted his head.

"What?"

"You're fucking perfect. And I refuse to let that stupid fuck be the first to make you come. That deserves to be me."

"Priest," I gasped, as he began to pick up the pace. "We need to stop. We've already gone too far. You're my—"

Priest bent down, licking my nipple, and drifted upward to my ear. "Will hearing me say it help you come, Laney baby? I'm your brother, and you fucking love this."

And just like that, my body exploded.

I stared down at Laney, panting, toes curling, smiling, as she came for the very first time. I had done that to her. My hands, my tongue, my words, had given her life's most ultimate pleasure.

Oh, I couldn't wait to do even more with my cock.

But that was for another time. Tonight was all about her pleasure, not mine. When her pussy stopped pulsing against my fingers, I pulled away and rolled her back into the spooning position.

"That was bad, Priest. We shouldn't have done that. I can't believe I just...we just—"

"That's what makes it feel so good. Knowing we shouldn't but giving in anyways." I ran my tongue along her shoulder. Her breath hitched.

"We can't do that again. It's wrong." She brushed my hand away from her breast.

"We can, and we will. We're going to get you through this storm."

"What are you talking about?"

My hand drifted back between her legs, pressing against her perfect little pussy, covered by her freshly dampened panties. "Did you not notice how little you paid attention to the storm while you were being pleasured?" I ran my fingers back up and down her slit, and she shuddered. "I told you I'm not going anywhere, and I wasn't lying. I'm going to spend the rest of the night, making you come over and over again until you forget where you are, what's going on, and why you were ever upset in the first place." I slid into her slickness. "All you're going to remember is that it's me making you feel this way, and you fucking like it."

"Ah!" She flinched when I pressed my thumb over her clit. She was still sensitive. I pulled my hand out and kissed her shoulders and neck. Tonight would be a slow torturous cycle for both of us.

"Priest, you can't tell anyone."

"Tell anyone what?" I teased, nipping her neck. "That I fingered my sister?"

She moaned.

"That you liked it?" I cupped her breast and then tugged at her taut nipple. "Or that after the first time, you wanted me to keep going?"

"All of the above," she groaned. "No one can know, like you said, it's our secret." Her hand reached for mine and pushed it down, past her belly and back into her panties. She was ready to go again. My cock throbbed, begging for attention, but I forced those thoughts out of my head and focused on Laney.

"Right. No one here can know that I'm your brother and that the first night here I did something naughty. But what about when we get back home?"

"No! Mom and Dad, they won't—"

Understand? Approve? Support? I'd spent the last four

years having that drilled into me each and every day. I was disgusting for thinking of Laney, my stepsister, the way I did. That I should be ashamed and find some other worthless cunt to fuck to oblivion. To take someone else. To save Laney's innocence, her purity. But that all went out the door when I saw her again. It was either me or no one.

"Sssh, baby, you're too tight, we need to relax you." I had to bite back the urge to tease her hole. I'd never been with a virgin. I'd never really cared about it before now, but the fact that Laney, my Laney, had waited, was incredibly hot. I would be the one to take her and claim her as mine.

My cock pressed against her ass, and I thought about that too. I'd take everything this week. Her ass, her pretty little cunt, and her mouth. As I peppered kisses all over her, my hand returned to her panties. I slid under them and with no hesitation spread her lips and dove in, she was drenched.

"You're fucking dripping, Laney," I told her with a kiss on her breast. "Do you always get this wet?"

"What do you mean?"

"When you're aroused, is it always like this?" I swirled my finger around, and she moaned lightly. She was ready for another orgasm.

"No, I don't think so. My undies have been damp, but nothing like this."

My cock wept at her answer. It begged me to take her now.

Now! Fuck waiting and letting her feel good. It took everything in me to stay in my boxer briefs and focus solely on her.

"I love that I did this to you. I wish it wasn't as dark. I want to see your pretty pussy, dripping for me. How does it feel, to know your big brother caused you to feel this good?"

"Wrong, bad, Priest."

My heart hammered as my fingers betrayed me, and I circled her hole. Just one deep, hard jab, and she'd be popped. Nothing to it, and then we can move on to the real fun.

Maybe even take that vibrator out and see how hard we could make her come.

No. I forced my fingers to focus somewhere else. Her clit was swollen and needy.

"I don't think we should keep going." She panted.

"Why, do I not make you feel good?" I picked up the pace, strumming her body like a guitar.

She responded with a low moan.

"I told you, Laney, you are going to spend the evening coming, over and over again, until your body can't take it anymore. Are you ready for number two?"

I nudged her dress up and took her nipple into my mouth, biting down just hard enough to get a gasp from her. I picked up the pace with my fingers and sucked on her breasts until I felt the familiar gush of wetness and the pulse of her body as she unraveled in my hand for the second time in an hour.

"I'm burning up!"

I laughed and opened the blanket for her to get some air.

"With the power out, the heat probably is too. Being hot is probably a good thing right now." I fanned her until she sighed and reached for my arm.

"Can you just... hold me?" Her voice was quiet, and for a moment, a low rumbling of guilt tightened in my belly. Suddenly, we weren't two fully-grown adults, doing what adults do when single, attractive, and alone together. We were kids again, and my little sister needed her big brother to make her feel safe. I could almost hear her thoughts as I pulled her to me and wrapped my arms around her tiny body.

Be here now since you weren't then.

I wanted to scream and remind her that I couldn't be there. I'd been at Risky Rush Overnight Camp. My first time. How was I supposed to know what would happen? It wasn't my fault.

Despite the rational side of me saying she couldn't blame

me for not being there, I understood why she did. I was her big brother, her defender, her savior. I was supposed to be there. There'd been no one to save her, to hold her and tell her everything would be okay. But tonight, and for the rest of our lives, there would be. I wasn't letting her go again.

Rule 16 - Priest
Don't trust anyone else to watch your final girl.

Eight years old.

"Did you have a fun time at Camp Risky, sweetie?" Mom asked. I sat in the back of the car with my damp bags and sleeping bag. The last few days of summer camp had thunderstorms so severe that we had to run and take shelter in the mess hall. All of our belongings that had been left in the cabins were soaked.

"It's Risky Rush Overnight Camp, Mom." I rolled my eyes. "I made a bracelet for Laney." I'd only made it because I'd been forced to do arts and crafts one of the afternoons because another camper had gotten hurt pretty badly and they didn't want anyone on the slides.

"You're such a good big brother."

I nodded. Sure, she was kind of annoying. She was six and I was eight. That was loads older. But despite having run out the door, so glad to be leaving for a week, I found myself missing Laney.

"Why didn't she come to pick me up at the airport?" I asked, looking at the empty seat on the other side of the car.

"She's with a nanny. We took a mini vacation ourselves." Dad and Mom shared a look, and I grimaced. I knew what that look meant. They wanted to make a baby.

"Which one?" I demanded.

"What was her name, sweetie?" Dad looked at Mom.

"Laurie, I think."

"That the Strode's girl?"

"Yes, darling."

"She had the fun one?" I crossed my arms and glared. Why couldn't I do something special and she just be stuck at home?

"Oh, it was just the weekend. I'm sure she misses her big brother. Don't worry, I don't think it was too much fun," Dad teased.

I napped at some point and woke up just as we were passing the welcome sign for town.

"Oh my god. I didn't realize the storm had been that bad," Mom gasped. I perked up and looked out the window. All over, people were standing in their yards with pieces of roof and wood in their hands. Firetrucks raced past us, and a few police cars were at various houses. People were crying and holding each other.

"What happened?" I asked.

"Well, they said a tornado touched down, but the news made it sound like there was barely any damage." Dad's face scrunched up.

"Ron, she didn't answer this morning," Mom muttered. She didn't want me to hear, but I had. He was talking about the babysitter.

"She was probably just busy with Delaney," Dad replied, but his tone made my stomach nervous.

"I'll just call her parents and see if they can get a hold of her." Mom pulled out her cell phone and made a call.

"Hello, hi. Yes, we just wanted to see if you've heard from Laurie today. She's not answering the phone back at home."

Mom visibly paled and her eyes widened.

"What? No, she was supposed to stay all weekend. Both nights! We paid her in advance! Oh my god, Ron, we need to get home." She hung up, and Dad floored the car.

"Laurie told her mom that we didn't need her for nights, and she came home and went out with her boyfriend. Both times!" Mom began to sob. "She called her mom last night to tell her she was sleeping at her boyfriend's and hasn't come home yet. Delaney has been alone almost the entire weekend!"

Dad was too angry to console her. His eyes lowered into slits and he gripped the steering wheel so tight his knuckles turned white. My stomach was a bundle of nerves as I tried to understand what was going on. Laney had been left alone during a tornado. I stared out the window at people holding their families and crying as they stood in front of their destroyed homes. What if ours had been torn down? With Laney inside?

We got home in record time and everyone flew out of the car and bound toward the front door, only to stop short all at once. There was a girl on our lawn, facedown, with a fence post going through her back. Her yellow sweater was a deep red all around the wood, and she looked like she'd been rained on all night. Mom's shrill scream caused me to look away from the body and Dad to take action.

"Go find your sister," he demanded as he pulled out his phone. I stormed into the house ran upstairs. I knew Laney more than anyone, if she'd survived, she was in her closet. Her door was locked. I shook my head and threw myself against the door.

"Did you find her?" Dad yelled up the stairs.

"I can't get the door open!"

Quickly, Dad joined me and pulled out his wallet. He slid a credit card down the slit to unlock it and shoved it open. Only, there was resistance.

"Delaney?" Dad yelled, panicked. "Delaney, it's daddy. We're here to save you. Are you okay?"

"Daddy?" A small sound came from across the room. "Is Priest with you?"

My heart soared as I heard her voice. She was okay.

"Yes, sweetie, he's right here next to me. I'm going to push the door open and you need to stay out of the way, okay?" All of the furniture her tiny body could move had been shoved against the door. The moment we were inside, Laney flew across the room from her closet and threw herself into my arms.

"It's okay." I hugged her tightly as we cried. "Everyone is okay."

"Not everyone." Dad sighed. I glared at him as I set Laney down. I didn't care even the slightest about that babysitter's death. She deserved it for what she did to Laney, *my Laney*.

Dad stared at me for a long moment. It was as if he was staring directly into my soul and knew my dark thoughts. He then looked from me to Laney. His face creased with uneasiness and he opened his mouth to speak, but Mom suddenly came into the room.

"Oh, thank god." She ran to Laney, scooping her up. "You're okay."

I saw the terrified look in Laney's eyes. She would never be okay.

Rule 17 - Delaney

Sleep finally took me against my will. With every kiss Priest planted on my body and every stroke on my wetness, my fears began to dissolve, leaving only lust for more.

I'd never felt like this before. I'd fallen asleep from sheer exhaustion, not being able to come anymore. My body was weak and my legs shook, but I felt... good.

Priest continued to tease me in my sleep. I knew because despite being so dead tired, I was still being petted and roused every once in a while. I kept my eyes closed and rolled to give him better access to my body, and he worked his magic on me, giving me another earth-shattering orgasm.

It wasn't until I finally woke up in the morning, shivering from the cold in the room, that it hit me. Priest, my brother, oh my god.

I flinched away from him. In the dim light, he looked so beautiful, so at peace. It was a stark contrast from myself. I felt disgusting and ugly and... insane. How could I have allowed this? I slid off the bed on the other side and put my feet firmly on the bone-chillingly cold floor. The electricity was still out.

I stood, and instantly my knees buckled. Jesus Christ. Priest had fondled me so much last night I couldn't walk. And yet, as much as I hated myself for it, my core ached for his touch. Arousal pooled between my legs at the memory of his fingers strumming my clit. I'd liked it. Each and every time he trailed his fingers across my thighs, I had liked it.

What kind of fucked up relationship was that? Steeling myself, I stood again and carefully walked to the bathroom. I still didn't like the dark, but it wasn't as bad. Priest had been right. Although I almost felt like Pavlov's dog. Instead of drooling at the sound of a bell, my body was seduced by what the darkness held.

Feeling the urge to pee, I shut the door softly and went to the toilet. With my panties at my ankles, I sobbed. What had I done?

I had saved myself for so long. I put sex up on this pedestal and had pushed away so many boys, only to let my stepbrother who I hadn't seen in years... How humiliating!

A cold knock on the door caused me to snatch my panties up and stand, flushing the toilet. "I'm about to shower!" I called. I couldn't look at Priest right now.

"Is the water warm enough for a shower?" he called from the other side of the door. I reached for the handles on the sink. Cold water sprang. I waited, but it didn't turn warm. Fuck. I sighed and sat on the rim of the tub.

"Go away, Priest."

"Laney, can we talk?" I was mortified. What if someone found out? "Laney, you need to open this door." He jiggled the handle.

"No! Just go! We shouldn't have done that."

"Laney," his voice had a warning to it. "open the door."

"No! I don't want to see you."

I relaxed my shoulders and then turned to look at my reflection in the mirror that stood from floor-to-ceiling and wall-to-wall. I looked like a mess. I stood and went to it, observing myself.

My makeup had been ruined from the crying, and I'd sweated off the remainder of the night. My face was flushed and my eyes were bloodshot. But I was more concerned with the rest of me. Did I look different?

I knew it was absurd. I hadn't actually had sex. I was still a virgin. While I couldn't give Moth my first touch or orgasm anymore, I still had my hymen. The clinical term wasn't sexy, but he wouldn't care. I was glad Priest had kept his massive package in his underwear last night. With how good I'd felt, I didn't know if I would have stopped him.

I raised my arms and my nightie rose so high you could see the round curves of my breasts. Oh, how stupid I'd been to invite Priest here! He was just a man, with the same urges as all the others. He saw me, wearing this ridiculous nightie, and couldn't help himself. With shaky hands, I undressed to stare at myself fully naked in the mirror.

My nipples were hard and darker than normal. I reached for one and winced. They were swollen and sensitive. I spun around, looking for hickeys or other love bites, and thankfully found none. I wasn't sure, as I reached for my pajamas if I was relieved or disappointed to see no change in me, other than simply being sore. Unlocking the door, I cautiously walked out into the living room where Priest sat, fully clothed, on the couch. He looked up at me with amusement, and I blushed.

"You should probably get dressed. It's a little cold." His eyes went to my chest, where my peaked nipples shone through the dress. .

"Okay," I said softly and rushed to my room to dress. Priest waited for me. I hadn't packed any practical clothes. We were going to be inside a warm hotel resort all week, not a rundown building with no power. I pulled on a dress and my winter coat, and together, we went downstairs.

Arden, the caretaker, was at the stairs, handing out flashlights to everyone as they came down. "Apologies. We lose power often during harsh weather."

"It's daytime, why do we need flashlights now?" Juniper complained a few steps ahead of us. "When will the power come back on?"

"Hopefully sometime tonight," Arden answered. "The path to town is blocked until the snow melts. There is no other way down the hill."

I shared a nervous look with Priest. Tristan waved us all into the banquet hall for breakfast.

"Well, we have a full week to let the snow melt. Until then, I say let's eat, then get started with the day's activities."

"Which are?" Annie joined us, sitting right beside Priest across from me. Jealousy flared inside me, and I blinked away the odd emotion. Why would I be jealous of my brother with a woman? That was how it should be. Not in bed with me, with his hands between my legs. Priest shifted away, putting an extra foot's distance between them.

"A haunted tour. Which is perfect with no power. We'll be able to fully experience everything the Vincent has to offer us. Perhaps we will see a spirit in the halls," Tristan said.

Gloriana came in, pushing a cart.

"Continental breakfast, as there is no way to heat bacon," she muttered, setting boxes of cereal on the table, along with pitchers of milk. I reached for the Froot Loops, and Annie snickered.

"How old are you, twelve?" She turned away from me. "You know, Priest, Delaney was telling Moth last night that she's still a virgin. She can't even legally drink. How lame."

"She's not terrible," he teased me.

"Well, if you ever get bored in your room with little Miss Froot Loops, come find me."

"Noted." Priest did something that made my breath stutter. Waiting for me to look up, he itched his nose and then inhaled. He made sure to maintain eye contact as he did so, stretching his arms afterward to make it look less conspicuous.

That was the hand he'd had between my legs for hours last night. My thighs clenched and my core ached as I recalled how skilled he was with them. Priest grinned wickedly at me, as if he could read my thoughts and reached for the Froot Loops as well.

"I don't think she's boring."

"It's cold, but we've got fires going in every fireplace," Tristan told us over our cold cereal.

"It's still pretty cold in here," Annie complained. "I can see my breath."

"Yes, well, put more layers on," Tristan snapped and turned back to the rest of us. "There will be brainstorming sessions in the Delambre room, and a write-in will take place in the Marion room, snacks and drinks will be provided in both. I personally plan on spending my morning in the Delambre room. Anyone else?"

Everyone looked around, but no one came forward right away.

"What are you going to do today, Priest?" Annie asked. He glanced at me, and I looked at my soggy cereal.

"I have some edits for a client due so I'm going to hang out in the write-in room." He shivered. "I'll grab my jacket too."

"Ooh, good idea. I'm on a deadline too. I'll join you and write for a few hours. If my hands get too cold, can I warm them in your coat?"

Priest stood quickly and offered his hand to me. "What are

you doing?" I looked around the table. Annie was glaring at me, Juniper had her eyes raised as if to say, 'Go with Priest', and Moth was... smiling at me.

"I'm gonna brainstorm. What do you say, Delaney? I can help you with your manuscript. Want to come with me?" The way Moth said that last question, with the double entendre, sent heat to my cheeks.

"Why don't you come with me?" Priest suggested. "Go put something warmer on and then decide."

I nodded and stood. "I'll see everyone in a bit."

Priest followed, and the moment we were on the stairs, he grabbed my wrist and spun me around. "You can't be alone with him."

"Who?" I said, knowing full well who he was referring to.

"Don't play stupid with me."

"You don't get to tell me what to do." I snatched my arm and hurried to our floor. I sped down the hall, with him quick at my tail. I pulled out my card and my hand shook as I opened the door and slid inside. I tried to shut the door on him, but he was fast and pushed his way inside. It was dumb to try anyway. Priest had his own key.

"He's bad news, Laney," Priest argued, following me to my bedroom.

"That's for me to decide. You can't just—" I let out a cry of frustration as I reached for my laptop bag.

"Can't what? Watch out for you?" he demanded.

"No!" I protested. "You can't tell me you aren't my brother and the next moment boss me around like one. So what if you went to school with Moth? Are you going to tell me he sleeps around? Newsflash, I know that already. I don't care!" I threw my hands up. "Moth isn't my one true love, but if I want to have some fun this Valentine's week, that's my right as an adult woman."

"You're not acting like an adult." He crossed his arms and

leaned against the doorframe. "Everything about you screams immature child."

"Really? Because if that's the case, then why did you..." I trembled at the memory of us in bed together just hours ago. Priest kicked off the door and came over to me, standing by the bed. He shoved the bag on the blankets. In the cold room, our breaths were visible and he stood so close they intermingled as he stared down at me.

"Did I not satisfy you enough last night? Do you need more?" His hand went to my hip, pulling me to him. His hard chest was warm against my freezing frame.

"No, but, it's wrong. We shouldn't have done that." I pushed him away. "I don't know what I'm doing," I admitted. "This whole thing is so fucked up. Some moments, it feels like we're total strangers, and the next you're the boy I grew up with. The one who sat under the tree at Christmas with me, who terrorized me. We shared baths together when we were little! Priest, you're—" I threw up my hands, and he slapped his palm across my mouth.

"Don't finish that sentence," he warned. He pulled me back to him, tightening his grip on my waist. "You're right. We were raised together, but at the end of the day, nothing is stopping us from feeling the way we do about each other."

We?

He smirked. "You deny being attracted to me?" His hand slid from my waist to cup my mound under my skirt. His finger pressed against my underwear, tracing my lips, wiggling deep, and pushing on my clit. "What are the odds that you're wet right now?"

His green eyes pierced into my soul, shattering it completely. My breathing became labored as I stared into them.

The odds were good.

I reached up and tugged on his fingers, and he let his hand drop from my lips.

"Why are you still treating me like your bratty little sister if you don't want people to know the truth?" I asked. "They'll figure it out."

Priest pushed my hair behind my neck.

"They won't." Tilting my head to the side, he scraped his teeth over my earlobe. Desire, need, *ache*, pooled between my legs. I gulped. No, this was wrong. Priest's hands drifted down my shoulders to my waist and hips. "You asked why I'm still treating you like my sister despite begging you not to tell anyone." His fingers tugged my top out of my skirt. "Maybe it's because I like how dirty it sounds."

I lost my breath completely when his fingers touched my bare midsection.

"How dirty what sounds?"

"Fucking my little sister."

"I don't understand," I said aloud, although it was more to me than him. "Why are you acting like this all of a sudden?"

Moments where we fought, and he picked on me in front of his friends, and was cruel in private—flashed in my head. Now, he suddenly flipped his opinion on me.

"All of a sudden?" Priest met my eyes with his dangerous ones. "Laney, why do you think you were sent away?"

"I-I can't remember." I shook my head. Flashes of doctor visits and harsh lights filled my mind. I stumbled out of his grasp. I put my hands over my temples. Why had I been sent away? "I don't know."

"Laney." Priest took a step closer to me. "Are you all right?"

I closed my eyes as my back hit a wall. "Yeah, I just... I don't remember a whole lot about..." The image of a female doctor with sharp features and cruel smile continued assaulting my brain. "I don't want to think about it anymore," I said quickly and swallowed.

"I don't know. But I take it my leaving had to do with you?" I shook my head, still in disbelief.

Priest nodded. "It did. I care deeply about you, and that's why I worry about you spending time alone with Moth. He's a pathological liar. He's a narcissist, who doesn't give a shit about you, and—"

"And what?" I had spent my high school years in Shelley Vale, a shitty, backward town, all because of Priest? What had he done? While I couldn't remember, I knew he hadn't touched me. He had done something even more sinister. Somewhere, buried deep inside my mind, I knew that he had hurt my soul more than my body. "What is so wrong with Moth that has you so insanely jealous over the thought of me being with him? I don't care if he's a liar, or likes himself too much or—"

"He's a psychopath, Laney."

Three years ago.

"**I** don't know, Priest. I could get fired." Chastity, the young, night nurse ran her hand through my hair and tugged lightly. "They already don't like me for befriending you guys."

I chuckled. Befriended? This pretty little slut just got done deep throating my cock. My cum was still on her tongue.

"Oh, come on, I thought you liked me." I pinched her chin. Chastity wasn't the first nurse I'd seduced while I'd been locked up in Cunningham's psychiatric facility. She was moderately attractive. I'd definitely had prettier and smarter, but none of them were who I truly wanted. None of them were Laney.

"I do," she whined. She'd come into my room to give me my nightly meds and took a break to blow me. She fucking loved sucking cock. I didn't even have to ask. "I do, but I also need this job. It pays well and it's so close to my apartment."

"Oh, right." I put on my false face. "I forget you have a life outside of here. Must be nice."

"Priest, don't be like that." She reached over and rubbed my back. I stiffened but forced myself to relax. I didn't like her enough to want her to touch me, but if I wanted her to do shit for me, it was a necessary evil. "It's not so bad in here. You have me."

"At night, sure. During the day, I have no one. And now we've got that new guy. I don't trust him. He's lying about himself. Chastity, you need to get me his file."

Chastity stood. "Fine. But I have to do it when no one's around. Some of these nurses love to catch people doing stuff they're not supposed to. Just the other day, Bridget told on Miranda because she'd offered one of the children her bag of chips! It was a whole big thing and a headache and I am not trying to have another memo sent out about being too nice to you guys."

"You are too nice." I stood and adjusted my soft blue standard-issue Cunningham pajama pants. I reached for her and moved in close as if to kiss her, getting her hopes up, just to dash them by quickly moving my lips to her ear to whisper. "But I like the nice nurses."

She swooned and then quickly left, promising to return later. She didn't, but when she came back the next night for my meds, she had a small packet of papers hidden under her shirt.

"Here. Read them and then give them back. I'll have to burn it or flush it or something once you're done. Bridget's suspicious of me. She saw me looking at the file last night. That's why I had to wait."

Timothy Burke, 19, admitted by family for violent behavior.

I skipped the family history and physical forms and quickly scanned the list of medicines he was on. Anti-psychotics, a lot of them. I'd been locked up in here with him for two months, I knew for a fact that the fucker wasn't taking any of them.

I continued reading and found pages and pages of incidents and statements from psychiatrists, all saying the same thing. He was a narcissist, a pathological liar, and based on the number of animals they'd found dead in his care, a psychopath. There had been an incident that went to trial, which wasn't fully listed, but the result was that he'd be doing a year here to pay for whatever he'd done.

I tossed the papers back at Chastity.

"Are you not happy?"

I stood and paced my small, beige room.

"No, I'm not fucking happy. How does he have a list that long and still get out in a year?"

"I-I don't know. His family must have some pull with the judges or something. Priest, he's really not that bad. He—"

"What, are you sucking his dick too?" She didn't answer, which told me enough. I laughed. "Wow, can't get enough crazy cock, huh? Do you like that? Bad boys?"

"Priest, you know you're not supposed to say that word."

I cocked my head to the side. "What? Crazy? Look around, sweetie, we're in a fucking loony bin. And good news for you, in ten months, you and that stupid little bug can be together on the outside." I went to the door and put my hand on the handle. It wouldn't open for me, but it was my way of telling her to leave.

"Priest, I don't want him. I want you. I love you." She rushed into my chest. I didn't touch her. She disgusted me.

"You're stupider than I thought if you love me." I jerked on the handle and it remained locked. "You'll have to wait a whole lot longer for me to get out. I'm a lifer."

"You never know," she said, but couldn't meet my gaze. She'd seen my file. We both knew I wasn't going anywhere.

"Leave, please. I need to be alone."

She left, tears falling silently down her face. I didn't give a shit about her feelings. I was tempted to tell someone what she'd done for me. If it weren't for the knowledge that I'd be put in isolation or given some more stupid therapy, I would have let her get fired.

That next morning at breakfast, a hard shoulder bumped into me. I turned quickly to see Moth glaring at me.

"I heard you had a visitor last night," he said. I looked down at his tray. Oatmeal in a paper bowl and a carton of milk, just like mine.

"What about it?" Much to my displeasure, he sat across from me and dug into his food.

"Oh, nothing. She was a bit upset. That you just threw her aside so quickly. She was so inconsolable, I had to choke her while I fucked her ass just so she'd stop crying over you." His eyes flickered with amusement, but mine were dull with boredom.

"Is that you bragging?" I snickered. "I don't give two fucks about the nurses. Take her."

"Oh, I will. Again and again. You see, Priest." He reached over and snatched the milk from my tray. He popped the tab open and drank it like a shot of alcohol, slamming it back down on the table when he was done. "I don't take kindly to people who can't mind their fucking business. What exactly were you looking for in my files?"

"You lied about why you were here. I knew it and wanted to see what the truth was."

"Oh, poor you." He frowned dramatically. "You're upset I lied in group? Must be weird, seeing a direct reflection of yourself, huh?"

His lips curled slowly upward, sending a chill through me. "You're not the only one who has some pull around here. I know what landed you here. No one believes your story, you know that. They know you did it."

"You're funny." I wiped my face with a napkin.

"No, you are the funny one, Priest Duvall." He kicked outward, hitting me directly in the shin. I winced, but didn't move anything but my eyes. They flickered to the guards and other medical staff walking around, watching us. If I reacted to Moth, I'd be sedated. "You know why you're so funny?" He laughed. "Because we're the same person, and yet I'm getting out, while you'll be here for the rest of your life. What a place to rot."

I had tried to explain to Laney, but she wasn't interested in hearing my words. She laughed off my concerns and fled the suite, running straight for Moth's violent arms. With no other choice but to follow and watch over her, I grabbed my laptop and headed down to the brainstorming group. Moth knew I wouldn't be able to participate, as I wasn't a writer. I was an editor. I cleaned up after the party. I wasn't actually invited.

When I walked into the Delambre room, I was confused to only find Moth inside, one leg crossed over the other, grinning smugly.

"What would an editor need to brainstorm?" he asked. I set my bag down on a side table and sat down in the chair across from him.

"Where is she?"

"Who? Oh, Delaney Duvall? Don't think that was lost on me. I remember your file well." He reached for a tumbler filled with amber liquid. "Why are you two lying to everyone?"

"I don't know what you're talking about."

"Really? Not a clue?" He glared at me and reached into

the cushion under him, pulling out a Michael Myers mask. "Just like you didn't put this in my room last night?"

I stared at it in confusion. He'd found one too? I shook my head in disbelief.

"I didn't. Moth—"

"Liar!" He leapt up and went to the doors, shutting them loudly and spinning back around to me. "I looked you up before the storm hit and we lost power. How'd you do it, Priest?"

I stood, my fists clenched at my sides, ready to finish what was started years ago. He snickered and sauntered closer. "Seriously. Cunningham's is tight. Even I couldn't get out early. How the fuck did you escape and not get caught?"

I wasn't going to indulge him. That was none of his fucking business. "You showed your hand too soon. I can't let you leave now. Be careful who you tell, or I'll have to kill them too."

He laughed. "You think you scare me?" Moth came closer and grabbed my shoulder, squeezing painfully. "That shit might have worked in the psych ward, but not here. You've got shit fucked up, Priest Duvall. We're not trapped here with you. You're all trapped in here with me."

I shoved him back, and he cackled. It made me cringe, remembering that same laugh from when we were together at Cunningham's. I hated him every second he was there and was so glad when he was released.

"Six months!" He clapped. "I'm genuinely impressed. And you kept your name and everything. Come on, I need to know how you did it. When they find your body after the storm passes, they'll want to interview me. I can see it now, man saves entire hotel from crazed murderer, escaped from asylum."

"You think you can kill me?"

"I don't *think* anything." He shrugged. "I would have let it go if you hadn't pulled that little prank. "You weren't the only one who could get whatever he wanted from those hot little nurses. I read your file too. They couldn't prove it, but your folks were so sure it was you that butchered that guy, they bypassed everything and got a judge to sign off on your sentence quietly, to avoid a trial. You got to leave that little town of yours quietly, with no media to know what you did, but they knew. Everyone knew, and they were embarrassed."

I grabbed my bag. If Laney wasn't here, I didn't need to be either. "I didn't do the mask. I don't know where that came from," I said and strode to the door. I wasn't lying, but now I was curious to see if the one I'd found was still in my room. Had someone taken it and put it in his?

"Really? It's an odd coincidence, don't you think? The guy your parents thought you murdered was killed by someone in the same mask. You don't think that's weird that me being the only one who could reveal your secret and send you back was given this in his room?" He went to it, picking it up and shaking it wildly like a real head. He tossed it at my feet.

"I don't know what you're trying to accomplish."

He put his hands on his hips and bobbed his head. "The only goal for this trip is fucking your little piece. Delaney Duvall. Your little sister. I knew you were twisted, but that's a whole new level of depraved." He chuckled. "I may be a killer, but at least I don't fuck my family."

He came over, picking up the mask. He slid it on and stared at me with his disgusting green eyes through the slits. "I spent a full year at Cunningham's being tortured by you. Now it's your turn." His voice was muffled through the mask. "Darling Delaney doesn't know what's in store for her this week. She wants to lose her seal, I can do that, but I'm not going to be nice about it."

I shoved him back but he only laughed as he caught himself.

"Jealous, Priest? I'm going to make that little girl scream. She's going to sob as I shove my cock into her dry, forcing her to tear and stretch."

Moth swung at me, his fist colliding with my jaw. I swung back, catching his shoulder.

"I'm going to take my cock, bloody from ripping her innocence, and shove it into her mouth. I'm going to force her to take me in every single one of her holes until she goes unconscious, and then I'll still keep going."

I caught the back of his calf and hooked his leg, dropping him to the ground. I lunged for him. I threw punch after punch, directly at his face, and all the while, he laughed. I was transported back in time, back to the asylum, where we'd go back and forth weekly, beating the shit out of each other, just for looking at the other wrong.

I grabbed his shoulders and lifted him so I could smash his head onto the floor. He grinned as his eyes glazed over. He was too far gone. He called me a psychopath, but he was worse than I could ever be.

"I'm going to make sure you never look at her the same way again. I'm going to make more than just her tight little cunt bleed."

I froze, which gave him the chance to roll us and he got in a punch. He raised his arm, and I knew his fist was aiming for my nose. I turned my head, and as his arm swung down, the door opened, and Tristan strode in.

"Woah, hold on now. What's going on?"

Moth shot up, brushing himself off. "I think someone is just a bit jealous of the attention my presence has on his suitemate."

"Is this so? Priest, this retreat is meant to be calming and pleasurable. Not some alpha show. While I do welcome you to join us, please be respectful of my guests."

I got up and snatched my laptop bag off the floor. "Got it. I'll go find something else to do." I rushed out of the room and jumped slightly when I turned and saw Carson lurking against the wall.

"Things not going as you planned?" My childhood friend smirked.

"Don't you have a fire to poke or something? It's pretty cold in here." I started down the hallway.

"There's not much we can do at this time. Still getting into fights over Delaney, I see."

"Fuck off, will you?" I started up the stairs to my room.

"Who knew such a small thing would trigger him so hard."

"What are you talking about?" I looked over at him and froze. "It was you! You put the mask in his room. Why?" I demanded. Carson grinned and shrugged a shoulder.

"I was bored. It's just a mask, right? A silly prank."

It was more than just a mask. Way more than he knew.

"What are you staring at?" The voice came from a beautiful Latina woman I didn't recognize.

After I left my suite, I'd gone exploring and found an empty lounge-like room. It looked more like a closet, but I needed to be alone, and this was perfect.

"Oh, I'm sorry. Is this your room?" I stood to go. We weren't the only guests this week, and I had forgotten all about the other people around the hotel. Had I stumbled upon someone's paid space by accident?

"No, although I do enjoy the view." She brushed past me and looked out the window, only to frown when she looked back at me. "Most of the time. I hate the winters here."

"You come here a lot?"

"Unfortunately. Do you? I've never seen you before."

"No, I'm just here with a group. We're doing this writing thing."

"Oh, I did see that in the lobby. Fun," she said with a loud layer of sarcasm. "If you're with a group, why are you up here alone?" She sat and patted beside her. Nervously, I sat back down.

"I had an argument with my b—suitemate," I corrected myself quickly. "He doesn't like the man I'm interested in."

"Oh? Does he have a say in that?"

"Not at all. That's why we were fighting."

"Maybe he's jealous. Is he attractive?" She brushed her long, shiny waves behind her shoulders.

"Who, Moth?"

"The one you're fighting with." She adjusted her shirt, revealing the edges of a tattoo on her collarbone.

"Oh, Priest. Yeah, I guess." Attractive was an understatement. Priest was probably the hottest person I'd ever seen in real life. Unfortunately for me, he was off-limits. Or, supposed to be, anyway.

"What's he look like? I wonder if I saw him already. I like to wander during the day."

"Dark hair, bright green eyes. They are stunning and deep. You can feel every emotion behind them."

"I think I did see him. Tall, built... Italian?"

"His dad is from Spain, actually, but yeah, that's him."

"Yeah, I saw him at the pool. He was in just his underwear..." A smile curled on her lips and she looked up at the ceiling. "It's been a long time since I've seen someone like that."

"Really? But you're... beautiful."

"Yes, but beauty is meant to be seen. No one sees me anymore, darling." She sighed deeply. "Except for people like you." She went to the bookcase, pulling a book from the shelf. "While I do kind of claim this as my space, consider it yours while you're here. I'll leave you alone to write or whatever you're doing. Feel free to read the books too. Some of them are pretty interesting." She waved the one in her hand at me and then set it back on the shelf.

I joined her and read the spines of the books. Most of them were classics or non-fiction.

"What are you writing?" she asked.

"Romance."

"I love romance. It's the greatest escape. What kind of romance? I always had a thing for men in kilts."

I perked up. "I love historical romance. But mine is more contemporary. It's a little dark."

"Dark?" She laughed. "What's that even mean?"

"She falls for the villain, not the hero."

"Oh, interesting." She nodded. "Is it spicy?" She crossed her arms and leaned against the bookshelf. "We need more of those on the shelves. Gloriana always takes them for herself when someone leaves them. Tell me about it. Actually, no, let me read it."

"I mean, I'm not published yet." I looked down at my feet. "I'm here to figure out how to write better."

"I see. So, no sexy book." She made a sour face.

"Not yet. Soon. Oh, you uh, your makeup is running." A black tear slid down one cheek. She rubbed it away, only to smear it across her face. "Oh, hold on." I turned around, looking for my bag. "I have a mirror."

"No!"

I fished my compact out, popped it open, and turned. "See, quick fix—"

The woman made eye contact with her reflection and screamed. I leapt back, confused as the beautiful woman burst into tears and her makeup began to seemingly melt off her face.

"Are you okay?" I shrank to the other side of the room. She was standing stiff as a board, sobbing and screaming as if she'd seen a ghost. She began blubbering through her screeching, but I had no idea what she was saying.

"Redrum! Nur! Won! Teg Tuo! Nur! Redrum! Redrum! Redrum!"

Unsure of what to do, I grabbed my things and bent down

to flee the room, but she caught me by the shirt and pulled me back.

"Redrum! Teg Tuo!"

"I don't know what you're saying!" Could no one hear us? "Let go of me!" I shoved her away and she fell back onto the bookcase. Books fell off the shelves and scattered all over the floor. She stopped screaming and fainted. I could not have pushed her that hard.

Silent and still, I reached out to make sure she was okay. I couldn't tell if she was breathing or not. I touched her hand and she bolted up. I leapt back with a yelp as she stood and fled the room so fast I didn't have time to fully comprehend what had just happened.

I shakily went to the open doorframe to peek down the hall. The hall was empty! I stepped out fully to double-check, but there was no one here.

What the hell?

A chill ran through me, but I forced myself to toss the feeling away. Maybe her room was on this floor, and she was so embarrassed she went back to clean herself up. I convinced myself of this before turning back into the little room I had found to gather my things.

Deciding I wouldn't be returning after I cleaned up, I picked up the books and set them back on the shelves. It wasn't until I started shoving them back into the empty spaces that I noticed how dusty the shelves were. If she came in here often, why did it look like no one had touched this stuff in ages?

I picked up a particularly heavy book and paused. It was large, like a dictionary, and bound in red leather. I turned it over to look at the cover.

Arachnophobia.

There was no author listed. I held it in my hands, even more curious. Arachnophobia, wasn't that the fear of spiders?

I began to flip through the aged, yellow, crackled blank pages, only to find nothing but more empty pages.

A flash of red caught my eye. I went back to find the page and found splotches of deep maroon all over the page. It was the color of blood, and it looked... damp. This was fresh.

I put a finger on a splotch and confirmed that it was still wet. As my hand rested on the book page, something small and black came from the center crease in the book. I pulled my hand back as I realized it was a spider. But it wasn't just one. A dozen of them burst from the center!

I screamed and dropped the book, only for it to cause a stir. A hundred tiny black beasts exploded out of the book and rushed over my feet! I backed up quickly, only to fall over the coffee table and land on my ass. The spiders seemed to multiply into a hoard, climbing over my legs and arms.

I screamed again and brushed them off me, but they kept coming. More and more spiders wiggled around and crawled over me. I grabbed my bag and turned to run out the door, only to freeze in horror.

It was a blank wall.

Rule 22 - Delaney

I clawed at the wall as the sound of hundreds of spiders scurrying around the small room filled my ears. Where had the door gone? I pounded my fists at the solid surface and sobbed, as I continued to brush the tiny, black, terrifying things off me.

The book.

I hurried to where it was on the floor, pages open, spiders continuing to pour out, and quickly slammed it shut.

For a moment, I thought they would all disappear. It was just a figment of my imagination. The girl who had come in before had spooked me, making me create this horrible situation all in my mind. But no. The book shook in my hands and then burst open, spiders spilling onto my hands, my arms, and crawling up my body.

I screamed and brushed them off, returning to the wall to pound, only to find a door handle now. I quickly turned it. The wall opened and I fled the room as fast as I could, screaming and continuing to rub my arms and kick my legs to get the spiders off.

I ran down to my room, sobbing. I tossed my bag on the

couch and stripped down in the living room, not caring if Priest was here or not, and hurried to the bathroom to shower.

As I ran the chill water, spiders tumbled to the tile from my hair. I stared at them in shock as they slid down the drain. I slid down and let the water run over me until my teeth chattered. The room, having no windows and no electricity, grew dark, and only when I couldn't see anymore, did I stand and turn the water off.

I'd washed my hair and body, but I could still feel them crawling all over me. Shivering, I dried myself as best as I could and went to the living room, where my spider-ridden clothes had been folded and sat on the couch, and a fire had been lit in the fireplace. I went to it, still wrapped in my towel, and attempted to warm what I could. The door opened a while later, and I stood just as Priest walked in.

"I wondered where you'd run off to." He gave me a fake smile. "Did you get any writing done before your laptop died? Mine just shut off."

"I—What time is it?" I asked instead, stepping away from the fire.

"It's almost six. Dinner should be soon. You want to get dressed and go down together? I heard they're doing a tour around nine."

"Sure, yeah." I dug through my clothes, looking for something warm. I huffed as I found nothing that would keep my teeth from chattering or my knees knocking together. I had planned for a week of seducing, not a week with no heat. I put on my red baby doll dress and the longest socks I had that went to my knees. I added my winter coat, but it did little to warm me.

Looking in the mirror, I felt utterly foolish. My cheeks were puffy from crying all afternoon, my eyes looked tired from the stress of the spiders. I was never going to get Moth or anyone else's attention looking like this! Glancing at the clock, I grabbed my makeup bag and quickly did what I could. Priest knocked on my door just as I was putting my setting spray on.

"You look nice. Cold, but nice," he said as we went down to dinner together.

"Thanks, you too." I looked him up and down. He wore a black button-up and jeans but had styled his hair to look a little messy, which made him even more... sexy. My stomach fluttered at the word. Could I say that? Could and should were two different things.

At dinner, I was distracted. I kept feeling the little legs of spiders on my skin. It was all so confusing. Who was that woman?

At night, I found myself agreeing to go on the ghost tour with the group. Priest, who decided not to go after all, tried to convince me to go back to the room, but the look in his eyes told me how he intended on spending the evening. What happened last night couldn't happen again.

"I'll keep an eye on her." Moth put his arm around me and pulled me toward the group before I could explain to Priest why it was a bad idea for us to be alone. Which, oddly enough, despite knowing better, I still wanted us to be alone. I didn't really want to go with Moth and the others. Was I losing my interest in Moth already? Because of Priest?

My core pulsed, remembering last night. No, it was a good thing to go with Moth. Moth was safe. I was allowed to love Moth. But I didn't.

I looked back as we started up the stairs for the tour, and saw Priest watching me with careful, yet sad eyes as I went with Moth and the others.

The tour was done with flashlights. Gloriana led the tour, telling us all about each person who had died in each room. Her tone was so deadpan, and her voice so dry, that I was catching myself dreaming about other things. So much so that

I found myself abandoned on the third floor. I looked around and called out.

"Moth? Annie? Juniper? Where did you guys go?" I stepped out of the room and into the pitch-black hall. "Hello?"

The fear of darkness crept back in. I didn't have Priest to save me tonight. I turned back into the room as shadows darkened everything, so I could see only shapes of things and nothing else. My heart raced as I hurried to the curtains, drawing them open, only to see nothing but black outside. I turned again, my body readying itself for a panic attack when a figure stepped into the doorframe. I squeaked as I jumped and fell against the wall.

"Moth?" The figure was male and large. I could see that. That left only a few people it could be. The figure cocked his head but didn't speak. Instead, he stepped inside the room.

My eyes were adjusting, but only slightly. Enough to see that whoever it was had a mask on. Was that...the guy from those Halloween movies? I laughed, despite my clammy palms and racing breath.

"Michael Myers? Where did you even get that? Did you bring it with you?" I asked Moth. Despite the mask covering his face, I knew who it was. No one else knew I was up here. He must have waited for me and then once the group had gone on, put the mask on and come looking for me.

Despite knowing who it was, the way he stalked slowly toward me, almost menacingly, was... thrilling. I pressed my back to the wall and shrunk into myself.

"What are you doing? Let's go find the group."

Michael Myers shook his head. I squinted, trying to see more of him. He was shrouded in darkness. He reached up, bringing his hand to my throat and squeezing gently. His other hand went to my sex, cupping me between my thighs.

I gasped and arched my back. I closed my eyes and focused

on steadying my breath. "What are you doing, Mr. Myers?" I teased. My masked man let me go and as I inhaled, he lifted me, cupping my ass and pulling me into the center of the room. I wrapped my arms around his neck. I could take the mask off right now and see who it was, but... I didn't want to. Moth wanted to be kinky? I could be kinky.

He sat me down on something hard and roughly pulled me to the edge. In a flash, he was down on his knees, shoving my thighs open.

"Someone is going to find us." I tried to shut my legs but he squeezed and looked up at me. I stared at the faceless man for a long moment. This was a dream come true. Moth, wanting me, and so quickly. I thought it would take more than one day for us to be like this.

He shook his head and reached under my skirt. His fingers found my panties and swiped them aside, diving into my wetness with an urgency that only made me hotter. I let out a sharp gasp and he pulled away. Standing, he reached into his pocket, pulling out a scarf. Without speaking, he brought it to my face, wrapping it around my eyes.

This didn't feel like a game anymore. "I don't know if we should do this. I don't like the dark."

My masked man returned to to his knees and pushed my thighs apart more.

"Do I know you?" I asked weakly. Silence. This was all part of the game, I realized. I inhaled deeply, bracing myself. The man took his mask off and dove under my skirt. His tongue found my folds and I shivered as he ran it up my slit.

"Oh," I gasped. He chuckled and used his fingers to spread me further, tasting me, teasing me. Keeping my eyes closed under my blindfold, I fisted his hair and pushed him deeper between my legs. I needed more. It felt so good. It was intense and I could feel my orgasm building as the unknown man lapped at my body like it was his job to make me come. He found my clit and focused on it, running his tongue in circles, and sucking. I screamed as suddenly my orgasm overtook me and my body erupted in warm waves.

The man continued to lick until I came down and shoved him away from my sensitive body. He snatched the mask up and shoved it back over his head before removing himself from between my thighs. He stood and removed my blindfold, stuffing it back into his pocket. I stared into the darkness in awe. Despite the ugly mask, this man was beautiful to me.

He put a finger up to his rubber lips. I nodded. I wouldn't tell a soul what had just happened. Something in me had been awakened, and I wasn't going to sleep.

Despite the lights having turned on shortly after Laney returned to the room yesterday evening, she had them turned off this morning and chose to let the fire brighten the room. She sat by it with a small smile on her face, holding a mug of warm cocoa that Gloriana had brought up to compensate for the power outage.

"What's got you so happy?" I cocked an eyebrow. I was just coming up from some morning laps in the pool. The water was freezing, but the pain felt good. It reminded me of when I was a teenager, taking tacks and safety pins and sliding them down my arms, pushing them just enough to hurt but not leave lasting damage. It was apt, that I'd want to feel pain like this again, as I'd started hurting myself right around the time I realized I had feelings for my sister. My stepsister. I had to constantly remind myself that little bit. It was the most important part of our situation.

"Nothing. I finally feel inspired to write." She sighed wistfully. "Hopefully the rest of the week will be just as productive. I wrote so much this morning."

"Is that so?" I sat on the chair across from her. "What were you writing about?"

She blushed. God, I loved making her embarrassed. She was so damn cute.

"I don't think I'm ready to share my stuff yet."

I leaned forward. "You're lying. Laney, were you writing smut this morning?" I grinned. "You were. I want to read it!" I eyed the laptop resting beside her on the couch. She saw my line of vision and snatched it up.

"Absolutely not. I can't. Not you. Especially not you."

"Why not? Reading smut is my job. People pay me good money to read their filthy thoughts." I stood and went to her. I pinched her chin and tilted her head up. "I'd love to read yours, Laney darling."

Her chest heaved as she stared up at me with her large, beautiful brown eyes. "I can't. It's too personal." She turned away. "I'm sorry. You can't read it."

"Personal? What does that mean? Is it a self-insert? I mean, that's not terrible. It could be done well if you know what you're doing," I rambled on, my editor brain taking over. "I really wouldn't mind taking a look at it and—"

She blurted out, "It's a real experience. I don't think it's appropriate for you to read it."

"Why?" I laughed. "I was there."

Laney, you dirty girl. It was on the tip of my tongue to ask if she touched herself as she wrote about us. My cock throbbed as the image of her in bed with her legs spread and her head thrown back as she fingered herself traveled through my mind. The idea was hot as hell.

"No, you weren't."

The words hit me like ice water. Harder than ice water. I'd just been in ice water and this was worse. It was like my body had been shoved into a glass window and I felt every last shred of sharp broken glass.

"What?"

Laney hung her head. "You weren't there, Priest."

"What the fuck are you talking about?" I demanded. My hands shook at the idea of someone else touching Laney as I'd touched her.

"I don't want to talk about it." She stood and ducked under me, clutching her laptop to her chest.

I spun her around. "Like hell, Delaney Duvall. Who the fuck has been touching you?"

She tugged, but I refused to let her go.

"You're hurting me."

"I don't give a fuck. Answer my question."

She continued to fight against my grip, and I squeezed harder. Growing more and more angry with each passing second, I grabbed the computer from her.

"It was Moth!" she cried out. I dropped my hold on her.

"Moth?"

Flashes of that blond bastard thrusting his cock into my beautiful Laney caused my brain to short-circuit.

"Yes. Moth. The man I told you I was interested in. The whole reason I'm here. I wanted to learn about sex and now I am. He's an excellent teacher, if you must know." She reached for the computer in my hands and I gave it to her.

"Excellent?" I laughed. "Was I not good?"

"You were, but that was different. That was—" She looked down at her feet.

I stepped toward her, pressing my chest against hers. "Was what? Was Moth able to make you come over and over all night long with just this?" I raised my hand and flexed my pointer finger.

"I'm not talking about this with you."

"Fine. Show me."

"What?"

"Show me. Show me exactly what was so captivating that you had to write about it."

"You're insane."

"Call the doctors and have them take me away." My hand went to her shoulder, rubbing it gently. "Come on, Laney, darling, my beautiful sister, show me what exactly he did that you liked so much. I want to see if I can do better."

"And what if I don't let you read my book?" She stared up at me with a mix of defiance and fear. It was beautiful. She had spirit. She wanted to fight this sexual tension between us, but I'd break her. By the time this retreat was over, she wouldn't be thinking of Moth. I'd be the only man for her. I'd have her begging for me to stop making her come while simultaneously pleading for me to keep going.

I didn't escape captivity for nothing.

"Then I'll just have to assume I was right, and that Moth isn't shit compared to me. So, are you going to let me read what you wrote?"

RULE 24 - PRIEST
MEMORIZE HER PASSWORDS.

"Fine." She clenched her eyes shut, and I opened her laptop.

"What's the password?" I asked.

"Figure it out yourself."

"Fine." I shrugged and typed in passwords she'd used as kids, finding 5980, still in use. The computer beeped, signaling that it was booting up for me. She paled.

"How did you—"

"I told you, I know you better than you know yourself. You like to use important dates as codes."

She huffed but said nothing as her screen lit up and the document she'd been working on popped right up without me having to dig.

"Oh look, it's right here." I began to read the words she'd written about the encounter that had inspired her so. It was only a few pages, but the prose... wasn't too bad.

"Happy now that you've humiliated me?" she snapped.

I shut the computer. Humiliated? She hadn't experienced anything yet.

"This was you and Moth?" I snickered.

"Yes. We were doing the tour and I got distracted and left behind. He came back for me."

"And ate you out while wearing a bunny mask?"

"No, I changed the mask. If you must know, it was one of those rubber ones you get from the Halloween store. I didn't want to write about exact details."

"Honestly, the entire chapter reads like pure fiction," I mocked. "I know Moth, and this isn't him."

"Oh, really? You sound so jealous right now." Laney stood and reached for her laptop. "Which is absurd, considering—"

I pulled her to me, crushing my lips down onto hers. Her eyes widened, but she didn't move away. The longer I pressed my mouth against hers, the more she softened, and her lips parted. She let out a small groan. My hands slid down to cup her ass, squeezing it tightly.

"It hurts that you think Moth is that good of a lover." I pulled away from her lips, only to kiss her jaw and then neck. "It's like choosing a finger-painting over the fucking Mona Lisa. Why not go for the masterpiece?"

"I never liked the Mona Lisa."

"Really?" My hand slid under her skirt and over the front of her panties. They were damp. "You aren't attracted to me? You don't want my tongue between your thighs like in your story?"

Like last night.

"It wasn't you in my story," she protested. "It was just a man in a mask."

"Moth?"

"Last night, for me, it was. In my story, it could be anyone."

"I find that hard to believe that Moth inspired anything like that."

"Stop." She sighed but didn't brush my hand away as I

teased along the edges of the fabric. "It has nothing to do with Moth. It's the darkness I liked."

The darkness? I looked past her, suddenly understanding. In the dark, it could be anyone she wanted. She turned from me, covering her face in her hands.

"It's embarrassing. I told you my writing needed work. You shouldn't have read it."

"I don't think that's it." I pulled her back, facing away from me. My hard cock pressed against her ass. "You just need more experience, like you said. Your words..." I paused. "It read like you barely knew the female anatomy." An idea came to me then, something to satisfy both our lusts. "I could help you."

"What do you mean?" She tried to turn back but I held her firmly, my hands gliding back down her body, pulling up her skirt. I drifted over her panties again.

"Why don't I show you how to get yourself off? Learn what feels good and figure out what exactly you want."

"I don't know..."

"I won't be touching you. Just watching."

"You want to watch me?" she gasped. I brushed her hair back to expose her bare neck.

"I do. What do you say, Laney? Let big brother watch you make yourself come?" There was a pause, where I could hear our hearts hammering, matching each other's rhythm, waiting for one of us to refuse. But the moment never came.

"Okay." Laney reached for my hand and led me to her room. I followed behind like a dutiful puppy. Finally, Laney was letting me into her world.

"What am I supposed to do?" she asked when she closed the door of her bedroom.

"Go to the bed and get comfortable." I found a chair in the corner and sat, choosing to keep it in its place, rather than moving it closer. Laney was slow, her hands shook as she climbed onto the massive bed.

"I can't just turn my body on and off," she said.

I gripped the arms of the chair. "Take off your panties, Laney." She did as told. "Good girl," I offered. "Now touch yourself."

"Like..." Her voice shook. "Like you did?"

"Exactly." She looked absolutely terrified, and it turned me on immensely. "Are you wet?" I asked, knowing she was.

"Yes, but I'm not..."

Another idea came to me. "Laney, would you like me to read to you?"

"What?"

I pulled out my phone and looked in my email inbox for my latest manuscript from one of my authors. "Grab the toy from your bedside table, and I'm going to read to you while you pleasure yourself." When I didn't hear anything, I insisted, "Laney, do what your big brother tells you."

As if those were the magic words, Laney leaned over and pulled the drawer open, grabbing the box. She pulled out the toy, a rose.

"Press the button." She did and it whirred to life. "Now press it to your clit."

She looked over at me, and I nodded. Slowly, she lowered the vibrating machine and then her head fell back.

"Oh."

I laughed and brought my phone to eye level.

"Gabriel's eyes drifted over Helena's body, ready and wanting. He'd waited years to touch her, and now, he was going to finally have his way with her."

Laney had relaxed in bed.

"Do you like it?" I asked her.

"It's... strong." She panted.

"I want you to turn it off and listen to my words. You're going to use your fingers to come today, understand?"

"Mhmm..." She turned it off and dropped it onto the bed, her fingers quickly diving between her legs.

"When I speak to you, I want you to address me as brother or big brother, understand?"

"Yes, big brother."

I cleared my throat and continued reading. "Helena slid down her robe, exposing her breasts to the cold air. Gabriel bent down, taking a nipple into his mouth, running his tongue along it until she groaned."

As if on cue, Laney let out a groan of her own. My gaze flicked to the bed for only a moment, finding Laney slowly massaging herself. My cock throbbed painfully in my pants. I wanted to play, but once again, I had to remind myself that it wasn't time yet. My hand drifted to my jeans and I massaged my cock through them.

Continuing to read, I tried to focus on both my phone and the beautiful girl, now a woman, on the bed, unraveling just by the sound of my voice. If my words did this to her, I couldn't wait to see what my cock did.

Laney whimpered as her movements sped up. It was beautiful, and I found myself rubbing my jeans at the same pace. I didn't care if it made a mess, I'd deal with it later. I was determined to come right with her.

"Gabriel, now satisfied that Helena had been teased enough, positioned his cock between her pussy lips and thrust into her."

"Ah!" Laney let out a deep moan as she came, and I froze as my orgasm was brought on by hers. Much like her, the sound of her voice had been my undoing.

Both of us sat breathless in the dark.

"How do you feel?" I asked. "Do you understand how to please yourself now?"

"Yes," she whispered.

"Yes?" I lowered my head.

"Yes, big brother."

"Good, now you don't need to bother trying to get with Moth or any other stupid piece of shit. You can do it yourself like a good girl."

She looked so peaceful, so beautiful. I left the room quietly, going to my own. I changed and cleaned myself up, wiping the cum off my thigh. It was noon, and I had shit to handle.

Heading to the exit door, I grabbed the Michael Myer's mask off the side table and left to find my competition.

"What the fuck do you want?" I found Moth in one of the many studies, with his feet propped up and reading a book. I stormed over and kicked his feet off the coffee table.

"Did you touch her?"

"Who?" He slammed the book closed and sat forward. "Oh, you mean that pretty little virgin? Not yet. Why? Is she asking about me?" He stood and reached into his pocket. "I'm going out for a smoke. I'm not going to continue pandering to your whiny bullshit."

"You better keep your hands off her."

"You better mind your own fucking business." He walked toward the exit, pulling out his phone. "She gave me her number last night. I should text her, see what she's up to. You think she's thinking about me?" He laughed as he left the room, leaving me to fume. I needed to see that phone.

The rest of the day I sat in wait. I watched him from the windows go out to the back of the hotel to smoke. I caught him a few times leaving from the same door. The maze loomed just ahead of him. While I waited for the sun to go down, I planned.

At dinner, Moth insisted that Laney sit with him. They laughed and whispered to each other. He would say something to her and then grin at me, knowing how much it was getting under my skin. But not for much longer. As I sipped my wine across the table, I wondered if Laney knew it wasn't him under that mask last night, if she'd still be giggling with him tonight.

It should be me she had her hand on. Me that she was texting. I was the one whose face had been buried between her thighs, after all.

She'd tasted so sweet...

After dinner, while everyone discussed their writing over drinks, I explored the hotel, gathering what I'd need for tonight. There wasn't much I needed. The mask was already in my possession, and I'd found an axe right next to a fire extinguisher on my floor.

Moth's addiction to nicotine and pussy that wasn't his was going to be his utter downfall. Watching the clock, I knew he'd be getting up to smoke soon. Concealing myself in the shadow, I waited for him to go through the doors. What a pleasant surprise to hear him tell everyone goodnight.

"I'm going to go do something artistic. Laney, you've inspired me. I'll text you later, sweetie." He spun around to leave.

Laney? That was *my name* for her.

He opened the door, and the wind was so loud, he didn't hear me follow him out. The door slammed shut behind him, and he didn't turn. Instead, he quickly lit his cigarette and began walking through the snow toward the maze.

Stretching my shoulders, I pulled the mask from my coat and shoved it over my head. The rubber shielded my face from the harsh weather. Moth peered into the maze as if unsure. I wasn't going to give him the choice. It wasn't until he finished his cigarette and turned to go back inside that he saw me standing there. He jumped and his eyes went wide.

"Jesus fucking Christ." He looked me up and down, his eyes landing on the axe in my hand. "What is this, some fucked up joke?" He snickered, but when I didn't move, he frowned.

"This isn't funny." He stepped back toward the maze. "I don't have a coat."

Oh, but he didn't need one.

I took a step, and he matched me, taking one back.

"Is this because I flirted with your sister?" He snickered. "You think scaring me is going to make me back off?" Moth straightened. "Nice fucking try. You don't scare me, Priest."

I lifted the axe and swung it. Moth jumped and fled into the maze.

Here we go.

I cracked my neck and strode into the maze after him. While he had the advantage inside the hotel, with everyone on his side and the speed to catch me off guard, I had the advantage here. I'd made myself familiar with every twist, turn, and wall. I walked slowly, listening for his heavy breathing and the crunch of his boots on the snow.

I turned and swung the axe, only managing to get a scream. His cries were lost in the howling wind.

"What the fuck is your problem?" he shouted, stepping out from his hiding spot. "You wanted me dead then too. I knew it. I could see it in your eyes every time you looked at me in group. They said our rap sheet was the same, but I knew you were far worse than I ever was."

I didn't answer. I was going to let him do all the talking. He backed away slowly, shaking his head. "No, it all makes sense now. It was because of her, wasn't it? The guy you killed, was he trying to get with her?" Moth stopped walking. "She's your sister, dude."

I shook my head slowly.

I didn't care if he knew the truth now. He'd be dead soon. Harsh wind paled his face even more. His lips began to tremble. I could see the recollection of my file in his eyes. It was all coming together for him. Marco Brandis, murdered by axe. They never found the killer, but I was the main suspect.

I lifted the axe and he took off again, tripping and scurrying back up. He knew I wasn't playing. He had to get out before I could catch him, but that wasn't going to happen. Hearing him on the other side of a wall, I swung my axe out, and this time, I felt the impact of metal on flesh. *Squelch.*

I let him flee, clutching his arm, now spurting blood. It wouldn't be long now. I followed behind, aiming for his legs this time. I caught him close to the exit but managed to trip him instead of maiming him. Moth fell onto the snow, staining the white ground red.

"Please, don't. I won't touch her. She's all yours, man."

I stepped over him, pinning him under me.

"I don't even like her. She's just a quick lay. I'm not going to take her from you." He pleaded.

I raised my arms and the axe over my head, poising to deal the final blow, when suddenly Moth's eyes went from panicked to overjoyed as he raised his good arm and clicked open a pocketknife, jamming it right into the back of my calf.

Grunting, I fell to my knees, sitting on his chest. Moth lost his breath but managed a cackle as he drove the knife deeper into me. I dropped the axe from one hand and swung my fist at his face, landing square on his nose. It crunched under my knuckles. Blood spurted from his face, causing him to fall back. I took the distraction to tear the knife from my calf and toss it aside. I could have stabbed him directly in the chest and ended it now, but I wasn't ready.

Taking a deep breath, I pulled the mask off. We both knew it was me, anyway.

"Out of all the people my little sister could have had a crush on, it had to be you."

"I always fucking hated you," he said, while still clutching his nose. "They kept saying we had the same mind, but even I'm not sick enough to fuck my sister."

"Oh right, you're just a serial killer. Killing the less dead, right?" My hand drifted back to the axe, and I wrapped my fingers around the cold, wooden handle. "Did you stop after you got out, or did you just get better?"

He chuckled, and blood spurted out and onto my jacket. "Do we ever stop? What do you think my real plans were for this week? To write a book? I haven't written shit my entire life. My parents hired a ghostwriter and I play the part. I'm just a shitty tattoo artist who's here because Tristan wanted to kill—"

"Kill who?"

"The virgin. I didn't realize she'd be that fucking hot."

"You're more deranged than I thought." He was going to kill Delaney this week? If I hadn't been there, he would have!

"They let me out, so they must have thought it was okay. But you'll never escape Cunningham's. Did you ever truly leave Priest Duvall?"

I brought the axe to my lap and then passed it to my other hand. Slowly, I began to lift it over my head.

"I wouldn't be too concerned about me, Moth. It's you who won't be leaving." I swung the axe down and split his head right down the middle. I stood, my leg shooting with pain from being stabbed, and then grabbed the mask, sliding it back on.

I stared at his body. He was still in the maze. He wouldn't be found for a while. Deciding to leave him there, I stepped toward the exit and then paused. I went back to him and dug into his pockets until I found his phone, keys to his room, and wallet. I grabbed his hand and used his pointer finger to unlock the phone. Just then, a text came through from Laney.

Delaney: Are you still up?

Did I want to keep this ruse up? That it was Moth she was with, and not me? I'd have to change the code on this asap if I did. Fuck it, I decided, and typed back.

Moth: For you, I can be.

RULE 26- DELANEY
KNOW WHO YOU'RE TALKING TO.

I rolled my eyes at his text.

All evening, after dinner at the bar, Annie and Juniper had been making comments about my age. Moth and I spent hours exchanging knowing looks. I was far from innocent. He'd made sure of that last night in the study.

My belly fluttered. Should I go for it?

My bedroom was dead silent. I could hear the crackling of the fire in the next room. The door opened in the other room and my eyes flicked to mine, checking again to make sure it was locked. If this were really happening, I didn't need Priest storming in. Especially after this afternoon. Another thing I'd have to talk to him about. I needed to draw clear lines for us. It was easy when he wasn't around to say we shouldn't do those things, but when he was here, right in front of me, it was a whole different ball game.

A second door opened and shut, telling me that Priest had gone to his room. A moment later, my phone lit up.

> Moth: I didn't think you could be dirty. Why don't you show me what you mean?

Was he asking what I thought he was asking?

> Moth: I'll show you mine if you show me yours.

Oh my god. I looked down. I was ready for this, I reassured myself. After drinks, I'd gone up and taken a long, luxurious bath. Then, I curled my hair, reapplied my makeup, and put on my sexiest nightie. I knew that tonight was the night based on how much Moth was touching my thigh under the table at dinner.

I turned the camera on my phone and aimed it to take a selfie showing off my ample cleavage. It was too dark to see anything. I stood and went to the window, opening the curtains to search for moonlight. I took the picture, and it wasn't until I sent it that I saw that my nipples showed very clearly through my dress. My nerves went crazy, but... this was what I wanted... right?

A picture for me came through a moment later, and I found my heart racing. I'd never seen... not one that wasn't in a movie before. This photo was meant for me. Or, was this one he sent to multiple girls? My paranoia and self-doubt washed over me. What if he still saw me as immature and silly? A text came through, pulling at my curiosity enough to click the photo.

Moth: I did something. Let me know what you think.

I clicked the photo and gasped. It wasn't the whole thing, just the base, which was... thick. But that wasn't what I'd been meant to focus on. I looked past his rigid length, past the well-groomed tussle of dark hair, and stared at the cursive tattoo on his lower hip. It said my name.

Laney.

I typed back furiously.

Me: You didn't.

Moth: I did. I knew bringing my equipment would come in handy. Do you like it?

My mind raced. I thought back to that first evening. He had said he was taking an apprenticeship. But he was meant to tattoo Tristan, not himself! And not... my name.

Moth: I've been practicing on oranges, but I had to do this. You inspired me last night, Laney.

Moth: Care to see the rest of me?

I counted my heartbeat. Did I?

Moth: Did I scare you off?

The second text brought me back to earth.

Me: No. I just... I'm nervous. In a good way.

Moth: How can I make it less scary?

I bit my lip and replied before I lost the nerve.

Me: Wear the mask?

It took almost five full minutes before my phone lit up again.

Moth: Kinky. You got it. Open the door when
I knock.

Me: When are you coming?

I sat in bed for forty minutes before I heard a knock and hurried to the door. I looked out the peephole and my jaw dropped. He was wearing the mask. I opened the door an inch and suddenly it was being shoved open and a hand was on my throat. My masked man squeezed firmly, but not enough to cause pain. I gasped as he pushed me toward my bed and tossed me onto it.

I felt just how trapped I was in here with him. But I wasn't scared. Nervous, yes. But ready.

"I thought you weren't going to come," I said when he pulled his hand from my neck, allowing me to breathe.

Michael, Moth, whoever he was, shook his head. He reached into his pocket and pulled out the long black scarf from the night before, and then another. He watched me carefully, and I didn't understand until he snatched my wrist and roughly tugged me upward on the bed, quickly tying me to the post. I was too shocked to fight as he did the other one just as fast and soon I was bound and at the mercy of Michael Myers.

I pulled on the restraints but it bit into my skin and nothing else. I wasn't going anywhere.

Michael lifted my legs into the air like I was a rag doll and tugged on my panties. This wasn't at all how I expected my first time to be, but I wasn't mad. My core ached with desire. I needed to be touched. My legs fell open after he pulled my panties off and brought them to his mask. He inhaled deeply and I shuddered at how... invasive that felt. He stuffed my panties into his pocket and moved over me.

His hands went to my breasts, fondling me over the night-gown, eventually tugging on it until it ripped, making my breasts spill out. He tweaked them with one hand, while the other went to the wetness between my legs and began to massage me. I groaned as he toyed with my body, bringing me close to the edge and then stopping, only to do it all over again.

"More," I gasped. "I can't do this anymore. I need more," I begged. Michael cocked his head and nodded. It felt so grim, so dark, so... sexy. The idea that he couldn't speak, and had to communicate with just his hands and body turned me on immensely.

Michael stood on his knees and began tugging on his belt. He slid his clothes down, and my eyes zeroed in on the tattoo of my name, right at the top of the V in his hips. He did that for me. Why? Had I made him feel so strongly? He had branded himself for me. What did that mean? The tattoo had me so enraptured, I didn't even notice the eight-inch, thick and stiff cock pointing directly at me.

"Do you have a condom?" I asked. Michael shook his

head. "I have them. In my suitcase." I nodded to the closet. He reached for my thighs, positioning himself between them and shook his head again. I laughed nervously. "Do you want me to get pregnant?"

He nodded, and butterflies fluttered in my stomach. I laughed, but when he didn't, I realized he was serious. We really weren't using a condom. He reached for his cock, stroking it as he positioned it against my folds.

"Don't hurt me," I whimpered, suddenly scared of how big his cock was. Michael thrust his hips, ignoring me completely. I cried out as he entered me. It felt like a weird bubble bursting and then pain. I was being stretched and it hurt! He waited a moment before pulling out some and then did it again. Tears slid down my cheeks as he ignored my cries and fucked me. And the crazy part was, I was happy. These tears weren't just ones of pain, but of pleasure too. It felt good to not be treated like a princess. To be treated like a toy that was meant for him.

He lifted my ass and pushed deeper into me, hitting something that felt... interesting. The pain of my first time soon disappeared as Michael used his hands to roam my body, pinching my nipples and teasing my clit. A different kind of pleasure took the place of pain, and I found myself gasping and moaning and then... exploding.

I'd heard stories and been told not to expect an orgasm my first time, but he'd done it. My masked lover had figured it out. He watched me unravel under him, and once I'd stopped shaking, he gripped my hips and thrust harder into me. I cried out, as he stretched me and fucked me into abandon, making me sob and beg to be let free, but he didn't listen. He continued to thrust until suddenly his body stiffened, shuddered, and his cock pulsed inside me. It took me a moment, between my own feelings, to realize he'd orgasmed.

He pulled out quickly, slid his pants back up, and then

leaned over, putting his hand around my throat. As I stared up at the masked man, a flash of something passed through my mind. Something I'd been told to forget. My brain squeezed in pain, and I gasped as I tried to remember. I closed my eyes and tried to focus on breathing, and then, it came to me.

The mask and what had happened to Marco Brandis.

Three years ago.

"Delaney, are you there?" Fingers snapped in front of my face, and I blinked out of my catatonic state. I looked up at the doctor. He'd made another house call.

"Yes. I'm here."

"It doesn't seem so," he said. "What's wrong this time?"

"I don't know." I squinted, trying to remember what I was doing before everything went black. "I was handing out candy. On Halloween." I looked down at myself. I was still in my costume.

The doctor nodded. I didn't like this one. I'd seen a handful since I'd been sent away. Doctors and psychiatrists and other professionals of the mind. They all asked the same questions. Why was I constantly blacking out? I'd like to know that answer myself.

"Yes, you were. And then your aunt came home and found you on the couch, candy everywhere, staring straight ahead. Now, we've discovered you don't like storms, but the weather is warm and clear tonight. Your spell must be from something else."

My aunt stood behind the doctor, her arms crossed and a scowl pasted onto her face. She reminded me of Carrie White's mom in Stephen King's *Carrie*. I remembered when I borrowed the book from the library and accidentally left it on the kitchen counter, she lost her shit. I knew I should have apologized, but I couldn't stop laughing at how similar she was acting to the character in the book. And here she was now, at it again.

"I think it's all got to do with—" she started but the doctor cut her off.

"I know. She's been with you for over a year now, correct?" She nodded.

"And still no change. I think the trauma of that event has caused her mind to create a shield. Any time she sees something that may trigger that memory, she shuts down."

"Well, it's a little hard to figure out what it is when she's still protecting the boy," my aunt snapped.

The boy? Who? Priest, my brother? We weren't close anymore. Hell, since I've been here, he hadn't once called or wrote to me. Why would I be protecting him? What had he done?

"I don't know what you're talking about," I told them. Both adults shared a look.

"We can take her to the facility if you'd like," the doctor offered. "There are some more tests we can run, but I'm almost sure this is what is happening, and we won't be able to treat it until she talks."

"I always said to my sister those two were too close. Stepsiblings should be just that. Step. Not raised together like blood. That's where they went wrong and look now!" She threw her hands up. "Both of them are heading to loony bins!"

"Priest is in a loony bin?" I stood. "Why?"

My aunt crossed herself and turned away. She waved to the doctor beside me. "Do what you need to do. I can't handle her. You have my full permission to do whatever you think will fix her."

Fix me?

"Well, ma'am, making her forget isn't always the best solution. Therapy can help her work through—"

"No! I am not spending thousands of dollars and hours of my time taking her to and from just to talk to someone about her sins. I am putting her mind in you and the Lord's care."

With a sigh, the doctor pulled out his cell phone, and moments later, two large men came into the house and beelined for me. My head whipped back and forth and I tried to run but they caught me before I could take a single step.

"Nice try," one of them growled. "Let's go."

I was taken from the house and put into an ambulance by force, with me kicking and screaming the entire way. My aunt rode in the front with the doctor, who had her signing form after form on the way in..

Signing my life away.

How could this happen? I was a good kid! I hardly ever talked back, I did all the chores she asked of me, and I was on the honor roll. I'd been brought here for... why had I been brought here? I tried to remember, but I couldn't. One day I was at home, with Mom and Dad and Priest. We were a happy family, going on family vacations and having large holidays. Everything was perfect. Then, it wasn't. I don't know what happened, but I'd been taken from home and put here as punishment for whatever it was. According to my aunt, it had to do with Priest.

When we got to the building that didn't really look like a hospital, they forced an IV into my hand and, whatever they pumped me with, caused me to fall asleep in the wheelchair I'd been strapped to. I woke up in a hospital bed, with arm restraints. Green light flickered above me, and the air reeked of... staleness. As if I were the first visitor in decades.

"Hello!" My voice echoed through the room. "What's going on?"

Someone's shoes clicked sharply down the hallway and a nurse came into the room. "Yes?"

"Why am I tied up?" I pulled on my arms.

"The doctor has to talk to you. I'll tell him you're awake." She left before I could protest, returning later with the doctor from before. He untied me, and I sat up.

"I don't think you're a threat, Delaney. You're just scared." His voice was calming. I was scared. Scared, confused, and hurt. While some of my memories were fuzzy, the ones of my aunt taking me here were not.

"Where's my aunt?"

"We took her home. She wants you to stay with us for a while. I wanted to discuss your options."

"Options?" I didn't understand.

"Yes. Tell me what exactly you're hiding about Priest Duvall. Why do children in costumes trigger you enough to black out?"

I shook my head. "I don't know. I'm not hiding anything."

He clicked his tongue. "Your aunt seemed interested in one of our treatments for people with trauma. It's fairly new to our facility, but people have been doing it for decades. You would be our first patient to undergo the procedure here."

A jolt of fear hit me and slid down my spine. "Don't I have a say?"

"You are sixteen, so no. However, I wanted to explain what it is and what it will do." He pulled papers off his clipboard, handing them to me. I stared at the paper.

Electroconvulsive Therapy

"What?" I quickly scanned the text underneath the title.

"We've tried other treatments. You've been seen by a dozen

other doctors, and nothing has worked. Delaney, your aunt is out of money and ideas. This is your last chance before she sends you to a permanent facility."

"She can't force me to go anywhere." I tossed the papers back at him and started to get out of bed. "I'll be homeless before I agree to let you zap my brain."

"Brian." The doctor's calm, kind demeanor shifted in an instant. He stormed out and an orderly in a Michael Myers mask came and grabbed me, tossing me back on the bed. I let out a shriek and fought as hard as I could.

"Get away from me!" I screamed and kicked him square in the face. Why was he wearing that mask?

"Stop kicking, little girl!" Suddenly, his hand was at my throat squeezing. I gasped and my eyes went wide as he kept tightening his grip. My vision developed black spots and I was out again. I awoke later, completely strapped down, and a large white light above me, blinding me.

"You hurt one of our staff, Delaney," the doctor said from somewhere I couldn't see. "I will give you one last chance. Tell us what Priest did, and why you can't handle seeing the mask."

"What?" Michael Myers stepped into my vision. Memories of Priest flashed in my mind. The fight we had on Valentine's Day... over what? I couldn't remember! I screamed and they shoved something in my mouth and jerked my chin up. I fought against my restraints as they explained that because I misbehaved, they'd be foregoing the anesthesia.

"I'm sorry it's come to this, Delaney, but it's time to fix you."

I screamed and burst into tears. My hands clawed at my head neck and hips. They had belted me down as they shocked me into unconsciousness. I remembered now. All of it. Shock after shock. Treatment after treatment, until I could hardly remember anything about Priest's past middle school. Everything about our lives together when I was fifteen had been shocked into oblivion. They wanted me to be 'normal' and forgetting Priest had done that. But I remembered now. My masked lover, grabbing my throat helped me to remember.

I was in danger.

I t felt so... invigorating. I stood naked in my locked room, staring at my reflection in the tall mirror. Blood covered my cock, evidence that I had taken Laney's virginity. Not Moth, not Marco Brandis, *me*.

The mask lay on the bed in a deflated heap. She'd been so into it. With her wrists tied to the bed and my hand around her neck, she'd had such a powerful orgasm. I'd never taken a girl's virginity, but even I knew it was rare for it to be pleasurable enough for them to come. I admired my cock, already stirring. The dried blood was a badge of honor. I'd done that to her.

And I'd do it again. I was sure of that. She liked the mask and what that meant. It could be anyone under it, and it was. She'd been texting Moth's phone, expecting him to come to her room. Right now, she thinks she fucked Moth, but that wasn't the truth. With great reluctance, I grabbed a towel and wrapped it around my waist to shower. Despite the sick fascination with her blood, I had to wash off the evidence of what I'd done.

As I was passing through the shared living room, I heard

crying coming from Laney's room. I paused. Did she regret losing her virginity to Moth? Or was she in pain? I considered going to her. I could be the hero. The man in the mask had abandoned her, but I would never do that. Not her big brother. I was here for her.

Realizing just how fucked up the thought was, I hurried to the bathroom to wash and decided that if she was still crying when I was clean, I'd go to comfort her. Much to my relief, when I returned to my room, she'd stopped sobbing. However, the guilt of knowing she was upset drew me to her. I dressed and went to her door. I tried the knob but it was locked.

"Laney?" There was no response. Either she was asleep or didn't want me to see her crying. I left her alone and returned to my room. I was too excited from this evening's activities to simply go to bed. I glanced at my phone. It was midnight. Most of the guests would have gone to their rooms already, but I wanted a drink and conversation. I didn't care with who. Just... someone.

Grabbing my wallet, I walked to my door and hesitated. I turned and went back for the mask, sliding it over my head. I knew I looked ridiculous. A long-sleeved flannel and jeans with a Michael Myers mask, but I was curious to see how long it would take for someone to realize it was me.

I took the stairs slowly, silently, as if truly embodying the famous slasher villain. I followed the piano music back to the bar and was surprised at how full it still was. I looked around, searching for the other writers, but found none. Carson sat at a table with two women. Skipping the invite, I went right over to them and sat. They greeted me warmly.

"Hello." A blonde offered me her hand. "I'm Steph. This is Polina, she's from Russia."

Polina, the brunette, tipped her cocktail at me and

continued the conversation with Carson as if nothing was out of the ordinary. Steph focused on me.

"So, Michael, I like the silent type. They make me scream the loudest." She laughed and put her hand on my thigh. I jerked away. She was sloshed. Carson recognized me. We exchanged looks, and I could see it in his eyes that he knew who I was, but instead of calling me out, he kept the charade and inserted me into the conversation.

"Michael and I went to school together. Actually, him, me, and Delaney did."

"Which one is that?" Steph asked.

"The Hispanic girl, young, beautiful," Carson described.

"The one every male here wants," Polina said, her accent thicker than I had imagined. "Including you." She nodded to me.

"I saw her. The one dressed in all pink and going around telling everyone how pure she is. I was like that, once. I have half a mind to kick her out into the snow and lock the doors!" Steph announced. "Save everyone from that."

"Calm down, no one's forgetting you," Carson told her. "You're still The Vincent's reigning beauty."

"Damn straight." She lifted her glass. "I've stayed here far too long to be anything less."

Carson flicked a glance at me. "How long has it been, Steph?"

"What year is it?" She slurred her words. "Because I got here in 1980. Right after my summer at that shitty camp. They wanted to fire me, for the accident, but I told them I quit! I was done with my community service. I was going to come here and spend the winter prepping for the Miss... whatever pageant, and then I'd be famous!" She grabbed her drink. "I guess I was wrong."

"Don't listen to her." Polina waved her friend off. "She

should be the one at your writer's retreat! Always with the stories."

"It's true!" Steph gasped, putting a finger up. "It's true. I had big dreams and this place took them from me."

I looked around the table in utter confusion. Polina and Steph went back and forth, with Carson interjecting occasionally while turning to me and asking how I was enjoying the hotel. I answered with nods and head shakes. Suddenly, Steph reached under the table and grabbed my cock. I shoved her hand away and she tried again.

"Oh, come on. Don't tell me you're hung up on that girl. After what she did to you? She put you in that place, practically locked the key, and swallowed it."

I turned to her curiously. Why did she know so much about me? She grinned, but I noticed it didn't reach her eyes.

"Didn't you stop to think of how surprised she was to see you? Almost as if she thought you were locked away forever?"

I gulped. I hadn't. Did this complete stranger know Laney? If so, that meant that Laney knew... everything.

"She knows what you did. She knows and that's why she was crying."

In a blink, everyone in the room was gone except Steph and I. The silence was deafening as she opened her mouth, and it began to stretch far past human capacity. I watched in horror as her jaw unhinged and her skin ripped away, exposing muscle and other red disgusting bits. I stood quickly, my chair falling to the ground. I didn't care. I needed to get away.

Steph's arms began to grow and stretch, just like her mouth had, stretching until it couldn't anymore and then it tore, her arms falling with loud thuds onto the ground.

"What's wrong? Am I not beautiful?" Her voice called out, despite having no mouth. An arm dug its fingers into the carpet and began to drag itself toward me. I fell flat on my back. "Do you want her more? Why? She's not special. *I'm special.*"

I rolled over, narrowly escaping capture.

"You can hide behind the mask, but we all know the truth. Your beauty hides darkness. She knows it. She knows the truth. Confess!"

Sweat poured inside the mask, and I ripped it off my head, taking in a deep breath of chill air. The monster lifted her head to look at me, and with a quick shudder, her arms and head flew back to her, pulling together and righting her back to her original state.

"Don't want to hide anymore?" she asked, pouting her lower lip. My chest heaved as I stared at her, trying to understand what I'd just seen. The chair I'd fallen over was still on the ground. It hadn't been my imagination.

"What do you want from me?" I asked.

"Not me. Her." She pointed her finger to the ceiling. "Confess to what you've done, before she catches on. You can't hide the truth forever. About yourself, about the man you killed. Secrets are what this hotel feeds on. You don't want to end up like me."

A figure walked from the shadows, hands in his pockets. My entire body chilled as Moth stepped into the light, the large gash where I split his head down the middle just hours ago still bleeding and pulsing. He waved as if he didn't know the wound was there.

"Or me."

RULE 29 - PRIEST
MOTHS ARE A DANGEROUS PEST.

Two years ago.

Moth sat across from me in the circle, his arms crossed and that shit-eating grin plastered on his face. Everyone left, including the therapist, leaving just Moth and I to stare each other down.

"Tomorrow is visitor day. Will your family come to see you, Priest?"

I grit my teeth. When he confronted me about looking at his files, he'd been right. Our diagnoses were very similar.

"I think my mom, dad, and my sister will be showing up tomorrow. My mom will cry, and my dad will sigh and apologize a lot. My sister will sit on her phone the entire time. She doesn't care that I'm stuck here. Sisters, am I right?"

I glared at him.

"Why is your dad apologizing? You're the one that killed someone."

"Yes, but"—he put a finger up—"it was a less dead. No one cared."

"Less dead?"

"People no one cares about. No one was looking for her. I made a few mistakes, but that won't happen again." He stood and stretched.

Again? He made eye contact with me and laughed dryly. "What, you think she was my first? No, just the first to be found. Now, come on, Priest. Let's go play chess."

I stood but went the other way. He asked me every day to play chess, and every day, I refused. I noticed that he never played with anyone else either, so the offer was just another game of his I didn't understand.

At dinner, Moth made sure to sit at my table and bring a few others along with him. He spent the entire meal discussing visitor day.

"What about you, Ricky? You got family coming?"

Ricky, a middle-aged black man with extreme OCD, nodded. He was one of the more tolerable residents here. He had his way of doing things and was soft-spoken. I knew from past visitor days that he would have at least six to eight people come, and they'd regale him with gifts to help his stay. He was one of the luckier people in here.

I tuned them out and ate my watery potatoes and bland carrots quickly. I finished eating, but there were still twenty minutes for dinner, and we weren't allowed to leave until then. Begrudgingly, I put my tray away and returned to my seat just as Moth started to talk about his sister.

"Tara, she's the worst. Two years younger than me. She put our parents through way worse than I ever did. Boy after boy, in our house. There was a tape that was thrown around at school. It was a fucking mess, and as the big brother, I had to always clean it up. My dad turned gray in just a year! What about you, Priest? What's Delaney like?"

The entire table's eyes shot over to me. My fists clenched under the table. How did he know about Laney?

"Who's Delaney?" Peter, a younger kid with pale skin and

freckles all over, asked. Moth, still grinning, looked around and feigned confusion.

"Delaney is Priest's sister. Did you not know that?"

"Priest doesn't have visitors," Peter said. "Not since I've been here."

"He's the only one who doesn't," Ricky added.

Oh, fuck off, Ricky.

"I guess that makes sense, considering what he did." Moth reached over and put his hand over my shoulders. I was on top of him in an instant, my fist going into his face, over and over again.

"You don't get to say her name!" I shouted as I swung at him. Orderlies came and pulled me off him. Two held me back, and another two were picking him up. Moth was grinning, as blood trickled from his nose. He managed to do exactly what he'd wanted. Now I looked like the maniac, not him.

"Fuck you!" I spat. He laughed, and they dragged us both out of the dining hall and tossed us into our rooms.

"You know better than to start trouble with the other patients, Priest," Jack, the orderly who'd been in charge of me, chastised. "I'm going to lock you in early tonight. I suggest you find some way to calm down, or they aren't going to let you out for three days. You shook Ricky up."

I gave him the middle finger and went to my small, square window with the bars on it. The night had just started to come. It was hours before lights out. Jack left and I heard the click of the lock on my door. It was going to be a long night.

The next morning, I was woken up by a doctor with calming meds. If I wanted to leave my room today, I'd have to assure them I was okay It took a full hour of assuring him I was fine. I lied about what Moth had said.

"He was teasing me about not having visitors."

"When you said, 'You don't get to say her name.' Who were you referring to?"

"His victim. He was bragging about it."

"I see, and you feel a certain protection over the dead girl."

I furrowed my brows in confusion. Did he not care that Moth was openly admitting to murder?

"Not really. I don't like being around someone who brags about killing people."

"Is it because you feel guilty about what you did?"

Hardly.

"I don't know what you're talking about." I wanted to roll my eyes but refrained. They'd been trying since day one to get me to confess to Marco's death, but I wasn't that easy. I especially wasn't being taken down by a guy who called himself Moth. "I can't feel guilt for something I didn't do. I feel anger that I'm stuck here, while he gets to go free just because his family has some ties to people in town."

The doctor sighed. "Have you ever considered that it's not solely that his family is wealthy, but that Moth acknowledges and admits to his crimes? He's taking accountability for killing that woman. They say the unknown is far scarier than the monster you do know. When Moth leaves Cunningham, he'll be monitored and given little opportunity to kill again. We know his triggers and how to help him not have the urge ." He stood, and went to the door, unlocking it. "With you, we have no idea where to start. So you might want to make friends. A lifetime can be very lonely here."

Rule 30 - Delaney
Don't get locked in… anywhere.

I woke up in the morning to my entire body stiff and sore. I stood on shaky legs and went to the mirror. I had bruises on my neck and thighs, but otherwise… I looked like I'd had the time of my life.

The bed had a big stain on it, which was embarrassing. I pulled the sheets off, tossed them in the corner, and called to request new bedding.

I was grateful that Priest wasn't around so that I could shower and change in peace. After what had been so brutally brought back to my mind last night after those moments of complete passion, I wasn't sure if I could look at Priest the same. He'd killed Marco Brandis because of me. I reminded myself as I put my makeup on to text Moth and ask what he knew about Cunningham's, and any details from him and Priest's time there.

I was exiting my room with my laptop in tow just as a maid was coming down the hall with new blankets. I hurried away, mildly embarrassed about what she'd find when she entered my room and ran straight into a hard, familiar chest.

"Priest!" I gasped as his hands went around me. I pushed

back, scurrying out of his arms. "You scared me!" I looked up into his eyes. They had large bags under them, and his smile was weak.

"Sorry. You okay?" he asked. I patted my bag on my side.

"I'm fine. I was just—" I paused, but then decided it was time to rip off the Band-Aid for good. "I'm going to go see if Moth wants to do some writing together."

"Fun," he said in a dull tone and went into his room as if he didn't care. Maybe he didn't, I realized, as I stared after him. Good. This was how things should be. He shouldn't care who I was sleeping with. I took a deep breath and went downstairs, texting Moth on the way.

> Me: Where you at? We should write together today.

The response came much later.

> Moth: Not feeling great. Gonna sleep in. Hit me up later.

"Delaney, are we still on for that today?" Tristan pulled me from my phone.

"On for what?"

"Our class on the human body. You were going to pose for us."

My heart skipped a beat as I remembered what I'd agreed to. He wanted me to be nude. "Oh, I mean, sure. We've been kind of relaxed with everything so I wasn't sure if we were still doing that."

"Yes, well, I'd like to get in a few of the things I had planned before the week is out. Although it looks like we may be stuck a day or two longer. We're still blocked in." He frowned. "How about after lunch? That'll give me time to prepare the room and run you through the details."

"Sure." I agreed and promised to meet him in an hour in the Delambre room for a briefing. My stomach churned with unease as I set my laptop up and attempted to write during that hour. I had so desperately wanted to write a passionate story during this week. Something to show off to that agent who told me I sucked, but everything that inspired me to write was so... dark. I couldn't show a soul.

By the time Tristan returned for me, I was still staring at a blank screen, with the memories of last night still running through my head. Was it bad to have enjoyed being tossed around so hard? Was there something wrong with me to crave being choked? Had they damaged my brain when they shocked me, or was this who I always was? I followed Tristan to the other room, and he closed the door behind us.

The room was a study, but had been rearranged to fit small, individual tables and chairs. In the center of the room was a short pillar with a black cloth draped over it. He pointed to it.

"That's where you'll be. We can have you sitting prim and proper at first as everyone walks in. Smile and wave, get people relaxed." We looked at each other for a long moment before I realized he expected me to go do it now. Nervously, I stepped over to it and climbed onto the pillar.

"I have a gown to drape over you." He went to a table and raised a red cloth. "Would you like to try it on now?"

I shook my head. "I'm sure it fits." I swallowed the lump in my throat. My eyes flickered to the door. If this was just a run-down of things, why had he locked it?

"Delaney," He clicked his tongue. "Don't be shy. We're all professionals here. We come to learn. Most of us are introverts by nature and rely on people like you who are willing to teach us." Slowly, he came toward me, stepping behind the pillar. He leaned in, his breath hot on my neck as he brushed my hair away from it, sending a chill through me. "And in return, I could teach you."

"What do you mean?" I shifted uncomfortably.

Tristan's hand went to my waist, and I jumped. With his other hand, he gripped my arm and squeezed, holding me in place. His hand moved lower. I pressed my thighs together.

"I know you're a virgin. And we don't want to ruin that," he whispered. I closed my eyes as his fingers tried to shove my legs open. "But there are other things we can do. Have you ever had your pussy licked?" His tongue slid up my neck, and I pushed him away and jumped off the pillar.

"No, thank you."

His hand caught my wrist and tugged me back to him. I fought his grasp but he was strong.

"Why not? I'm handsome, smart, and have connections. You want to be a published author one day, don't you, Delaney?" He squeezed me against him and forced his tongue into my mouth. Out of reflex, I bit down, and he yelped, finally releasing me. He winced but then chuckled. "I like a girl with a little bite."

I hurried to the door and found it locked. I tugged on it, hoping at least someone would hear and come help me. "Why are you doing this?" I demanded.

"Why?" He laughed. "Because we're stuck up here for god only knows how long, and Summer, the girl I had planned on fucking, didn't show up. I need someone to blow me, so if it can't be her, might as well be you." He reached for his belt and I turned back to the door and pounded my fist into it. "We can have a lot of fun without popping that cherry."

Tears began to streak down my face as I continued to fight with the door to open. Then, just as Tristan was squeezing my ass, the handle jiggled from the other side.

"You need a key, and I'm the only one with it," he snarled. "It's okay, little virgin, I won't hurt you."

"I'm not a virgin!" I screamed just as the door burst open and both of us flew back. I scurried up and ran toward my rescuer, throwing myself at them. I looked up and found Priest. Flames filled his emerald eyes as he stared past me at Tristan.

"Care to explain why this door was locked?"

An angry Priest loomed over Tristan.

"How did you get a key? This is a closed room until after lunch," Tristan said, crashing into a set of desks.

Priest stalked toward him, grabbing him by the shirt once he was within reach and lifting him in the air. Priest was trim, with a swimmer's body, but he was strong too. Tristan kicked and struggled to get out of his grasp, but Priest wasn't letting go.

"Closed, sure, but locked? Doesn't that feel a bit predatory?"

Tristan scoffed. "It's only predatory if you make it so. I did nothing wrong."

"Priest," I gulped. "It's fine. I'm okay."

"What's going on in here?" Annie's voice came from the hall, and she appeared in the doorway. Priest dropped Tristan quickly and he fell to the ground with an *oomph*. Annie crossed her arms and shook her head at the scene. "Someone get a little too handsy with the virgin?"

I rolled my eyes. It was on the tip of my tongue to

announce again that I was no longer a virgin as of last night, but, when my eyes flicked to Priest, guilt pooled in my belly. I hadn't wanted him to find out like this.

Tristan didn't read the room, and as he stood and brushed himself off, he waved his arm in my direction and scowled. "According to her, she's not anymore."

"What?" Annie's face paled. "Since when?" Her face turned from smugness to shock to anger in just a matter of seconds. Something about her face irritated me.

"It's no one's business besides mine and the other person involved." I turned to Tristan. "I'm not doing this anymore. Find someone else to get naked and assault. Kick me out of the retreat for all I care. I'll continue my stay separately from all of you if need be." I started out of the room, and as I left, Annie began arguing with Tristan.

"Go get her!" she hissed. "I don't believe her, and even if she is telling the truth, maybe it won't matter. We need her!"

I paused just outside the door. Why did they need me? Tristan ran out and, seeing me standing against the wall, his face changed. His hardened gaze shifted to a sympathetic one.

"Delaney. I need to apologize for my behavior. I don't know what came over me. I think it must be a bit of cabin fever." He chuckled and nodded to the room. "You don't have to pose, nude or otherwise, but I'd like you to still participate in the retreat. Come to the talks, the write-ins, and meals just as you have been. You and Priest both. I've read your writing, and you've got such potential. It'd be a shame to not get what you came for." Tristan pinned me with his arms against the wall. I shrunk down into myself. Priest stepped out of the room, and Tristan dropped his arms immediately.

"Are we going to have problems?" Priest asked.

"No. None at all. I was just telling Delaney that I was sorry for my behavior and to make up for it, not only will I beg her to stay for the rest of the retreat activities, but I'll help get her manuscript into the hands of all the agents who represent romance at Garden Bell Publishing. I've been with them for a few years now and I can call in some favors." Tristan reached out and brushed my cheek with the back of his hand. "What do you say? Let's finish that book this week."

I slapped his hand away and stepped out of his reach. "Sure, whatever, just... don't ever touch me again." I hurried away, and when I heard Priest calling after me, I turned and waved him away. "I just want to be alone for a bit, okay?"

I returned to my room, where I shot Moth a text.

> Me: Tristan is a complete creep. You would not believe what just happened.

I didn't get a reply but considering he was resting, it didn't bother me. Unsure of how to spend the rest of my day, now that I wasn't doing today's class, I found my swimsuit and decided to try the pool. Priest had gone down every day since we'd been here, including the day without power. Maybe it could give me some peace and clarity.

The water was cold, and I shivered as I slid into it, slowly, inch by inch. I shuddered, and my teeth chattered as I plugged my nose and went underwater. It was better to get the discomfort out of the way rather than to have it looming over you. As I swam with my eyes shut underneath the water, I thought about how often I did just that. Put off uncomfortable things in hopes it'd disappear, and every time, it seemed like it did more harm than good.

That was exactly why the doctors and my aunt had done what they'd done. Because I couldn't admit the truth about what I knew. That Priest...

I came up for air, gasping and spinning around. While all the clues were there, I had no real proof that Priest had been the killer. Just that we'd argued and he had the same mask the murderer did. That meant nothing. Those masks were everywhere. He and Carson both had them that year for Halloween.

Carson.

My blood ran cold. Could it have been one of his friends setting him up?

As I floated in the pool, staring up at the green glass ceiling, I thought about Priest. I chose to get my brain completely fried rather than tell them what I knew. Or rather, what I couldn't acknowledge. My brain had been blacking it out, but it was because I was forcing it to. Deep in my soul, I had remembered it all, and it scared me. Not that Priest would come after me, but who would come after Priest if I told them what I knew.

I did more laps and enjoyed the calm afternoon away from everyone. Eventually, I got out and as I was drying off, a man walked in. I looked up and squinted. I knew him.

"Carson?" Priest's best friend, all grown up, stood before me in a hotel uniform. "You work here?"

"I do. How are you, Delaney?"

I blinked, still in disbelief. "I'm good. Does Priest know you're here?"

"I have spoken to him. How are you, Delaney?" he asked again. Something about his tone sent chills through me.

"I'm good," I repeated. "Did you need something? Am I not supposed to be in here?"

"No, you're allowed anywhere in the hotel. You've already been to the top floor, I heard you saw a spider." He laughed.

"How did you know that? Did you speak to that woman? Is she okay?"

"Everyone goes a little mad when they stay here. She'll be fine. She's already back in that room, as we speak, looking out the window."

Carson had yet to make direct eye contact with me, and

with how glossy they were, it gave me a sense of unease. I reached for my clothes. "Well, I'm going to go back upstairs. I should shower and get the chemicals out of my hair." I put my skirt and blouse over my wet suit and slipped on my pool sandals.

"Ah yes, that's why I came in here. I remember now." His smile was unsettling and far too big. "Guests were complaining of wet carpet, coming from the pool up to their rooms. I wanted to point out the secondary exit that will take you to tile flooring, which we can keep mopped up. Come, I'll take you now."

"I'm not that wet," I protested. Carson shook his head and motioned for me to follow him. We went around the pool and came upon a door I hadn't noticed. It blended with the walls.

"It is a bit chilly, but nothing you can't handle. I hope you enjoyed your stay here at the Vincent." He nodded to the door.

"My stay?" I stiffened.

"Your swim. The pool is open all hours."

I blinked. I could have sworn he'd said *enjoyed* your stay. I finally reached for the door and pushed it open. All I saw was pitch-black darkness.

"Is there a light?" I flinched away. I couldn't go in there.

"It'll brighten," Carson said and shoved me into the darkness, closing the door behind me with a loud slam. I shut my eyes, turned back, and pounded on the door. A gust of wind blew threw me, and I shuddered. Wind? Slowly, I turned, and despite everything telling me not to, I opened my eyes. Carson was right. It did brighten, and it was cold. That was because I was outside, and it was snowing.

Rule 32 - Priest
Knowing the rules is key, but you need to know the players too.

"You're riding a thin line," I warned Tristan when I returned to the room he'd locked Laney in just minutes ago.

He smirked as he picked up the furniture and began righting everything again. "I'd say you're the one that should be worried, not me."

He had no fucking clue who he was trapped in this hotel with. "And why's that?"

"Because if what she said is true, that she isn't a virgin anymore, then there's no reason to baby her. She's worthless to us."

"What are you talking about?"

"Tristan, stop," Annie interrupted, stepping between us. "He's just pissed that someone else got to sleep with her. Ignore him. He'll be fine." She shot him a dirty look. "I'll go talk to Delaney and see if she's okay." She hurried out, and I left too.

The phone in my pocket vibrated and I pulled it out, seeing a text from Laney. I rolled my eyes. I thought replying this morning to her text with an excuse would get her to stop texting Moth, but nope, here she was, looking to him for comfort. I ignored the text and shoved his phone back in my pocket.

By the time I made it back to my room, Laney was gone, and I decided to try to get some of my own editing work done. I was already behind due to the power outage. An entire afternoon passed before my eyes, and when I finally shut my laptop, I realized I hadn't seen or heard from Laney since early afternoon. I stood and pulled out my phone, and after a few rings, I heard a click.

"She's not here anymore, Priest." Carson's voice came from the other side. My stomach tightened.

"Carson? How did you get Laney's phone?"

"She doesn't need it anymore. She's probably unable to speak anyways, her tongue frozen solid."

"You're not the friend I once knew. You're..." I didn't want to say the word, it sounded absurd, but after last night at the bar and now this? Carson was evil.

"Dead?" The call clicked off and, sensing someone in the room, I spun around to find Carson feet away from me. I leapt back.

"How did you get in here?"

He rolled his eyes. "Honestly, it's disappointing. I didn't think I'd have to feed it to you. You were smart. What happened?"

"Fuck you," I spat. "What did you do with Laney?"

"She is of no use to the hotel now, so I got rid of her."

"No use?" Tristan's words flashed in my mind. "What do you mean you got rid of her?" I stepped over to him and grabbed him by the shirt. "Tell me what you did!" I roared.

"I did what we do with everything that has no use to us. I put her outside," he said simply.

"Outside?" I fled to the door, grabbing my winter coat. "You're gonna pay for this," I threatened. I looked back at him and froze in horror. Carson was sitting on the couch, blood pouring from his face. His jaw was gone, as if...

"Pay more than I already have?" Carson's words came out muffled and gargled as he spoke through the shotgun wound.

"You really did it." I could barely say the words.

He laughed. "No shit, Sherlock."

"But you're alive."

"Try again." Carson stood and raised his hand to look at his watch. "I'd give her an hour before she freezes to death."

I fled the suite, tossing the horrific sight of Carson post-suicide out of my mind and focusing on finding Laney. I pulled my coat on and took the back door, shoving it open and screaming her name.

"Laney!" The wind howled in response, covering my screams. It was snowing and blowing so hard, panic for Laney's condition set me forward. I braced myself and sprinted into the darkness, calling her name as I went. I went through the maze, skipping over Moth's body. I looked at the trees surrounding the hotel. Perhaps she'd gone to them for shelter from the wind. I ran in that direction and continued my search. Carson had given her an hour, and it was getting close.

I was moving into full panic mode when suddenly, I heard a small, croaky voice.

"Here."

I turned, looking for the source of the sound. "Laney!"

"Here."

I continued calling, moving toward the sound until I found a dark mess of hair covering a body that had huddled against a tree for warmth. Without a second thought, I pulled off my coat and put it over her. She lifted her head weakly. Her eyes were tired and her lips were blue. Her hair was frozen, and her eyebrows had begun to ice over. I bent down and lifted her into my arms.

"It's okay, I'm here."

"Priest." Her voice came out so small, so... exhausted. I had to get her inside. Tired, I pulled through and exerted myself, pushing through the wind and snow. I reached the back door I'd come out of and found it locked. Despite Laney having my coat, she was still in need of actual warmth and shelter. I went around the building, trying every door as we went, only to finally burst through the front.

The lobby was surprisingly busy, with people heading to the banquet room. They stopped and watched us with curious eyes as I stormed up the stairs and hurried to our room. Laney's teeth rattled and her breath came shallow as I unlocked the door and flew to the bathroom. I lowered her into the tub and looked at her. Would it be better to keep her clothes on or off? Fuck it! I turned the bath on with her still clothed. She groaned as the warm water began to thaw her body, and slowly, her eyes opened.

She was going to be okay. I turned to look for soaps or something to fill her bath and then stopped when I caught sight of something in the mirror. I gulped and tried to move slowly, to not disturb it. It couldn't be. It made no sense. I stared at the reflection, waiting for the figure to do something, and finally, it turned and waved. The blood ran from my face.

Laney. Laney looking healthy, dry, and happy.

How could it be? Quickly, I spun around and a scream escaped my lungs. The figure standing in front of me wasn't Laney at all. It was a rotted corpse, and when my eyes flicked to Laney in the tub, her eyes were just as wide as mine.

She saw her too.

I stood, frozen on the bathroom floor. The rotting corpse turned her head to Laney, still in the tub, and then back to me. Her skin made a sickening wet sound as she moved. Getting a grip, I straightened and took a step toward it. Then, as if I didn't even exist, the corpse walked forward, going right through the wall and disappearing.

"Priest?" Laney's voice came weak and confused. "I'm scared."

I hurried to her, sitting on the edge of the bath. "It's fine. I mean, it's not, but I'm here. I'm not going to let those... things hurt you." I shuddered inwardly, thinking about... everything I'd seen in the last twenty-four hours. What was going on in this hotel? None of it made any sense.

"I think this place really is haunted."

I remained silent. She was scared enough. I didn't need to make it worse. I swallowed my terror and turned to her. "How are you feeling? Warm enough?"

She smiled softly. "Getting there. Thank you. I think I would have died if you hadn't come."

She would have. Carson had made it clear that was his

intention when locking her out. But why would someone already dead want to kill someone else?

"How did it happen?" I asked. She sat up, her clothes, now soaked from the bath, clung to her skin. I could see every curve, dip, and point. Despite being in the hot bath, her nipples were cold and poking through her clothes.

"I'd gone swimming, and when I got out of the pool, Carson was there. You know, your old friend from school?"

I stood and went to the back of the tub, urging her to sit forward.

"I've seen him. He's one of them."

"Well, he came and told me I had to take a different door because I'd get the carpet wet. Then when I went to the door, he shoved me out and locked it. I was outside, in just this." She lifted her arms and then shuddered. "My toes are still frozen."

I dipped my hands into her bathwater, now lukewarm. Her temperature must have diluted the heat in the water. I reached for her shirt and slowly pulled it upward. Realizing what I was doing, Laney lifted her arms and allowed me to take her shirt off. I tossed it on the ground and reached for the strings on her swimsuit, pulling them loose. It dropped into the bath, and I scooped it up, tossing it in the pile.

"The clothes are not helping," I explained. Laney put her hands over her breasts, but then slowly stood on shaky legs and turned to me. I unzipped her skirt and caught her bottoms, pulling them both down and tossing the rest of her clothing out. Laney was fully naked, my head inches from her bare pussy. I hated how despite the dark situation that got us here, my body reacted. My mind responded. I looked her up and down, and for the first time in the light, I was seeing all of Laney.

Her arms were still crossed, and cautiously, I reached up and tugged on them to lower. She was beautiful. I'd loved her body in the dark, but now, she was breathtaking.

"I'm cold."

Her words gave me a chuckle, and I stood, heading to the front of the bath. "Let's get you fresh, hot water and maybe some bubbles or something." I drained the tub and began to fill it again. I was nervous when turning to look for the bubble bath, scared that the ghost would return, but she didn't, and I turned back and dumped the floral-smelling soap into the water. It began to lather and bubble immediately, and soon Laney was surrounded by bubbles and sinking into the hot bath, looking less blue and more flushed pink.

"Aren't you cold?" she asked as I sat on the edge of the bath and watched her.

I shrugged. "Nothing compared to what you were. The adrenaline kept me warm." I grinned. "But I might be a little chilly." I dipped my hand in the bath, reaching for her foot. "Can you feel your toes yet?"

She moaned as I began to massage her foot. "Getting there."

My cock hardened as I watched her breasts rise and fall under the water. They were slick and shiny and I wanted to kiss them, bite them, leave marks on them, and claim her as mine.

"Priest." Laney's voice brought me out of my lustful thoughts. "Do you want to take a bath? Your hand is freezing."

"Is that an invite?"

She sat up, pulling her foot from my hands. "Priest!"

"What?" I laughed. "I'm not a bath guy, but if I have a toy to play with, I might be inclined to get in the bubbles."

She put her hands over her face. "You're terrible."

"You're still not saying no." I stood, then and pulled off my shirt. Laney's eyes drifted over my muscles, tracing each line, right down to the...

I made a mistake.

She couldn't see the tattoo on my lower hips. She'd know the truth about last night then. My stomach tightened, and I reached for my pants. Laney turned her head quickly and relief flooded me. Still bashful, thank fucking Christ.

"Don't look," I warned, teasing her. Even though she was turned away, I could feel her rolling her eyes.

"Just get in the bath."

I stripped and went behind her. She shifted forward, and slowly, I slid into the oversized bath. I pulled her between my legs and hugged her to my chest.

"Oh!" She let out a small gasp as our bodies collided. In an instant, my cock was rock hard and pressing against her. I rested my head on her shoulder and reached for a wash rag.

"The soap makes the skin so slick," I whispered, and taking the rag, I ran it over her shoulder, down her arm. "But I love how it feels." I kissed her neck, and she relaxed into me.

"Priest." Her eyes closed, and she lightly pushed my hand off her thigh. "I have to tell you—"

"I heard. This morning, as I was saving you from that bastard. You've had sex." My hand drifted up to her breast, cupping it in my hand. I rolled her nipple between my fingers. "How was it?"

"It hurt," she admitted. "But... I see why people like it so much."

I chuckled as I continued to tease her nipple and nuzzle her neck. "Oh yeah? Do you think you'll do it again soon?"

"Maybe. You aren't mad?"

"Should I be? You kept saying you were holding off, and now, you're free to play, am I wrong?"

"I don't know. It feels..."

"Good. It feels good, doesn't it?" I interjected. I reached my other hand around to tease the other breast. "You can deny it all you want, but you like it when I touch you. Did your lover from last night make you feel this way?"

"No," she moaned. "With him, I was nervous. With you, it's..."

"Scary?" I grinned and bit her neck. She threw her head back. I sunk lower into the bath, taking her with me. "Are you scared you'll like me more than anyone else touching you? Does it frighten you to think it could have been me all along?"

My hand drifted down her belly, and her thighs opened in response.

"Does getting you scared make you wet, Laney?" I parted her lips and ran my fingers down her slickness. "It appears it does." I teased her clit, rotating in slow circles over it. She arched her back in response. "I'm glad you're not a virgin anymore. You want to know why?"

"Why?"

"Because now I can do stuff like this." Finding her opening, I slid a finger inside. Laney shuddered, and her pussy clenched around my finger tightly. "Relax and let your big brother take care of you." I pushed deeper into her, hooking my finger. She lurched forward and I pushed her back against my chest. I moved my finger slowly back out, and then in again, finger fucking her slowly.

"Ah," she winced at first, but the more I thrust, the more she relaxed. I continued sucking on her neck and shoulders while pinching her nipples. I ran my thumb along her clit while I moved my pointer finger inside her. She was so fucking wet and tight and the closer she got to orgasm, the more my cock strained and pleaded to be touched. I bit back my desires and focused on hers. Knowing I'd get mine later, I was able to calm down and chase her release.

"Come on, Laney, you don't have to be scared anymore. It's natural to feel this good. To want this. I want this too. I want you. I need to make you come."

"Ah!" With a cry and a shudder, Laney exploded. She gasped and panted and jerked against the finger buried inside her. I watched in awe as she came, and only when she collapsed again did I remove myself from her.

"How does it feel?" I asked, bringing my finger to my mouth and sucking on it. Her arousal was a mix of her and the soap from the bathwater. She pulled my arms around to embrace her. "Your big brother being inside you?"

"Like I shouldn't like it as much as I do," she confessed. "If anyone knew..."

"What? You want to keep this a secret?"

"Yes."

"And what if I don't want to?"

"Please, Priest," she begged.

I kissed the top of her head and returned my hand to her pussy. "Fine. For now, it'll be our little secret."

"That wasn't like the baths we'd had as kids, but I kind of like this more." Priest nuzzled my ear, and I let out a small giggle.

"Stop!" My stomach fluttered nervously. I shook my head. "What are your plans for when we get back home? We can't be like this in front of..."

"People who know the truth?"

We stood in the bathroom, with towels wrapped around us. Just hours ago, I'd been about to die of hypothermia, and then when Priest saved me and put me in the tub, we saw... a ghost? A spirit? I was unsure, but before I could process it, Priest joined me in the bath and proceeded to... maybe I'd been hallucinating?

I should have been more concerned with the ghosts and Carson trying to kill me, but my mind was elsewhere, thinking about Priest. I hated how good it felt with his hands between my legs and his mouth on my neck. I shouldn't like the dirty things he whispered in my ears just as I was reaching my peak, but I'd be lying if I said they didn't assist in getting me there.

I came so hard with Priest.

"I'm tired." I sighed, and after drying my hair, I padded out of the bathroom and to my bedroom. "I'm going to go to bed. Goodnight, Priest."

I turned at my door to look at him. He was standing in the bathroom doorway, a towel hanging low on his hips. This wasn't the first time I'd seen him just like this, but it was still incredibly hot. It was on the tip of my tongue to invite him to sleep in my bed, but I knew that was taking things too far. The look Priest was giving me with those sinful green eyes right now told me that he had no intention of sleeping if we shared a bed, and I wouldn't be strong enough to refuse.

"Goodnight, Laney darling."

I shut my door softly and rested my forehead on the wood. What the fuck was happening to me? I locked the door again, finding comfort in it. However, it felt less like locking Priest out and more like locking me in. I pulled out another lacy, pink nightgown and then turned the lights off. I wanted to be tired, I should be tired, after my day, but I wasn't quite there yet. I went to my bag, pulling out my Kindle. I paused at the table with the book page roses. I picked one up and sighed. How fitting for a writer's retreat set during Valentine's Day week. I set it down and flicked to the book I'd been reading and climbed into bed, almost instantly getting lost in my dark romance novel.

There was always something about the push and pull, the long gazes, and secret touches before finally giving in to the heat and tension. I'd been reading for almost an hour, fully immersed in the secret society of hot, wealthy, sex-crazed men, when a ping rang out through my room. I blinked and looked at the clock. My phone went off again, and I reached for it. I must have left it up in the room when I'd gone swimming. My stomach fluttered when I saw Moth's name on the screen.

Moth: You up?

Moth: I have something to show you.

Me: I am now. How are you feeling?

I wanted to roll my eyes at the fuckboy message. Texting late at night? We both knew why he was messaging me, but still, I squealed like a schoolgirl and clenched my thighs together. Moth was texting me. Me! I'd mentally prepared myself for a one-night stand, especially after he'd confessed that he was married.

Moth: Better. I've been exploring. So much better than Gloriana's tour.

Moth: You want to see what I've found?

Me: Sure.

A picture came through, and my heart skipped a beat. There he was, in a blue jumpsuit and his mask, taking a full mirror selfie. My body reacted unnaturally. Why was I attracted to that suit?

Moth: I found the rest of the costume.

I tried to contain myself. I'd said just earlier tonight I couldn't keep going back and forth but... A video came through, and I eagerly pushed play. Moth turned the camera around to show me the room. I gasped. The walls were all mirrors, from floor to ceiling. The furniture was minimal, with just a grand piano and a single chair.

Me: Where did you find that room?

Moth: Third floor. You should join me.

It was late. I knew what he wanted and that it was wrong. I shouldn't be attracted to someone who only wanted me while wearing a costume, but I couldn't be that angry when I was using him myself. My eyes flickered to the door that led to the suite, where Priest was. Despite how good it was with him, the moment we left the hotel, we'd be forced to return to how we were. I needed to move on. Slowly, I climbed out of bed.

> Me: I'm putting on my robe. Where on the third floor?

> Moth: No robe, come in whatever flimsy little nightie you're wearing and nothing else.

> Me: No bra?

I glanced at myself in the standing mirror. My nightgown was sheer. In the light, everything was visible.

> Moth: Absolutely, Laney.

> Moth: Be a good girl and do what I tell you to do.

I stared at the words for a long time.

> Moth: I'm waiting.

> Me: Okay.

I searched for my heels and slid them on. My hands shook as I reached for the knob. What if someone saw me? How mortifying it would be? My phone pinged.

> Moth: What did I tell you?

Moth: If you don't come to me, I'll be forced to come to you. Do you like to be punished, Laney?

His words sent my pussy spiraling. Did I like to be punished?

Me: I'm on my way. You didn't tell me where on the 3rd floor.

Moth: Figure it out.

Me: What are you going to do to me if I'm late?

Moth: Don't be.

I bit down on my lip until I tasted blood. Taking a slow, deep breath, I opened my door and crept out into the hall. My hands went over my chest instantly, and my phone pinged. I tilted the screen to see Moth's text.

Moth: Put your arms down. I want anyone that comes out to see your perfect tits.

Moth: Laney, be a good girl.

Slowly, I lowered them. Where was he viewing me from? I walked down the hall, praying no one came out of their rooms for a midnight snack. Every creak made me jump. I pressed myself to the wall when I heard a door, and Moth texted me instantly.

Moth: If I have to come get you, I'm going to make your ass very pink.

There was a picture attached of his hands holding a belt. I gasped and clenched my thighs together, imagining it.

Yes, Michael.

My brain shifted, just as it had the past two nights. I wasn't going up to see Moth. I was going to meet a stranger, a man in a mask who gave me as much pain as he did pleasure. A man that I wanted to keep seeing, to keep pleasing, and to keep riding the line of good girl and bad girl with. I took the elevator, despite hating every squeak and jerk the ancient machine gave out, and soon, I was on the third floor.

Moth: Down the hall, to the left.

My heart beat fast. The air was eerily quiet. I was waiting for someone to pop out and scare me, but I continued on down the dimly lit hall. I turned into the room I'd been directed to. The lighting in here too, was low. Just dim enough to give my masked lover, standing in the center of the room, an air of mystery and excitement; even more so, now that he'd found the blue jumpsuit.

The video was accurate to what the room offered. It almost felt like an old dance studio, with wooden flooring and scarce furniture. Michael stormed over to me, shutting the door. I flinched as he pinned me to it. I looked into his eyes; it was too dark to see perfectly, but the hunger was evident. And then, a low, guttural growl came from under the mask, and one last text came through. I gulped, and with shaky hands, brought the phone to my face.

Moth: You're late.

I stared at the eyes inside the mask. They didn't look like Moth's. But they had to be. It only added to the thrill of it all. What if it wasn't Moth under the mask? What if it was one of the hotel's ghosts?

"What are you going to do, Michael?" I rolled my eyes. He talked a big game, but would he actually hurt me?

He tilted his head, just like the character did, and my heart picked up speed. We stared at each other, and now, I wasn't entirely sure it was Moth under the mask. Lust was overtaking me, and suddenly, he was just Michael.

He squeezed my cheeks, pinching my lips together. I writhed under his grasp.

"I'm sorry!" I muttered through my squished lips. My masked lover's eyes lit up as the other hand went to my throat again. He squeezed, and I melted. I let my eyes roll into the back of my head as his thumb ran over my lips, and then drifted to my chest, cupping a breast. He let my neck go, and I gasped for air. Little black dots appeared in my vision, and I moaned as he reached for my neck again.

While he choked me against the door, his other hand

fondled my breasts above the thin fabric. He pinched them while he alternated between choking and letting me breathe.

"Is this my punishment?" I gasped. "Just teasing me?"

Michael shook his head. He was taking his role seriously. He let my neck go and snatched my wrist. He tugged me to the center of the room. Dozens of us reflected back from the walls. What an odd pairing. I giggled. Me, in a pink nightie with bows and ribbons that matched my stilettos, and him... Michael Myers.

He motioned to the chair. It was just a chair meant for a dining table. He reached into his pocket and before I could protest, he flashed the silver handcuff and snapped it around my wrist, pulling it to the arm of the chair and connecting the two.

"Hey!" I tugged but only moved the chair. I glared up at him, whose eyes sparkled with mischief. "What's this for?" I put my free hand on my hip. Michael sat in the chair and motioned in front of him. What did that even mean?

"I can't dance." I pulled on the handcuff.

He shook his head slowly and reached forward, tugging on my nightgown. When I didn't move fast enough, he slammed his hand down on the other arm of the chair. I let out a cry of surprise. His hand found my thigh and ran up it, my skin getting goosebumps with each inch. My legs were shaking by the time he reached my core. He cupped my sex and ground his palm against it. I groaned and parted my thighs to allow him access.

He tugged on my nightgown again. I nodded and pulled my dress down. It slid off my shoulders and went to my waist. Only to get stuck at my handcuffed wrist. Michael reached into his pocket again and pulled out a switchblade. He flicked it open and cut the strap off my dress, allowing it to fall to the floor. Without giving me the chance, he leaned forward and cut my panties on my sides, letting them drop as well. His hand went to my sex and his fingers pushed past my folds into the wetness pooling there. I moaned as he swirled his finger around my clit, but then pulled away.

What was I supposed to do? His erection was pressed against his pants so tightly I was sure it'd rip a hole in the thick fabric.

Michael saw my gaze and shook his head. He wagged a single finger and then reached for the zipper on his jumpsuit. He pulled it down from his neck and, keeping eye contact with me, slid it down his body. His abs were spectacular. I reached out to tug the suit off his shoulders, but he swatted me away and continued sliding the zipper down just past his belly button.

This would be the first penis, cock, whatever, that I'd ever seen. Sure, I'd felt Priest's in the bath on my backside, and this same masked man just last night had been... inside me, but I'd been too deliriously high off pleasure to pay attention. Michael must have seen my reaction and paused just where I knew hair would start. He then pulled out a second pair of cuffs and grabbed my free arm and tugged it to the chair, snapping it over the second arm.

Hunched over, naked in just my heels, I glared at him. Michael was smiling underneath the mask, but as I tried to get him to look at me, I realized he was looking past me at the mirrors. I looked up at the mirror in front of me and blushed. He was staring right at my exposed ass.

Michael lifted his switchblade and ran it across my skin, sliding it down my shoulder. I shuddered as he brought it between my breasts and then back up, tracing my jawline. He squeezed my cheeks again, holding me in place, and with his empty hand, he finished unzipping his pants and then patted his lap.

My belly swarmed with butterflies. With a deep breath, I raised my leg. I climbed onto him, and his cock jerked between my thighs. Finding difficulty with my hands now behind my back, Michael held my waist and assisted me up. I couldn't move my hands more than an inch or two, causing my back to be arched forward and my breasts to be thrust into his mask. Michael urged me up and positioned his cock between my wet, swollen, needy lips. He found my opening and pushed inside just an inch.

I gasped at the still unfamiliar feeling. It was pain mixed with excitement. I was frozen, afraid of the sharpness that came with being stretched for the second time. Michael let out a low growl and shoved me down, filling me with his cock.

I screamed, and tears slid down my cheeks. Michael moved my hips and lifted me. I could barely breathe. I pleaded for him to let me go, to stop, but he continued forcing my hips down and around until slowly, the tears stopped, and something began to build. My gasping turned from fear and hurt into excitement and hunger. Michael's hands abandoned my hips as I began to bounce and figure out the rhythm I needed. He moved to play with my nipples with one hand and my clit with the other. I watched us in the mirrors, and it was even more erotic and depraved than I could have imagined. Everything about this was wrong but felt so right. I threw my head back, completely at Michael's mercy, ready to explode, and then suddenly, I felt an eager tongue slide over my nipple, and I came undone.

Michael continued sucking on my breasts until I came down from my orgasm. I opened my eyes and he pulled back, slipping his mask back on. We made eye contact then, and a flash of recognition hit me but went away so fast I couldn't catch it.

"I love you," I gasped, and then he came. With a loud groan, Michael thrust inside me, his cock pulsed against my walls, spilling his seed, and I watched from the mirrors, thinking it was the most beautiful scene I'd ever witnessed.

Rule 36 - Priest

Four years ago.

"Priest, are you coming?" Laney whined from the bottom of the stairs. I rolled my eyes and glanced over at my friends, Carson and Kaleb. They were not excited when I told them Laney was coming tonight.

"Your mom knows it's an upper classman party, right?" Carson got up and went to the mirror, adjusting his jumpsuit.

"I told her. She thought I was being too dramatic." I played with the large, plastic knife in my hands.

"Yeah, well, it'll be real dramatic when your sister realizes she has no friends and she's all by herself in the corner." Kaleb stood and grabbed the masks, tossing one to each of us. "Let's fucking go."

I joined my friends, shifting uncomfortably in my stiff costume, and together, we stormed downstairs.

"You're all Michael Myers?" Laney scoffed.

I gaped at my sister, my *stepsister*, in her costume.

"Damn, Delaney, you don't look like a freshman." Kaleb whistled.

I shot him a look that made him clamp his mouth shut.

"You like it?" Laney beamed and raised her arms, showing off the full ballerina tutu. "I borrowed it from my mom's closet."

"I love it," Carson said. "Are you wearing makeup?"

I was going to murder my fucking friends.

"Yeah, bacon grease." I sneered and elbowed him. "Stop looking at my sister, you jackass." I waved my mask in the air. "Come on. I don't want to fight for a parking spot." The four of us piled into my car.

"Laney, sit in front of me," I ordered.

"Really?" She perked up. I'd always made her sit in the back when I had my friends around, but I couldn't trust either of them.

"Yeah. Hurry up," I said gruffly. While I drove, Laney asked question after question about the party.

"I've never been to a real high school party." She spun around to speak to the guys. "Is it as crazy as the movies?"

"How so?" Carson chuckled.

"Well, like, people jumping in pools and dance-offs and stuff." Her questions made me bite down on my lip. Her wide-eyed innocence was having the same effect on me that it was having on my friends. It was as if we were all sharing one mind, and that mind was filthy as fuck.

"Will you turn around? You've got your ass hanging out." I snapped.

"Sorry." She plopped back down. I turned the radio up, drowning out her annoying questions with System of a Down. I turned down a dirt road.

"We're here." I followed the other cars and parked in the giant yard. Laney threw her door open and bounced out.

"Okay, thanks, bye!" She waved and turned.

"Hold up!" I barked. She turned back. Carson and Kaleb got out of the car and looked at me, just as confused as she was. I swallowed, and thanked god it was dark and my hard-on was hidden by the car door. I did what I always did to get it to go down, and thought about the 1985 Chicago Bears, listing the players off one by one until my dick went down.

"Let me talk to my sister a second. You guys go."

Her face fell as the guys shook their heads and started toward the barn that was lit up and exploding with music.

"What?" Laney threw up her hands. "You gave this long speech just this morning about how I was to pretend you didn't know me and that as soon as we got here I needed to disappear because you weren't babysitting me."

"That was before I saw your costume," I snarled. I walked around the car and stood in front of her. "Laney, you can see..."

Everything.

"My cleavage?" She rolled her eyes. "Grow up, Priest. What, are you mad because your friends were checking me out? Who cares? They're pervs. I'm not interested in them."

I looked toward the dark, inky sky. She wasn't getting it. "This party has a lot of older people with more... expectations. I only agreed because I thought you'd be—"

She crossed her arms, making her look even more voluptuous. "Dressed like Scooby Doo?" She referred to one of her old costumes from elementary school. The photo still hung in the living room. "Well, I'm not. You go find your friends and I'll go look for some of my own. You're not my babysitter, remember?"

She stormed off toward the party, and I reluctantly followed, waiting until I was at the barn to put on my rubber mask and go find the guys. The barn was full of almost a hundred kids from school, dancing, drinking, and having a good time. I was halfway to the keg when I was stopped by a girl in a sexy, killer clown costume. "Priest Duvall? There's so many Michaels here!" She giggled and grasped my arm. I nodded. She was a pretty brunette.

"You're in my geometry class, right?" I lifted the mask and flashed a smile.

She let out a sigh of relief. "Yes! Jennifer Lesnicky. Are you going to the keg? I'll go with you." She pulled me through the dance floor. I looked for Laney, and when I didn't immediately see her, my heart sped up. It wasn't until we reached the keg did I spot her in the crowd, dancing with a group of girls, and I relaxed some.

"I was hoping you'd be here!" Jennifer shouted as she poured me a beer. "I've always been too nervous to talk to you at school."

"Yeah, why's that?" I asked, not fully invested in the conversation. She began to rattle off something about how she had a crush on me, but I tuned her out, watching Laney have the time of her life on the dance floor. Carson and Kaleb came over and saw where I was looking.

"Do me a favor." I tilted my head to them. "I'll give you twenty dollars each."

"What do you want?" Carson asked, and I nodded to the dance floor.

"Don't let any guy dance with Laney."

They exchanged looks.

"What's that mean?" Kaleb asked.

"Figure it out. I don't want to see her dancing with any assholes."

"So, babysit?" Carson rolled his eyes. "No thanks."

"Fifty." I upped my deal.

"A hundred," Carson countered. "If I'm going to spend my time beating up assholes instead of trying to get laid, then I want to be paid for it."

"Fine." I pulled out my phone, sending them both a hundred each, bleeding my bank account. Minimum wage didn't pay shit. They slid their masks back on, and headed into the crowd.

"Is everything okay?" Jennifer tugged on my jumpsuit. I blinked and looked down.

"Yeah, fine. So, you've always had a crush on me, huh?" I slid the mask I wore in front of others back on and worked my charm on her. I had a few beers, and as I flirted, I watched my friends misdirect guy after guy all night.

Sometime during all of this, Jennifer ended up on my lap in a chair, slobbering all over my neck. She chewed on my ear and I tried to get into making out, but I couldn't focus. All my thoughts kept returning to Laney, in the pink, skin-tight leotard and pointed shoes. I looked at Jennifer's red lips and saw Laney's shiny pink ones, and as Jennifer lifted my hand to her chest, all I could think about was touching Laney's breasts.

Jennifer reached for my flaccid cock and pouted. I gently pushed her off me.

"Look, Jennifer, I—" I stopped talking to her when something caught my eye. Laney was storming away from the dance floor in tears. "I've got to go." I flew after Laney, following her outside.

"Are you okay?" I asked. "Laney!" I called when she didn't turn around.

"No, I'm not okay!" She burst into tears and screamed at me when she turned. "I've spent all night with guys giving me grossed-out looks and turning me down for dances."

Those fuckers. They were supposed to divert dudes, not crush her spirit. "They're stupid."

"All of them?" She scoffed. "Not a single boy would dance with me all night. It was mortifying!" She sniffled and threw up a hand in my direction. "But you wouldn't understand. Girls throw themselves at you."

"No, they don't," I objected, but even I knew I was full of

shit. "Laney, it's nothing against you. They..." I had to think on the fly. "Guys just don't like younger girls."

"Sure. That's it." She rolled her eyes again. "It has nothing to do with me."

"It doesn't." A slow song came on, and tears pooled in her beautiful brown eyes again. Smiling, I extended my hand. "Could I have this dance?"

The look on her face would be forever ingrained in my memory. Hope, relief, love.

For a moment, I felt that connection. I took her hand and pulled her into my arms. We did slow circles with the music, and suddenly, we weren't stepsiblings anymore. We were...

I looked up and saw someone creeping in the shadows. One of the many Michael Myers. Carson took off his mask, stared at Laney and me, and shook his head slowly. I could see the realization in his eyes, and it filled me with guilt and shame.

He knew.

Rule 37 - Priest
Learn the house rules, not just your own.

"You found the mirror room." Carson snickered from behind me.

I blinked and looked around. Everything felt... fuzzy. As if I'd dreamt it all, but I knew I hadn't. I'd been here, fully aware, and... with Laney. I stood up from the chair and ripped the mask off. My cock hung out of the jumpsuit absurdly. I tucked myself back inside.

"I don't remember putting this on," I said, gazing at my reflection.

"You don't? How odd. Must be the Vincent's doing."

"What's that supposed to mean?" I turned around and reluctantly brought my eyes to his face. He looked normal again, the gunshot wound gone.

"I knew. The whole time. I knew about your feelings toward her. Kaleb did too. It was obvious. Even more so after that guy's murder. They tried to get us for it, did you know that? Because everyone remembered us at that Halloween party, pushing guys around who talked to your sister. No one believed us when we told them it was because you told us to."

"I didn't know that." A small twinge of guilt hit me but

then I recalled what he'd done to Laney earlier today. Or was it yesterday? My days were so blurred. I wasn't sure what was going on now. "You seemed to fair all right. For a little bit anyways."

"Ah, yes, my big finale!" Carson made a gun with his hands and pretended to blow off his head. "How dramatic that was. I shouldn't have done it that way. It was a gruesome scene. I'd much rather have... frozen in the cold." His eyes darkened and he chortled. The room echoed with his laughs, causing me to flinch.

"You bastard!" I started forward, catching him by the shoulders. I threw him to the floor, and he continued laughing.

"What are you going to do? Kill me? Newsflash, asshole, I'm already dead!" He lifted his legs and kicked me with his boots, sending me across the room. I hit a mirror, and it shattered, shards of glass rained down on me, and I clenched my eyes closed. A loud smash came from the other side of the room, and I peeked an eye open and then leapt to my feet. Carson had an axe and was smashing the mirrors.

"No one escapes the Vincent once you've been picked. Not me. Not any of those girls. and not you."

"What do you mean? I haven't been picked for anything. Carson, stop!" I lunged for the axe and he swung at me. I dodged just in time. His brown eyes began to glow gold.

"You have been picked, you idiot. Otherwise, we wouldn't be talking. You only see us if the Vincent wants you to. And the hotel only wants you to see us if it wants you to be one of us."

"Is that why you killed yourself? Man, that's—" I paused and laughed. This was all so absurd! "You could have gotten out! Me and Laney are getting out as soon as the storm—"

"Ha, you think that storm was accidental?" Carson shook his head. "The Vincent did that. It controls more than you know. More than any of us realize. We're all at the mercy of this fucking place. Even if they were considering letting you leave, you've no doubt made it angry by fucking her senseless. The Vincent doesn't like that." He lifted the axe and turned to the other wall, swinging against the mirrors again.

"I can't do this." I put my hands up and started walking backward toward the door. "You're not making any sense. I'll find you later."

Carson took a break and spun around, his face still maddening. "Yes, you will. And you'll be confused about how you got there and why you didn't feel quite yourself. Don't you see?" He waved up and down, and I realized he was talking about my jumpsuit. "It's already started. The Vincent is going to slowly take over your mind until it kills you. And if you die here, you stay here."

I found myself wandering the halls, holding my ruined nightgown to my chest, handcuffs still on both wrists and disoriented. I paused at a door and knocked.

"Moth?" I called. Everything felt so hazy. One moment I was in the throes of passion with a masked man, handcuffed and forced onto his lap. The next, I'd been set free, but... I didn't remember much else. I knocked again. The metal handcuffs rattling against the wooden door made my knock louder, but no one answered. I trudged back to my room, suddenly exhausted. I paused at my door and realized then that I was holding my keys and phone. Had I been drugged? No, I couldn't have been. I hadn't had anything to eat or drink in hours. Was the sex just that good?

I crept into my room, unsure of the time. But all of that was tossed out when I turned around and let out a small shriek. Moth was standing on the other side, grinning like a madman.

"How did you get here before me?" I asked quickly as he put a finger to his lips to shush me. I looked him up and down. "You changed your clothes." Seeing Moth in my suite only made me more confused. How did he get down here so fast? I put my hands to my temples and closed my eyes. A headache was forming fast.

"Are you okay?" he asked.

"Yeah, I'm just..." I thrust my arms out. "Can you unlock me?"

With a chuckle, Moth took my wrists and dug into his pockets for the keys. "Better?" he asked after releasing me.

"Yes, thank you." I blushed. "I never realized you were that kinky."

His eyebrows shot up in amusement. "Yeah? What made you think I wasn't?"

I put my arms over his shoulders and pulled him to me. I inhaled deeply and paused. He smelled different. He smelled like mothballs.

"Are those your clothes?" I asked, pulling back. "You smell old."

"Sorry. I should ask if they have laundry service. Who knows how long we'll be here."

"What do you mean? The storm isn't supposed to last for more than a week."

Moth didn't answer me, instead, he went around the bed and found my laptop, pulling it from my bag. "I got curious, waiting for you, and read some of your stuff. It's dark."

"You read my manuscript? How long have you been here?" How long was I roaming the halls?

"Not long, and I wasn't reading your manuscript. I found a recent document. Where you talk about what they did to you. After Priest killed that guy."

"Priest didn't—" I shook my head and joined him on the bed. "What recent document?" I didn't recall writing anything. He turned my laptop on and once it was loaded, showed me the document. I read through it quickly, my blood growing colder with each word. Those were my words, my memories, my story. When did I write this down?

"They treated you no better than a criminal. Shocking your brain until you were drooling and couldn't think for yourself. They should be in jail."

"I'm fine," I lied. "They only wanted to block certain things."

"Sure, but what about your life now? Delaney, you've been wandering the halls for hours. And before that, you went outside in the storm in just a shirt and skirt. I'm worried about you." He put his hand on my bare shoulder, and I shuddered. He was so cold.

"Why didn't you come find me?" I looked away from the screen to find his expression darkened. His soft, playful eyes were cold and hiding something.

"Delaney, what you've gone through, no one should ever have to experience. What does Priest have to say about it?"

I closed my laptop and pushed it away. "Nothing. I haven't told him. He doesn't need to know. That was private, Moth. You shouldn't have gone through my things."

"I had to. You're so closed off. I don't know anything about you other than how flirty you are, that you like to write, and that you're Priest's sister."

"What?"

A slow grin spread across his lips, and it sent a chill through me. "What, you didn't think I knew? I told you, we go way back. It was almost like seeing a ghost, that first day we got here. I never thought they'd let him out, and then when you said your name, I was just as surprised." He reached for my hand, bringing it to his ice-cold lips. He kissed the top and then began trying to kiss up my arm. I pulled away.

"What are you talking about? You said you knew him

from school. Cunningham's." I scooted off the bed. I found my robe, abandoned on a chair, and quickly put it over my exposed body. This wasn't the man I'd spent my evening with in that mirror room. Something wasn't right.

"I never said school. And if he did, he's lying to you." Moth stood and hurried over. "Cunningham's is a hospital for the mentally unwell."

The words were like a clap of thunder across my mind. "What?" I whimpered.

"Yes. An asylum for the members of society that have money to not be abandoned on the streets but not quite right in the mind to be allowed to exist with the general public. They're hidden there instead. Priest was what they called 'a lifer'."

"No." I shook my head. "No, no, no. Priest isn't insane."

"Isn't he? He murdered your boyfriend, Delaney. He ran him through with an axe and then came home like nothing was wrong."

I started to back up. The look on Moth's face was... murderous. He stalked me, pushing me back until I hit the wall.

"He confessed to me while we were there. After I saw his file. He told me all about how he had to do it because that guy was going to take his little Laney away. Priest is insane. I never really believed it until I walked in on him tattooing your name on himself."

My mind went blank, and then every moment since we'd arrived at The Vincent flashed through my mind all at once. "No, that was you."

"Me?" Moth laughed. "You think I wrote your name on my body forever? I don't even know you."

Tears slid down my face. "You're wrong. It wasn't him. It was you!"

Moth pulled away from me. "Look for yourself." He lifted his shirt and pulled his pants down just enough for me to see the bare skin on his hip. My heart pounded in my ears, so loud it was deafening.

"You faked it," I accused. "You are an artist in training. You have the markers and other equipment to make it look real."

"Nada. Wasn't me. You've been duped. But couldn't be all bad. You seemed to like it both times."

Both times? Was he saying... "You're lying. Priest would never—"

"Never what? Break out of an insane asylum and track down the woman who got him there? Of course not, that'd be absurd. But yet, here we are." He put his hands out and then let out a loud, belly laugh. It startled me so much I slid down the wall and broke into sobs.

Priest wasn't bad. He wouldn't have lied to me like that. Right?

"If you don't want people to know about us, just say so!" I spat.

Moth crouched and reached for my chin, pinching and tilting my head up. "I wouldn't care if people knew we had sex, darling. But we didn't. It's easy to fool someone when they don't want to accept the truth."

"He couldn't fool me. I saw you behind the mask."

"No, you didn't."

"Yes, I did!" I shoved him back and stood. "You have no proof that it wasn't you." My hands balled into fists. My entire body shook with rage. It was one thing to sleep with me and go our separate ways. But to make me believe it never happened was insulting.

"Proof?" Moth scurried up off the floor and laughed dryly. "You want proof. Okay, fine. Put on some warmer clothes. I'll show you proof." He nodded to the dressers. I quickly changed into my clothes. I couldn't believe I was playing along with his absurd ruse. "You'll need a coat."

"Why? Where are we going?" I asked.

Moth's expression darkened. "To the maze."

It was still night, but Moth's insistence that it wasn't him under the mask gave me strength to leave my room with him. The wind howled outside.

"Do we have to go outside?" My mind went back to just yesterday when I almost died in the freezing weather. "You're not even wearing a coat."

"I don't need one. Come on. I want to know more about your therapy."

"My what?" I followed him down the stairs.

"Your shock therapy. What did it feel like?"

"Pain."

"Yes, but where? Did your body light up like a Christmas tree? Was it so strong it almost felt good? Did you come?"

I stopped in my tracks. "Excuse me?"

He laughed. "Oh, sorry. I just thought we were past polite, awkward flirting. The whole, *will we, won't we* thing is over and done now."

"Yes, because we did." I pointed out and started walking again. "And no, I didn't... come." I shuddered. "It was just pain. Lots of it. I couldn't think."

"That's the point, isn't it? To make it so you can't think. So you don't remember damning pieces of evidence. Wouldn't want that coming out, would they?"

"Who?"

"Your aunt, your parents, everyone who covered up what your brother did. Cunningham's is for people with money. A large number of them should have been in prison, not in a mental institution. Your brother is one of them."

"And what about yourself? Should you have been in prison as well?" I snapped back. I didn't like how he talked about Priest as if he was this atrocity. He didn't know Priest the way I did.

"Absolutely, I should have." Silence thickened the air. Was he saying that he too had...

We reached the doors that led to the back of the hotel.

"Why do we have to go outside?" I asked again.

"Are you scared I'll hurt you?" Moth tilted his head to the side.

"Yes," I confessed.

"I can't. Come with me and you'll see why."

"Why you can't hurt me?"

"That, and why it wasn't me you've been having sex with."

It felt so... vulgar when he said it. Maybe I wasn't cut out for writing romance. If I couldn't say sex, could I write it? Moth seemed to read my thoughts.

"Come on, Miss Aspiring Author. You want to be able to write more detailed, realistic prose, here's how."

Cautiously, I stepped outside with him, wrapping my arms around myself for extra warmth.

"You ever seen one of these in real life?" he called over his shoulder, heading to the maze. It was dark, but floodlights attached to the building lit the ground enough to lead us there.

"No." I looked up at the tall walls. "Is there light inside?"

"No, but you'll be fine. Here." He reached for my hand and squeezed. I shuddered. His hand was colder than the weather. "Now tell me more about the shock treatment. What exactly were they trying to get rid of inside your brain?"

"Why are you so interested? I don't want to talk about it."

He stopped short and let go of my hand. "Tell me, or I leave you here."

"I'll just go back inside."

"Can you find your way back before I do? Because I'm a bit faster and I have no issue watching you die in here."

My body shook from the cold. Or was it the fear? Both were fair assessments. "They wanted me to confess what I knew about Marco, and when I wouldn't, they decided it was best for me to forget everything about it altogether."

"That doesn't make sense." He stepped forward, taking us deeper into the maze. "Why would they want you to forget a crime, instead of torturing the truth out of you?"

"Because I couldn't remember it exactly, but I was constantly being triggered by things. It was becoming worse and worse. They did it for my own good."

"Yes, but why didn't they do it for everything? You're afraid of the dark, aren't you? Because of that tornado you experienced as a kid."

How did he know that?

"You wrote that down too. It's all there in your laptop," he explained. "Every little detail." The way he said it made my face warm. "But big brother made it all better, didn't he?"

I ripped my hand from his, which only made him laugh out loud.

"He's good at that, isn't he? Priest. Making all your problems go away. Or maybe they're his problems. What did you say to him after he came home from killing Marco?"

"I—" My mouth parted. "I didn't say anything. He was never proven to have done that. Marco's killer was never found." I'd said that so much over the years it was ingrained in my brain. It was an automatic response.

"No wonder they fried your brain. You can't even acknowledge what he is. You have to accept it, Delaney. Your brother is a psychopath, determined to make you his. He'll do whatever it takes to make that happen, including murder."

I put my hands over my ears and closed my eyes tight. "Stop!"

"Fine by me." Moth stopped walking, and I ran into his back. I took a step back and opened my eyes, slowly lowering my hands. "You wanted proof, right? Here it is." He kicked his foot out and it hit something under the snow with a thud. Something black came uncovered, and I leapt further back.

"What is that?" I stared at the boot. The black boot, that looked eerily similar to the one Moth was wearing.

"Take a look for yourself." He stepped away and motioned to it. "Look at what your brother, your lover, did." My body shook with terror. I couldn't move. Moth shoved me forward and I tumbled to my knees, right beside the lump in the snow.

"Look at it!" he screamed so loudly I jumped into action, swiping my hand over the mass. It was hard and frozen solid. A chest. I had known, in my heart, when I saw the boot, that it was a body. I knew, but touching it gave me no choice but to accept it. The male in the snow had been wearing a black shirt with a red snake on it. I looked back up at Moth. He stood there smugly, wearing the same exact shirt.

"Keep going." He demanded. I shook my head as hot tears slid down my cheeks. I didn't want to. None of this was making any sense! "I said, keep going. Find out exactly who your brother killed two nights ago."

"Two nights ago?" My voice came out hoarse as if I'd been screaming for hours. I'd been having the perfect night, and Priest had... murdered someone because of it? "Priest didn't do this."

I stood, but Moth kicked my back, forcing my face into the snow, right by the frozen corpse's head, still buried. I crawled away from the body and scrambled to my feet on the other side.

"You're just trying to frame him," I accused. "You said so yourself, you're just like him. If he's a murderer, then so are you. Who is it?" I asked. I pointed to the body. "Who did you kill to try to get Priest in trouble?" An evil grin spread over his face.

"Oh, I'm so glad you phrased it like that. Who is it, you ask?" Moth bent down and swiped the snow off the head of the body and then looked up to see the horrified expression on my bloodless face. "It's me."

RULE 40 - PRIEST

GHOSTS DON'T HAVE TO FOLLOW RULES.

"Where's Laney?" I demanded when I made it to our suite and found it empty. I knew one of the many ghosts in this fucking place was listening. I had to suspend my disbelief and accept that this was the fucked up world I was living in right now. A moment later, a young woman appeared against the wall.

"The romance writer?"

"Yes. Do you know where she is?" My patience was nonexistent. If what Carson said was true, that we'd been picked, then we needed to leave before they found out and tried to stop us.

"I might. The Vincent is a big place. It's hard to navigate. Is it important?"

"How long have you been here?" I demanded.

"Too long." She stepped forward. "Why are you looking for her so frantically? There's all the time in the world."

"No, there's not," I snapped. "You can disappear now. Or float away, whatever you do, but you can leave if you're not going to help me."

"I couldn't help you even if I wanted to." She laughed. "I

saw you talking to Carson in the mirror room. For someone who hates that room so much, he sure visits it more often than anyone else. He told you the truth, so now you know. The Vincent calls for blood, and someone wants her."

"Chosen her to what? None of this makes sense."

"Paint it red." She shrugged.

"Paint it red?" The more I dug deeper into this hotel's secrets, the more confused I became. I looked away for one moment and when my eyes returned to the ghost woman, she was gone. We had to get out of here.

I turned around and found Laney's suitcase. I'd pack us both up as best as I could and we'd leave in secret. We'd bundle up in warm clothes and walk until we found a car that could get us to an airport. I tossed shoes, makeup, and whatever I could find into her suitcase.

I found her laptop buried underneath clothes I'd tossed around. Had she been working before she left the room? Something about it called to me, and I paused to open it and see what she'd been doing last. The screen opened right up to a document, and as I scanned it, the blood drained from my face.

Paint it red.

All down the page. Paint it red. Over and over again. I pushed the computer away from me in disgust. What was this? Were we in the fucking *Shining*? I stood and paced. I'd been startled, which didn't happen often. That had been the goal of whoever had typed that document. It had to have been one of the ghosts around here. But were they truly ghosts if they could manipulate objects?

I picked up her laptop again and closed the document. I went to her Recent folder and found one that was titled:

For Priest.

I clicked on it and found a video with Moth's face in it. I rolled my eyes. Even in death, he annoyed the fuck out of me. I clicked on it.

"Hello, Priest." Moth's face was the only thing on the screen. His pupils were dilated and his smile looked absolutely deranged. "Did you lose something?"

Oh god, no. He had her.

"She's alive." Moth stepped back and revealed his entire frame. I looked around, trying to figure out where he was, but it was unfamiliar to me. "I took her to my room. You see, once you die here, The Vincent is generous enough to give you a room that's just for you. I wonder what yours is gonna look like?"

A low growl stirred in my throat.

"Mine is a psycho's wet dream. You see, they caught me before I could truly have fun with any of my victims. They sent me to Cunningham's not just to prove to the judge they were punishing me but also in hopes that the doctors there would fix me. We all know that's a joke. That place doesn't fix anyone, does it, Priest?"

Moth's boots echoed in the dark room as he walked to the other side. It was too dark to see anything but him, until suddenly he flicked on lights, and the room was bathed in bright, sterile lighting. The room was hospital green and it made my stomach roll. A muffled scream sounded, and the camera jerked to—

Laney.

Everything around me stopped. Sound, air, my heart, my lungs. Laney was strapped to a standing table and gagged. She was struggling against the leather belts holding her arms, legs, and torso down. Moth stepped into the video again, going over to her. My entire body tensed with rage. I was going to kill him again.

"Did you know that Little Laney over here was so fucked

up after you killed her valentine that they had to give her electroshock therapy just to be able to stop her from screaming at night? You traumatized her so badly, she couldn't even look at a Halloween mask without shutting down completely?"

"What?" Was this video live, or had he kidnapped her hours ago?

"When she found out it was you under the mask, not me, she blacked out again. As much as you want it to be so, your little sister doesn't want you, bro." He laughed dryly and pulled a rickety table toward him. It was a surgical tray.

"This chair is pretty fun. I tried it on myself a little bit before strapping her in. Just a sponge in the mouth." He removed her gag just long enough to shove the sponge into her mouth, putting it back quickly. "And then a quick flip of this switch." He picked up a box with a light switch on it off his table. "And she lights right up! How long do you think it will take to get her to forget what you did to her this time? I say, not much."

He flicked the switch and my eyes clamped shut. Laney howled and began to sob. The buzzing was loud. It mixed with the sharp clanging of metal on her restraints as she jerked around. Finally, he shut it off. I opened my eyes. Laney was slumped over, unconscious. Moth grinned.

"You better fucking come quick, before I get bored and end it for everyone." The camera shut off. I had to fucking find her now. I stormed out of her room and into the hall. Where the fuck were they?

I ran down the hall, taking the stairs up. He had to be on the third floor. That's where that mirror room had been. I reached the top of the stairs and sprinted to the other end of the hall, but nothing. There were no doors at all. I spun around.

"Where is she?" I demanded. "I know one of you fucking ghosts is listening. You better tell me where he has her before I burn this fucking thing down with everyone inside."

"So dramatic." Carson appeared beside me. "What are you looking for exactly?"

"Moth has Laney in a room somewhere. I need to find her."

"I don't see why that's any of our problem."

"It will be," I threatened.

"I'm already dead, none of what you say has any real bearing on things for me." He shrugged. "However, if you care to make a deal, I may be inclined to help you find her."

A deal with the dead? Nothing about this was right.

"Oh, come on, this isn't the first time we've made deals about your sister. I'm not going to ask for much, I promise."

"What do you want?" Every second I sat here with Carson, Laney was stuck with Moth. If I didn't find her soon, he'd attempt a lobotomy.

"Put this on." He reached behind his back, pulling out a Michael Myers mask.

"Why?"

"Because that's the deal. You put on the mask and I'll show you where to go."

I donned the mask again. "Happy? Now where is she?" I demanded. Carson snapped his fingers. A loud creak came from behind me, and I spun around and watched a trap door open from the ceiling and a wooden ladder slide down.

"There you go. Have fun, *Michael*."

I turned but he was already gone. I didn't have time to wonder why he wanted me to wear the stupid costume. I had to get to Laney. I climbed the steps and found myself on a fourth floor, identical to the ones below it. As soon as I was on solid ground, the trap door shut, and the ladder disappeared. I swallowed and began searching.

The first door I went to, the door was unlocked. I opened it, finding two young girls, playing with dolls on the rug. The next door had a group playing poker. Each door I tried had people from various time periods, doing seemingly normal activities. Were these the rooms that ghost was talking about? If so, Moth had to be here too. I reached the end of the hall and shoved the door open. Laney's scream pierced my ears and I stormed inside the pitch-black room.

"Don't fucking move." Moth's voice came from the darkness. I stopped. A light flicked on and I squinted as my eyes adjusted. Laney was still strapped to the table, but her eyes were red and sweat drenched her entire body.

"That's right, Michael came to save you, Laney." Moth hunched over her shoulder and smiled at me. "Not Priest.

Michael. He's not a monster like your mind wants you to believe. He's your savior. Priest is the bad man."

Moth's expression was that of pure evil. Chills ran down my spine as I continued to stare at them. What was he doing?

"I know the truth. About your escape. You didn't do it alone. There's no way you could have. Getting transferred to a new facility. That's genius. Who helped you?"

My eyes flicked to Laney. Her eyes were glazed over. I wasn't sure if she was paying attention, but I wasn't going to risk it. I didn't want her to know the truth.

"From mental patient to up and coming editor in the book world. That's not a trajectory I could have predicted, but hey, I thought you were going to rot in Cunningham's. Who would have guessed you'd find a way to get out?" He cackled.

I reached for the bottom of my mask, and Moth shook his head. He rose and lifted the remote that controlled the shocks that would go to Laney's head.

"Keep it on. I'm retraining her brain. When Priest killed her high school boyfriend, it scared her so badly that she couldn't handle the truth. She became a shell of her former self, running from men in masks, into the arms of the real monster. But I'm going to fix that."

My fists clenched at my sides as I took in everything around me. What could I do? I had to distract and then knock him out. Could I hurt someone who was already dead? Moth reached for Laney's head and forced her to face forward.

"Look at Michael, sweetie. He's the good guy, remember? Not Priest. Priest is bad. Priest is scary. You run away from Priest."

She shook her head in denial, and Moth pushed the button. Her body jerked as she screamed in pain. I lurched and pushed Moth to the ground. The remote flew out of his hands and crashed onto the floor on the other side of the room.

"You stupid fuck," he spat. "You think you can save her?"

We rolled around on the floor, both of us struggling for power. I didn't understand it. He was dead, and yet, I fought with him like he wasn't. I kicked off him and hurried to the remote. I pressed the button frantically, but nothing was happening. She was still being shocked. Moth laughed. "That's just for show. The machine doesn't turn off until I want it to, and I don't want it to."

I fought the urge to tackle him and instead hurried to Laney. I tugged at her restraints, but they were glued together.

"You want to save her? Make me a deal." Moth walked slowly around us, stopping behind her head.

Ghosts making deals to save a life? What was this place? Laney's mouth was dripping drool and her eyes were rolling to the back of her head. I didn't care what they wanted anymore, so long as they let her go.

"Let us into your mind, Priest."

"I don't know what that means!"

"It means, if you take that mask off, your body is ours to control. We need a host to help paint the Vincent red. Do this, and I'll set her free."

"Fine!" I screamed. Laney was going to die if I didn't say yes to whatever he wanted from me.

"Hold on, there's more." He stepped closer to me. "Why don't we make things a little harder for you? While in the mask, you can't speak."

"I don't care!"

"Starting now."

And just like that, the electric current shut off, Laney's body slumped, and the restraints loosened. My fingers worked quickly to pull her from the chair, and once she was free, she fell into my arms. I clutched her tightly to me, and I broke. My tears turned to hard sobs as I tried to listen for her heartbeat. It was slow but steady. Carefully, I laid her on the cold floor and stood. Moth leaned against the wall.

"There you go, she's still alive, she's still yours."

I opened my mouth to speak, but suddenly my tongue felt swollen and no noise was coming out. Frustrated, I began to lift off my mask. Moth clicked his tongue.

"Be careful," he warned. "Remember our deal. You take that mask off, you're ours, motherfucker."

I lifted it anyway, needing to know more.

"What does that mean?" I asked, my voice was released from the odd curse.

Moth left the room, pausing at the door. "I'm just going to let you fuck around and find out. If I were you, I'd put the mask back on, *big brother.*"

Rule 42 - Delaney
Sometimes secrets do make friends.

Four years ago.

"We can't. My parents will find out." I took the remote from Camryn and quickly turned the channel.

"Oh, come on," she whined. Her head turned toward the stairs leading up from the basement. "No one's going to know. It's just us girls." She motioned around the room, where all of our friends lay.

"Your parents aren't even here," Kat argued.

"Yes, but Priest is." I crossed my arms over my nightgown. "He's right upstairs with Carson and Kaleb and they'll hear it and know what we're doing."

"No, they won't." Sophie stood and stormed over, taking the remote from me. "And if they do, who cares? They'll probably watch it upstairs when we're done." She pointed the remote at the TV, went back to the pay-per-view channel, and began scrolling. "What should we pick?"

Pizza Delivery Sluts XI
Riley Needs a Lift and Lick

Badly Behaved Babysitters

My stomach twisted at the names.

"I'll go make popcorn!" April shot up. "Delaney, come with me. You guys keep looking, but don't pick without me!" She pulled me upstairs, and we went to the kitchen to microwave some snacks. I leaned against the counter.

"I hate this. I'm going to get in so much trouble."

"Kat said the same thing last week when Brady and Jake came to the slumber party, remember? It's fine. What's the worst thing that could happen? Your parents are way too nice."

"Really? Because I'm the only girl in ninth grade who still has a babysitter." I rolled my eyes, just as Priest strode into the kitchen, followed by his lackeys.

"What are you two losers doing up here?" He opened the fridge and pulled out three of Dad's weird Spanish beers and passed them to his friends.

"Making popcorn for the movie we're about to start." April giggled. She had a crush on a lot of boys at our school, but Priest was her current obsession.

"What movie?" Priest popped the cap off his bottle.

April and I shared a look.

Don't you dare tell them.

She giggled again and I let out a deep sigh. She was lovestruck.

"Ooh, is it a naughty movie?" Carson teased.

"Must be, for how red Delaney's face is right now," Kaleb added.

I put my hands over my cheeks, instantly realizing that I'd just incriminated us.

"I knew it." Carson smirked. "What is it? I may have already seen it. I can give you the highlights."

"Stop." I sighed. I looked to Priest, who was watching us

intently, but not saying anything. A small smile twitched at the corners of his mouth.

"You want company? I could go for a movie." Carson chugged his beer and gave it to Priest, who I assumed was going to hide them in his room and dispose of them Monday on the way to school.

"No!" I shook my head. "Absolutely not."

"Why not?" Kaleb asked.

"Yeah, why not?" April chimed in. Was she turning on me for a boy? For Kaleb Tomlinson, the ugliest out of the three? She elbowed me in the ribs. "It'll be fun."

I threw up my hands and stormed up the stairs to my bedroom, where I slammed the door and leaned against it. A knock on my door caused me to quickly turn the lock on the handle and step away from it.

"Go away, April. I need a bit to calm down." There wasn't a reply, which I took for her leaving me alone and going back down to flirt with Priest and his friends. I threw myself onto my bed and looked up at the pink canopy, wishing I hadn't lost my cool down there. A clicking sound and the twist of my door handle caused me to sit up quickly. The door opened and Priest came in casually, as if he hadn't just picked the lock to my room.

"What are you doing?" I crossed my arms. "Get out."

He shut the door and came over to me. "Tell me what's going on."

"What do you mean? I just don't want to get yelled at by Mom and Dad for buying porn."

"We order that shit all the time. What's the real issue?"

"I'm not comfortable with it. It's gross." I peered up at him, watching his reaction. He stared blankly at me for a moment and then nodded.

"It is kind of weird, getting hot with other people around. I get it."

"Priest!" I gasped.

"What?" He shrugged. "I'm just trying to do the big brother thing and relate. I don't like doing it either. Who wants to sport a woody with a bunch of other guys?"

I laughed, and the energy around the room relaxed. We weren't exactly best friends. We spent more time arguing than not these days, but maybe this was the start of a new leaf for Priest and me. I mean, we only had two years before he graduated and went off to college.

"I know, I'm weird. I'm the only one out of my friends who doesn't watch that stuff."

"I don't think you're weird. I get it. Porn isn't exactly aesthetically pleasing." He stood. "Come on." He waved for me to follow him as he went to the door.

I slid off my bed and hurried after him. "Where are we going?"

"To get you lady porn."

"Lady porn?" I giggled. "What's that even mean?" We walked down the hall, stopping at our parents' room. With a sly grin, he pulled out his switchblade and dug it into the keyhole.

"Is this how you unlocked my door?"

"I'm not telling you my secrets." With a few clicks, the door unlocked and he pushed it open. "After you."

Hesitantly, I went inside. We weren't supposed to be in here, hence the lock. Priest strode in like this was common for him and went right to the closet, throwing open the doors.

"You're being loud!"

"Who cares? Mom and Dad won't be back until Sunday night. I come in here all the time, calm down."

"You do?" I joined him in the closet. "Why?"

"Because of Mom's lady porn." He dove into the closet and pushed aside racks of clothing, revealing a hundred or more stacks of thick paperbacks.

I frowned. "Mom doesn't read."

He laughed loudly. "Oh yes she does. And this stuff is dirty. See for yourself, pick one."

Tentatively, I looked at a stack and picked the first one on top.

"Prisoner of the Scoundrel's Desire." I read aloud.

"Oh yeah, that's a good one."

I looked up at Priest in surprise. "You've read it?"

"I've read most of these."

A giggle escaped my lips at the thought. "No!"

"Movies aren't my thing; books are." He shrugged, unashamed.

"You steal Mom's porn." I couldn't believe it, yet, as I read the back of the book in my hands, I was tempted to steal it myself.

"I try not to think about it that way, but if you're insisting on saying it like that. Yeah, I guess."

I shook my head in disbelief. "I mean, I always knew you liked to read but..."

"I read just about anything. Not just this stuff. I've actually been looking into the other side of things. Publishing and stuff."

"You want to write books like this?"

"Not write but be a part of the process. An agent, or editor. I don't know, maybe I'll go to college for it or something." He rushed. "Hurry up. Pick a few out, then we'll lock up. I'm ready to get out of here."

I grabbed a small stack and turned away from the closet.

"Promise you won't tell anyone?" I shared a look with Priest.

"It'll be our little secret."

Rule 43 - Delaney

It's okay to fuck the slasher if he's your stepbrother.

I woke up in my bed, with a headache so sharp I cried out the moment my eyes opened. It was dark, the only light coming from the crackling fireplace. I sat up and looked around, screaming when I saw the figure to the right of my bed.

"Michael? I mean, Moth." The man in the Michael Myer's mask shook his head slowly. My blood chilled. "Where's Moth? What did you do with him?" I closed my eyes, trying to recall... anything. How did I get into bed? The last thing I remembered was... Moth was here. He accused Priest of...

"Priest is a bad man."

"Priest killed Moth," I said to Michael. "Priest is a bad man. Is that why you're here? To save me from him?" The figure, half-hidden in the shadows, didn't move. "It's okay. You don't have to talk. I know the truth. Moth told me everything."

Memories of Priest flashed in my mind. I'd almost liked him. I was so close to forgiving him for all the nasty, cruel things he'd said and done to me as teenagers, but Moth had exposed him for what he was. A monster. I was safe with Michael.

Moth was dead. He had become one of the many ghosts stuck here in The Vincent. Whoever was behind the Michael mask was Moth's gift to me. He was my protector, and I had to trust him.

"If I asked you to take off the mask, would you?" I asked him. He shook his head.

My core pulsed. Dirty thoughts ran through my mind, and I found myself lifting the blanket. "You must be cold. Even if you don't take the mask off, come lay with me. We can share warmth."

Michael stood. He was wearing the blue jumpsuit. That couldn't be comfortable. My mouth filled with moisture. I sat up on my knees and crawled to the edge of the bed. I grabbed his suit and pulled him closer to the bed.

I ran my hand along his erection. I went for the zipper on his suit and pulled it down, exposing his chest and boxers. Was this the same man who had been texting me? The one that came to my room and took my virginity while keeping me tied up? The one with my name tattooed on his hip?

Michael fisted my hair, and I took it as encouragement to keep moving. I continued exploring, tugging the suit down. When it reached his hips, he began to pet my hair, and although he'd yet to speak, I knew what he wanted from me. I needed to be a good girl and suck his cock.

My fingers curled around the elastic of his boxers, and with one quick motion, I tugged down, exposing his hard mast, and the tattoo two inches to the right of it.

Laney.

If this wasn't Moth, who else could it be? I closed my eyes and tried to think, but pain shot through my head and words were screamed at me.

Priest is the monster! Michael is your savior!

I looked up at the masked figure, and desire pooled in my belly. I'd do anything for Michael. I loved him.

Michael gripped my hair and urged me toward his cock, standing at attention. I opened my mouth and kept my eyes upward, watching his blank, white face. Was I being a good girl?

His cock was warm and massive in my mouth. I spread my lips further apart and tried to relax my jaw and throat to take more of him in. I wanted to take every last bit of him into my throat. The scent of his cologne filled my nostrils, making for an intense feeling of need and want. When I finally got down to the base, Michael tugged on my hair, pulling me back, almost to the tip, and then pushing me back down. Understanding what he wanted, I moved, swirling my tongue around and sucking his cock as I moved up and down, taking him in and out as far as I could.

My core ached from need, and I wanted to stop so that I could take his cock into my greedy pussy, but I was enjoying the feeling of him inside my mouth too much to do anything but continue sucking. Michael's cock pulsed as I worked it, and he began to thrust his hips, driving himself deeper down my throat.

I looked up at him, begging him to tell me I was doing what he wanted. A moan, a whisper, a growl, anything to show me I was doing this right, but nothing came from the masked figure. Instead, he cupped my face. It was a tender gesture that only made me want to please him more. I drove on, now determined to have him fill my throat with his cum.

I thought about the character in my manuscript, and how she could only dream to be living such a fantasy as I was right now and then Michael threw his head back and shoved my head deep onto his cock. Hot spurts of liquid burst inside my mouth, and I swallowed every last drop.

Michael pet my hair as I did so and finally let me go. I sat back on my knees and looked up to him for some sort of praise. He pinched my chin softly and urged me to lie down. Michael removed everything but his mask and joined me in bed. He pulled me into his warm body and trailed his hands down mine.

My legs parted as his hands came closer, but he shook his head and continued teasing me, getting just close enough to make me scream for more, but pulling back to not allow me release. He did that until his cock rose again, and the moment he was at full mast, he flipped me over onto my back as if I weighed nothing and climbed on top of me, pushing himself between my legs.

Michael tore my panties off, discarding the torn rags on the floor, and without a single word, shifted and then shoved his cock into my wet and wanting pussy. I cried out as the pain mixed with pleasure. He was so large, and I felt so full. He thrust into me, ignoring my screams and tears as I tried to manage all the feelings flooding through my body with each of his thrusts. He reached under my nightgown and pinched my nipples, going harder and harder.

"It hurts!" I whimpered, but he continued to pinch. Tears streamed down my face and my body wound so tight. It was then that I realized why he was intentionally hurting me. I had to relax.

Forcing my body to unclench and my thighs to fall open wider, Michael began letting pressure off my breasts and soon turned to massaging my breasts. My cries turned to moans as I closed my eyes and focused on the good feeling.

I couldn't believe myself. For the third time this week, I was allowing an unknown man inside me, without protection, and he was making me feel... good.

I began to roll my hips as pleasure rose. Michael ground against me, his fingers strumming my clit as he thrust. He lifted my legs in the air and then moved from my clit to press on my mound, and suddenly I exploded. My body gushed as my orgasm overtook me. Michael's cock pushed against something deep inside me, causing my legs to shake as floods of pleasure rushed through my body. He waited until I came down and then picked up the pace. I was growing familiar with this now and knew he was going for his orgasm. It didn't take long, and my second explosion came with his. We came together, his seed spilling into me, and as he pulled out to lie beside me, I clenched my thighs together, almost protectively.

I loved this strange man and hoped that this evening, this week would result in more than just a fun story. I wanted his child in my belly.

I lay beside her as she slept peacefully.

What the fuck was going on? Moth had me by the balls, and there was nothing I could do about it. I'd gotten Laney out of his horrible room and into bed to rest, but it was too late. Her brain had already been jumbled too much. She thought I was the bad guy.

And Michael made her insanely wet.

I could see it, the struggle her mind was going through as she tried to piece things together. The moment I took my clothes off, she knew who I was. But the brainwashing refused to let her acknowledge it. She was blind to everything that was Priest. As long as I had the mask on, I was Michael, her savior.

After she'd been put in bed, I went to my room, locked the door, and removed the mask. I was unsure of what Moth had intended when he made the deal, so I had to be on the safe side, away from Laney. There was a change in the air as if someone had opened a window, and then suddenly, warmth flooded through my chest, quickly turning to ice. And then, I heard a voice inside my head that chilled me to the bone and sent me flying back to the mask.

"Hello, Priest."

I shoved the mask back on. The feeling of... sharing my brain eased instantly, and I sighed, leaning against the wall. What had I done?

I repeated the questions over and over as I lay with Laney that night. She slept peacefully, as a woman who'd just been thoroughly fucked would. It was beautiful to watch. I wished I could do so without the rubber mask between us, but something deep inside told me it was dangerous to be unmasked around her. Whoever had joined me before in my room... wanted blood.

I tried to sleep but was restless. I left Laney's bed and went to my room. I locked the door and went to my bed, where I slid the mask off. A warm and cold feeling filled my body, but when the voice came, I spoke to it in my head.

"I need sleep."

I closed my eyes and felt the weight of the spirit leave my body, allowing me to rest, and thankfully, not dream. I awoke hours later and quickly reached for the mask, shoving it back onto my head. I could feel an angry energy in the room, but I ignored it. I was safe under the mask for now. I went for my laptop and turned it on. I was going to have to call in a favor if Laney and I wanted to get out of this fucking hotel.

Moth was right. I hadn't acted alone to get out of Cunningham's. I'd brought along a friend. He was across the country by now, but he owed me one. I had intended to flee far, but the draw to return to where I last saw Laney was too tempting. But now I was glad I did go home. She would have been dead already if I hadn't caught her that night before her flight.

I sent an email but was far too impatient to wait. I started perusing the web, looking for him. He had to be here somewhere. The first search pulled articles about our escape, but no leads. I went through pages and pages, trying to find something, anything, but then, something occurred to me.

I typed in the name, Elliott Spencer, and there he was.

Elliott Spencer, his pen name. The name was different from legal filings, but all the photos were of my old Cunningham friend, Les. I quickly made a dummy account on Facebook and shot him a message.

> Me: I thought we had an understanding. No SM.

> Elliott: What you mean? Who dis?

> Me: Let's not do this, Les. I need a favor.

Dots appeared and disappeared for a long time before finally, my laptop lit up with a call from Elliott Spencer. I sighed. Should I answer with my mask on or risk it? I answered the call and waited to see Les appear on the screen before removing the mask.

"Priest?" Les, a short, but stocky blonde man stared back at me, his blue eyes large and in shock. "How did you find me?"

The spirits that inhabited the hotel invaded my body and began screaming commands at me in my mind. I blinked and fought to listen and speak to Les.

"I need a favor."

"Sure, of course. Are you okay?"

"No." The spirit began trying to use my limbs, and my protest caused my arms to shake violently. "I'm trapped at the Vincent Hotel, in New York. I need you to bring a car close, down the hill from it, and wait. Me and Laney need will come down."

"Laney, your sister? Priest, I thought you weren't—"

"Fucking listen to me!" I snarled. "How far away from me are you?"

"Uh, hold on." He raised his phone and began to type. The entire time, voices screamed in my head, telling me to shut the laptop, that I wasn't going to escape, and Laney would be punished for this. "The Vincent, I can drive, but it's gonna be like three days. And Valentine's Day is Friday."

"Do this and I'll forget I ever knew you." My body trembled, and I reached for the mask. I needed to get it on now before it was too late.

"Fine. Okay. The Vincent, bottom of the hill. I drive a red Plymouth Fury. I don't know how good it will be in the snow, but I'll be there in three days. If you don't come in twenty-four hours..."

I swallowed the heavy lump in my throat as sweat dotted along my brow. "Assume I'm dead." I slammed my computer closed and shoved the mask back on, falling back onto the bed as the pressure lifted.

Fuck.

"I warned you." I turned my head to see Moth laughing at me from the other side of the room. "Not fun, is it?"

I tried to speak, but nothing came out, so I resorted to thought. Surprisingly, he heard me.

Fuck you. I'm getting out of here.

"Are you? Because based on that call, it sounds like you've only got three days to live, and I'll have fun with every second before I make you like me."

What was the point of killing you, if you can do everything you did in life?

"Everything but leave." Moth kicked off the wall and walked around the room. "The spirit inhabiting your body will only grow stronger each time you take the mask off. You will eventually be unable to do anything but surrender. We'll use you until our task is done, and then we'll make you one of us."

I can last three days. That's nothing. I did way more time at Cunningham's.

"Yes, about that. I'm still fascinated by it all. How pissed would you be if I inhabited your body and called them? You, turning yourself in, how hilarious. I think I might just do that. Is there a monetary reward? Hmm, I guess I don't need money anymore. I'll do it just for spite. That way, if you managed to get out, we'd both be locked away for eternity."

I stood to go.

"Tell me how you did it," he snapped.

I twisted the doorknob.

"Tell me how you did it, and I'll tell you his plan."

Whose plan?

"Mr. Vincent's."

RULE 45 - PRIEST
AN ESCAPE PLAN TAKES TIME.

One year ago.

"You like to write?" I motioned to the notebook in Les's hands. He'd been here six months and had already gone through three of them that I'd seen. The shaky man with tattoos covering his body looked up and flinched. I wasn't entirely sure when it happened, but over the years, I'd developed a reputation at Cunningham's. The female orderlies loved me, the male employees treated me like shit, and all the other wards were scared of me. Moth had been the only one to stand up to me, but he'd been gone for a while now.

"Yes," Les said softly. He was here because he'd had a mental break while on a meth binge. He'd woken up with tattoos all over his body and a fear of the outside world. Supposedly, he'd done the art himself, according to his charts. "And draw."

"Write and draw." I pulled a chair out and sat down across from him. "I like to read. Can I read your work sometime?" Most of the other patients came and went without so much as a second thought from me, but Les was interesting. Something drew me to him, and I wanted to figure out what exactly that was.

He pressed the notebook to his chest. "You'll just make fun of me."

"I won't," I answered honestly. That wasn't my style. "I'm genuinely curious about what you feel the desire to write down. Is it fiction or non-fiction?"

"What?" His brows furrowed.

"Real stories or made up?"

"Fake." His voice grew quiet. "When I was a kid, I used to tell stories. My therapist says it will help keep my mind active."

"Are you going to publish it when you're done?"

"Publish?" Les looked at me like I was crazy. "You don't even know if it's any good."

"Any story can be good if you have the right tools." I extended my hand. "Come on, let me read your story."

"No one will want to read a book from someone in here." He hung his head.

"That's not true. And even if it was, you just use a pen name. No one would have to know."

"A pen name?"

I explained to him that oftentimes authors chose different names to put on their books rather than their legal ones, and encouraged him to come up with one for himself. We spent a good amount of time going back and forth before he finally said, "Elliott Spencer."

"I like it. Now, Elliott, let me read your story."

He stood. "You'll have to start with the first notebook," he said and took me to his room, where he revealed almost a dozen of them, fully written in. He handed me one and his face turned serious. "Let me know what you think."

I stayed up all night reading Les's epic fantasy. There was so much to it, but it flowed well and kept me captivated through the next morning. I handed it to him at breakfast and demanded the next one.

"You liked it?" He seemed surprised.

"Yeah. I mean, you could use some help with spelling and sentence structure, but it's got good bones. Get it cleaned up and I think you could get an agent."

"Cleaned up?"

That afternoon, I tried to show him what I meant, but it only confused him. He ended up giving me the second notebook and insisted I mark it up for him. I took a nap and then went to work, my first real editing job. I made it my mission then, to help Les get his story published. I told my therapist this, and he started to help too. He provided me with books on grammar and how the traditional publishing industry worked. He allowed me access to a computer to research agents and publishing houses.

That was his mistake.

That was the spark.

The moment I realized I couldn't keep waiting for someone to let me out. For them to see I wasn't a danger to society. I wasn't getting out of this place. I needed more from my life. I wanted to do something meaningful. Not just rot in a bed at Cunningham's Mental Health Facility. No, I had to escape. And maybe, once I was successful enough, I could find Laney and convince her to run away with me. But could I?

I looked around the rec room, my books strewn across the table. They had no proof that I belonged here or anywhere locked up. I'd been tricked. Given the choice between prison and Cunningham's, scared, my parents sent me here. But I was done playing the good guy. I stood and stacked all my books and notes for Les's book.

"I can't wait to see your book on the shelves at a bookstore, Les," I told him. His deep brows furrowed in confusion. He and I both knew what they called me.

A lifer.

But they were wrong. I wasn't going to spend my life here. Striding over to the reception counter, I leaned over and smiled at Tatum, my most recent toy. Cunningham's was so short-staffed that she was the only one watching us today.

"Hey, sexy. You want to take a smoke break?" I winked at her. That was our little codeword. She nodded eagerly.

"Sure, it's about time for my lunch." She stood on her tiptoes. "I'll be back soon!" she said to the other patients. Tatum took me to the staff break room, which was just an oversized closet. The moment the door closed, her hands were ripping down my pants and reaching for my cock.

"I've been wet all morning," she moaned into my ear.

The pretty brunette slowly morphed into an adult Laney. Or, how I imagined she looked now. Would she still remember what I looked like when I got out? Thinking of Laney was the only way I could maintain an erection.

"I need a favor," I said.

"Me too, a favor." She giggled and dropped to her knees. "What do you want, more computer time?"

"No, I want to leave."

"After I come, okay?" She licked the tip of my cock. "Then you can go wherever."

"I mean, leave leave. I need you to help me leave Cunningham's."

She stopped mid-inhale and looked up at me. "You want to..."

"Escape," I finished her sentence. "And you're going to help me."

"I am?" She pulled her mouth away from my cock and stood.

I nodded slowly. "You are."

"But we're gonna have sex before?"

I fought back the eye roll. I swear, this one was the most

cock-crazy out of all of the ones I'd bedded so far. If rolling on a condom and plunging inside her for fifteen minutes while I thought of Laney got me out of here, I'd do it. I smiled and pressed my hand to her cheek.

"We are."

Michael gave me something to dull my headache and then left me to rest. I slept most of the day, missing breakfast, lunch, and dinner. I just made it out of bed and downstairs to find Annie, Juniper, and Tristan at the bar, huddled together and talking. They looked up and stopped when I came over.

"Hey, how's everything going? The writing classes still on?" I greeted them cheerfully.

Tristan scowled. "Not really. After your childish behavior about the nude modeling, I lost all inspiration to write. I've been focusing on other things."

"Such as?" I sat down at the small circle table and ordered the pink drink from the bartender when he came over.

"Well, no one has seen Moth," Juniper said. My stomach twisted as a flash of his body, frozen with his head bashed in, went through my mind. "Have you heard from him?"

I couldn't tell her the truth. Instead, I reached for the drink handed to me and shook my head.

"You don't think he tried to leave, do you?" Annie asked Tristan.

"He'd be stupid too." Tristan scoffed. "We're still snowed in. There's no way anyone is getting down that hill. I asked Gloriana this afternoon. She thinks it might end up being another week, especially if we get another storm like predicted."

"Another week?" I squeaked. I couldn't stay another week here! It was filled with spiders and ghosts and things that wanted to hurt us.

Tristan looked over. "Is that a problem? I thought you didn't work." The trio looked over at me, all mirroring the same look of irritation.

"No, I don't have a job right now, but I only had the money for one week. I can't stay another. Especially not in the suite." I rattled off lame excuses, and Tristan waved them away.

"There is an act of god clause in our contract, you're fine. As long as we're stuck here, once your agreed-upon stay is over, we're covered. I double-checked today as well. Besides, I thought you brought Priest along to help you with the cost."

"I did, but still." I paused, trying to come up with another reason to get out of here. "He's ready to leave too."

"Well, good luck getting down the hill." Annie smirked. "Maybe Arden has some sleds you can use. Or those innertube things. The big, black, rubber ones?" She nudged Juniper playfully.

"This has nothing to do with money," Juniper responded to me. "You're wanting to leave because you've seen something."

"What? No!" I knew as soon as it escaped my lips that it was too forced. They knew I was lying. All three of them leaned forward in interest.

"What did you see?" Annie asked.

"Who did you see?" Tristan asked.

"When did you see it?" Juniper asked.

Just then, Moth walked into the bar. The air chilled, and my gaze flickered over to the others. Could they tell he was a spirit?

"Moth! Thank god, I was so worried!" Annie leapt up. "I was sure you'd been attacked or something." She looped her arm in his and pulled him to our table.

Moth chuckled. "Why would you think that?"

The table grew quiet, and I could hear the unspoken word between us.

Ghosts.

"It's late. I should go," I finished my drink and stood.

"Wait." Moth grabbed my wrist and squeezed. "Stay a while. Tell us about the ghosts you've been seeing. Anything interesting?"

I shook my head furiously. " I should really go. Priest is—"

"Priest is working. I was just up there a little bit ago. Let him be." He squeezed me tighter. I was starting to second-guess myself. Had I really seen Moth's dead, frozen body outside?

Yes.

"Come on, Delaney," Juniper whined. "The otherworldly is the sole reason I'm here. Tell me everything."

"Yeah, come on, Delaney, tell us." Moth let me go and leaned forward. "Did you see a ghost?"

I licked my lips. "I don't know for sure. Maybe. There was a girl in a room on the third floor. She was really... odd."

"Odd how?" Juniper demanded. I looked around the table. Everyone was hanging on to my every word. Annie seemed skeptical, Juniper excited, Tristan surprised, and Moth... Moth was amused. That bastard.

"She didn't seem to know stuff about the modern world. Almost as if she'd been here a long time. But not too long, her clothes were relatively normal."

Juniper bent down and pulled out a large binder from her bag. "I think I can guess who it is. Was she Latinx?"

I lifted my shoulders. "Maybe? Her complexion was a little darker than mine. Her hair and eyes were dark brown."

Juniper flipped through the book like a madman, until she stopped and thrust the book up at me. I took in the photo she was showing me.

"Was this her?"

It was.

I paled.

"Holy shit, look at her face." Juniper laughed. "What did she say to you?"

"Nothing really. Just that she liked to read, and that Gloriana was mean to her." I tried to remember exact details of our conversation, but all I could think about was the spiders. I shuddered.

"I wonder if you can see other ones." Juniper's eyes glazed over. "What does this mean? That you're being allowed to see them?"

"You can too!" I blurted out. A hard kick came from under the table, and Moth glared at me.

"I haven't seen a single ghost." Juniper sat back and crossed her arms. "It doesn't seem fair. I come up here every year and nothing."

"Poor you," Annie said. "I am super glad it's not me seeing them. I enjoy peaceful sleep."

"You should write about it," Moth commented. "Tell the world all about the horrors of the Vincent Hotel."

"Oh, I wouldn't say horrors." Tristan scoffed. "So you saw a spirit. Don't be dramatic."

"I'm going to go try to write or something. Maybe reread what I've been working on so far." I left the group.

"Want some help? I'll join you." Moth followed me out of the bar.

"What do you think you're doing?"

"I could ask the same of you. You can't tell them what you know." Moth stepped up to me, pressing me against the wall. He pinched my chin.

"Why not? Eventually, someone's going to find you. When the snow melts and people start going outside..."

"That's a problem for another day. You can't tell them because they'll panic."

"Shouldn't we be panicking? If they knew about you, then they'd be figuring out a way to leave."

"That's exactly it." Moth's eyes darkened, and the familiar green irises turned orange, like flames. "You're not leaving."

How a dead spirit could hurt me was confusing. Had I imagined his body in the snow? I tore myself from his grip and slid under his arm.

"You're insane. We are all getting out of here. I don't care what you think. There's no way we could all die and no one catch on to things. I'm going to call my parents. They'll have some way to get me and Priest out of this place."

Moth snickered. "You really want to tell them you've got Priest here?"

My confidence wavered. "Why wouldn't I?"

"Because according to the internet, he's one of the most wanted men in the country."

I shook my head. "What? No. That's ridiculous."

I turned to look for the stairs but found them too far away. If I tried to bolt, he'd catch me. He read my face and laughed.

"Oh no. See, Big Brother has a lot of secrets he's not telling you."

"No. He went to school. He's a professional editor. You're the liar!" I pointed and continued to back away. I couldn't make it to the stairs, but the elevator was close.

"Oh, Laney, Laney, Laney." He clicked his tongue.

"Is everything okay?" We both turned to see Tristan storming down the hall. "Delaney, why don't you come with me? With us. Me, Annie, and Juniper were going to go up to the third floor and do some Rapid-Writer Prompts."

Tristan reached me and put his arm across my shoulder. "Let's take the elevator." He pushed me forward, and I followed him into the iron death trap. Moth stared at us from the hall. As Tristan pushed the button and we jolted upward, an eerie smile spread across Moth's face, and he raised a hand to wave goodbye.

"What was that about? Was your romp a little rougher than you wanted or something?" Tristan asked as we ascended.

"No, I didn't—" My blood ran cold as a sudden thought dawned on me. Moth had been able to touch me. I knew it hadn't been Moth, but what if I'd slept with a ghost? I gulped. "I don't want to talk about it."

"Well, I've got your back." Tristan put his hand around my waist and pulled me to him. "I know I was a little forward before, and I apologize for that. I think I had a minor case of cabin fever. It won't happen again, Delaney."

I stepped to the side. "Thanks. And I'm sorry for Priest's outburst. He shouldn't have attacked you like that."

"He shouldn't have." Tristan nodded. "If he'd given me time to explain, I probably would have come out of my little spell anyway. Maybe we should try to keep the classes going. It might help our sanity some."

I realized I had barely been to any of the things Tristan had planned for his retreat. I'd been too busy canoodling with ghosts and trying to fight the tension between Priest and me. I wondered what he was doing right this minute. I hadn't seen him since... when had I last seen him?

The elevator stopped on the creepy third floor and the

doors screeched open. Tristan offered his hand as he left the elevator. "Come on, the girls are waiting for us."

I stepped out and followed beside him rather than take his hand.

"I don't have my laptop," I said.

"It's fine, we're just going to shout our ideas." The farther down the hall we got, the more nervous I became. This didn't make any sense. Shouting out things we should be writing? Tristan stopped at the door at the end of the hall and pulled out a key from his pocket. There was loud chatter coming from the other side of the door. He grinned.

"See, they are already going at it. Let's go see what they're doing." He unlocked the door and flung it open. I peered inside and didn't see Annie or Juniper. It was dark in there. I started to turn but was shoved inside.

I was pushed so hard my knees collided with the hard floor and my palms scraped as I tried to catch myself. I let out a small scream, but before I could get up, the door was slammed shut and the telltale click of the lock being turned echoed throughout the room.

"What are you doing?" I screamed and banged on the door and jiggled the handle, but it did no good.

"You fucked everything up." Tristan's voice was muffled, but I heard him through the door. "You weren't supposed to have sex. Now, you're going to pay for what you did."

"What did I do?" Tears began to stream down my face. It was pitch black inside the room, and I could hear loud, yet unclear voices coming from all around me. "I don't understand." I sank to the floor. Darkness consumed me. I sobbed as I thought of Priest. How he'd tried to save me from my dark thoughts, but they'd returned so hard and so fast I wanted to vomit. Where was he now?

"You fucked us all," Tristan said, and while I couldn't see, I knew he'd walked away, leaving me in the terrifying darkness. Who would help me now? Michael, Moth? No.

"Priest?" I called out meekly. Would he be able to find me here? I needed my big brother now. For the first time since we'd reunited last week, I truly needed him.

I opened my eyes and stumbled to my feet, keeping my hands on the wall. It wasn't Priest I should be mad at. Or frustrated with. This entire time, he'd done nothing but save me from monster after monster in this place. It was Moth who'd put me in that chair and zapped my brain into mush. He wanted me to forget Priest, but somewhere, deep in my soul, my love for my big brother was too strong to simply be abandoned.

"Who's there?" I called out into the darkness. "Moth? Michael? I'm done playing with you. I'm not going to fall for anything else in this god-fucking forsaken place."

Suddenly, a single candle flicked on from the far end of the room. I shielded my eyes. Despite it being such a small light, it hurt my eyes. A large figure was holding the candle. He lifted it to his face, revealing a handsome, yet scary male face.

"Hello, Delaney." A second candle flicked beside him, and the second figure mimicked the first exactly, revealing twin brothers. "You're done playing?"

They took a matching step forward. They wore matching leather underwear; their tight, detailed muscles fully revealed. My heart beat furiously as I stared at them, and it wasn't until I noticed all the blood that covered their arms and legs that I grew truly frightened. Knowing I'd noticed, they both cocked their heads to the opposite sides and smiled.

"I don't want to be done playing," Twin A said.

"Yes," Twin B followed. "I think we're just getting started."

"Come play with us, Delaney."

RULE 48 - PRIEST
DON'T WEAR SCARVES WHILE RUNNING FOR YOUR LIFE.

I stared up at Moth's ghost after I finished the story of how I escaped Cunningham's. It had taken a lot of planning and lining up things just right, but no one got hurt. As soon as I was done, I slid the mask back on. The spirits fled and I could breathe again, but could no longer speak.

"If your parents knew, they'd call and have you hauled away again."

They would, but they didn't have to know. I stormed out of the room. I couldn't keep this up anymore. Laney had to know it was me under the mask, and why I had to keep it on for now. I pushed through her bedroom door and found Tristan.

He turned around quickly. He'd been digging in her suitcase and drawers. He had Laney's rose toy in his hand and he stuffed it into his pocket.

Where was Laney?

My tongue refused to move, so my pleas remained silent.

"She's not here. I took her upstairs to the twins. Is that you, Priest?"

The twins?

"The twins were a pair of identical brothers in the eighties who enjoyed booger sugar and hardcore sex. A little bit of both got them in a whole lot of trouble. Delaney had one thing to do this weekend, and since she couldn't keep her fucking legs closed, she's being punished. The twins will handle her."

Anger swelled inside of me to the point where I couldn't hold it in anymore. I ripped off my mask. I was so fucking angry, I couldn't feel the shift as the spirit took hold.

"What was it that she was supposed to do?" I gritted my teeth.

"Stay a virgin so we could sacrifice her to the hotel," Tristan replied in such a callous way that I was confused for a moment.

"What?"

"Have you heard the hotel say, 'Paint it red'?" He stepped toward me, stuffing his hands in his pockets. I had. "Years ago, when this hotel had been built, they discovered a dark spirit already here. It was constantly trying to hurt guests and finally, after a few limb removals, they asked it what exactly it wanted."

Blood.

Tristan grinned evilly. "Blood. You guessed it. Once a year, to keep the hotel relatively safe for other guests, we must sacrifice a virgin to the hotel. My grandfather did it, my dad did it, and now, I'm doing it. The retreat is the perfect explanation as to why we're here."

"But isn't it suspicious when one of the retreat guests goes missing every single year?"

"It would be if people cared about them. Haven't you ever heard of the phrase 'less dead'? No one cares about your sister."

I opened and shut my mouth quickly. Tristan smirked.

"Oh, yeah, I know. A quick search and some phone calls

revealed quite a bit about you, Priest Duvall. Locked up in an insane asylum after a man was brutally murdered on your block. And her, little innocent Delaney. Practically tossed to the wind as soon as she was eighteen. I did my research on her too before inviting her. I'm surprised she can still talk without drooling after how much ECT they did on her. She was the perfect pick for our ritual."

"If she needed to be a virgin, why did you try to rape her?"

"That was the spirits in this place. You've felt them, haven't you?"

I swallowed. More than he knew.

"They make you do things that you would never want to. I'm not a sexual predator. Hell, I'm not even that interested in your sister. But the spirits are growing more and more angry that we haven't painted it red, and they took it out on me."

"Paint what red?"

Tristan smirked. "The walls, of course." He spun around and looked toward the door. "But I'm finished with her. I'll figure something out. Otherwise, we'll all be murdered by the Vincent." He drifted over to the table, where paper flowers lay strewn across the surface. He picked one up. "I had these specially made for the retreat. Roses that won't wilt. I figured, since she wouldn't get real flowers ever again, she could enjoy these for eternity." He stuffed a flower into his pocket and strode out of the room.

The voice was growing louder inside my head. My limbs were blazing hot from the power it took to still move them myself and not allow it to seize my entire body. Despite the massive amount of resistance, I fought to put the mask back on, and relief washed over me when I could think straight again, but, for someone like me, thinking straight wasn't exactly a good thing. I returned to my room, finding the axe

I'd used before and then I went into the hallway to find Tristan.

The whistling sent me toward the stairs, where Tristan leaned against the railing, playing on his phone. He looked up at me, saw the axe, and smirked.

"You think that scares me?"

It should.

"If you kill me, you'll never know how to get your little sister back from the twins. They've probably already got her tied up, stripped down, and big rubber cocks shoved into all of her holes. The little cunt deserves it after damning us all. The hotel isn't going to let anyone out until it's received its sacrifice."

Moth could use some company, I decided, and raised the axe over my shoulders.

Tristan's face paled, and he slid to the side just as I swung down and the axe collided with the staircase railing. Wood splintered and cracked loudly, and I pulled back. Tristan took the second he had and fled the other way, sprinting back down the hall.

Knowing I could find him wherever he went, I strode at a slower pace down the hallway, letting him tire himself out. At some point, he pulled his room key out of his pocket but then dropped it. I scooped it up and flashed it at him.

"Help! Somebody, anybody! Wake up! Help!"

Moth appeared, and Tristan's face morphed into one of true terror. There had been nowhere for Moth to have come from. He'd appeared from thin air.

"How did you—"

Feet away from him, I swung my axe again, narrowly missing him.

"Moth, are you—" Tristan dodged my weapon again but rolled onto the floor. We'd been going all the way around and finally had made it to the other side of the hall and identical staircase. He pressed himself against the railing and frantically swiveled his head, looking for an escape, but there was none.

"Dead? Yeah, and it looks like you're next." Moth smirked.

"What?" Tristan looked at him, and I swung to the side. He once again was able to dodge the axe, but he turned and ran so quickly into the railing he flipped over it completely.

But there was no splat.

No loud thump as he hit the ground.

Moth and I shared a look and then stepped to the rails, looking over them and down.

Tristan's body hung limp, slowly rocking back and forth in mid-air. His scarf had caught on one of the large hooks used to decorate the lobby and had snapped his neck.

"Should we cut him down?" Moth asked me. I stepped away from the railing and walked toward the elevator to save Laney.

No, let them find his body like that.

RULE 49 - PRIEST
Don't let the ghosts fuck with your head.

We walked silently, me still clutching the axe, and Moth grinning happily that he had another friend to spend eternity with, until a voice called to us from behind.

"Hey, you fuckers!"

We turned to see Tristan standing by the railing, looking from us to the other side of the railing, where his lifeless body hung from a decoration hanger. I turned back around and continued walking. I didn't have time for a meltdown as Tristan's spirit or ghost or whatever came to terms with his death. A blink later, Tristan was right next to Moth and me, following us.

"You fucking killed me!"

"Did he? Because technically, that dumbass scarf you were wearing was what choked you. If you had just fallen to the ground floor, you could have survived," Moth argued in my defense.

"I wouldn't have tripped at all if I hadn't been being chased with an axe by a guy in a stupid Michael Myer's mask. Take it off, you fucking coward."

I paused and looked at Tristan through the rubber mask.

"He can't. He's cursed," Moth answered for me, his voice almost bored.

"Interesting," Tristan said and directed us upstairs to the third floor. It wasn't until we reached the landing that he thought to mention something. "You can't get in without the key."

I held out my hand expectantly, to which he simply laughed. "Why would I have it? You're gonna go have to steal it from my dead body. Isn't that a crime?"

"Out of all the crimes this guy's committed, desecrating a corpse doesn't really touch the top lists." Moth snickered, then turned to me. "Might want to go grab it. He's not going to do it for you."

Furious, I lifted my axe, which made them both laugh.

"What are you gonna do, kill me?" Tristan laughed.

I huffed and stormed back down to get the key from Tristan's corpse. The two ghosts followed behind me like my own personal hecklers.

Tristan addressed Moth, "You know he and Delaney are siblings, right? It's so fucked up."

"Step. But still, I never wanted to bang any of mine," Moth agreed. Reaching over the splintered railing, I hauled Tristan's heavy body up and dug into his pockets. I pulled out the paper rose from one pocket, the vibrating one from the other, and then found the key.

"Can you set me down?" Tristan said sharply. Turning up to look at him, I lifted his body up, returning it to the railing, and dropped him over it. The body made a sickening slap as it hit the marble floor below, and there was a beat before a female let out a blood-curdling scream from down below.

Oh well.

I abandoned the ghosts, standing still with wide eyes, and fled to the third floor again, key in hand and both roses in my pocket. I hurried down the hall, trying the key in every door, but they all remain locked. Panic set in as my mind went wild, thinking of all the things they could be doing to hurt Laney. Were they sexually assaulting her, as Tristan had mentioned, or were they more into gore-porn and currently cutting into her with a buzzsaw?

A door on the left unlocked and I shoved it open, revealing... darkness. A dull drum sounded throughout the room like a heartbeat. It was warm and moist and just under the drums, I heard whimpering. I stepped inside cautiously and the door swung closed. With a sudden whoosh, all around the room, candles flickered to life, and after my eyes adjusted, I saw Laney.

She was crouched on the floor with her eyes shut and hands over her ears.

"Who are you?" a voice asked. I looked around and found a tall man in leather gear talking to me.

"This room is for invited guests only," another voice said. I turned and saw the other twin. "I don't remember inviting you."

My fingers twitched, pleading for me to remove the mask. I wanted to speak, but I needed my mental facilities to be my own here. Something in here, while not directly frightening, was off.

I spun back to Laney and hurried over, knocking candles as I moved through the room. I crouched down, dropping my axe to the floor for just a moment, and reached for her.

"I wouldn't do that."

"She's currently in a very fragile state."

I needed to be able to communicate, but how? My hand grazed Laney's cheek and she opened her eyes. They were calm and then when she saw my face, she screamed! I stumbled back as she scrambled away from me.

"It was you! I saw you! You—" She stammered. "You killed

Marco, you killed Moth, and you convinced me you were my protector! I let you..."

What was going on? I shook my head, but she continued to cry. She looked toward the twins, who nodded.

"We showed her the truth," Twin A told me.

I leapt to my feet and swiped my axe back into my arms. They shook their heads in sync.

"This will not help your case. The truth has been revealed. She knows the masked man is the monster. If you want her to follow you, you must reveal your true identity to her."

I lifted the weapon. I knew it was pointless to aim it in their direction. They were already dead. But I could destroy the room.

"Priest..." Laney's soft, sobbing voice came from the corner of the room. I turned. She had her head tucked into her knees. "Priest. I need Priest to save me. Where is he?"

They were going to force me to take the mask off. I couldn't do that and keep my sanity.

"She's fought it for so long. Even went through tremendous pain and hurdles to refuse what she knew was true, but it's time to confess to her. Show her exactly what she's been denying for so long, and we'll make it stop," Twin B said. The music beat louder in my eardrums. The room grew warmer, to the point where I could barely breathe through the mask.

Twin A clicked his tongue.

"Every night for years, she has had nightmares about the man in the mask, coming to hurt her. They had to manipulate her brain just to alleviate some of the deep-rooted fear, and yet you stand here, allowing her to go through it all again! Tell her!"

I spun around and dropped the axe to the floor. Laney looked up from her knees and stared in horror as I took the mask off, revealing myself as the true monster of her nightmares for all these years. It was no masked man who had done those things. It was me.

"Priest?" It didn't make sense. How could it be? Priest wasn't the one who murdered Marco or Moth. He didn't come into my hotel room and— "No."

I stood. My feet wobbled on the floor, and I stepped back. I couldn't take my eyes off the man in front of me, dripping sweat. His chest heaved, and the familiar green eyes bore into my soul. It couldn't be. Not Priest.

A sharp flash ran through my brain, and I cringed as the memory returned to me. Priest, grabbing the mask from the end table right before going upstairs. It had been him. I had known, when they told me about what happened to Marco, I had known who'd done it, but I couldn't accept it at the time.

It all came back to me in one hard rush. Every last bit. I'd been an inconsolable mess. Every night, I'd cry and scream and demand they tell me where they took my brother. I had to be sedated more often than not just to not lose my voice and mind. They'd made me forget just how attached I was to him before...

I reached out, and Priest leapt back as if I were the dangerous one. His body began to shake and his eyes rolled into the back of his head. I pressed myself to the wall and watched him twitch for a long moment before he stiffened and then drew himself back to a normal stance.

"Laney," Priest's voice came out in a low growl. Without taking his eyes off me, he lowered himself and slowly picked up the axe he had dropped. My blood ran cold. What was he doing? "Baby, love of my life."

I looked around for the door. I had to leave this room. I wasn't sure exactly what was going on.

"Priest, please," I begged. He put his hand up and stepped toward me.

"You interrupted me." His eyes were cold and chilling. This wasn't the Priest I knew and confessed my love to just nights ago. No, something had come over him. Something sinister. I sidled to the door and turned the handle, and thankfully, it unlocked. Priest's expression changed so quickly that it startled me. He was almost two different people. He lifted his empty hand. "Nothing's going to happen."

I opened the door and fled down the hall. I glanced back to see Priest coming after me, seeming to struggle with his walk. He lifted the axe and glared at me, his face back to the monster from before. "Well, now I might just have to slice you through the middle. Right in fucking two!" he screamed and began to run.

I flew down the stairs, past the second floor, and then past the first as well. I kept going until I reached a door that was labeled the boiler room. With each step, I could hear Priest's heavy ones behind me. I turned the knob and ran inside, slamming the door behind me. I took a moment to breathe, but a large thump against the door got me moving again. It was dark, and the roll of the boiler terrified me, but the man with the axe scared me more.

I found another door labeled as an emergency exit and pushed it, setting off the alarms. I didn't concern myself with the loud alert, I blinked, shuddered from the cold, and took off running into the night. There was nothing but snow on the ground, but I kept pushing through. I turned and saw Priest storming out into the weather. My legs ached from the running, and my body shivered from the cold, but it was literal life and death, and I wasn't going to die this way.

The maze was visible and I turned toward it. It was uphill. I fell over and over, my knees stung from the snow, but finally, I made it to the maze, and steeling myself, I went inside. Moth's frozen body lay at the end. I wasn't going to let mine be the same.

"Laney," Priest called to me through the maze. I couldn't place where his voice was coming from, so I drudged forward. My legs were beginning to weigh me down, and soon each step was laborious. I turned a corner and hit a hedge wall head-on. I stumbled backward, but something grabbed me through the bushes and pulled me forward and tight to the wall.

"Stop!" I screamed out. The hands latched onto my wrists and squeezed, holding both of my arms firmly inside the bush. They ran something across my pointer finger and then poked it sharply. I gasped.

"Let me go!" I whimpered, and then suddenly, Priest was behind me. I felt the warmth of his breath on my neck. I could smell the familiar scent of his cologne mixed with sweat. The hand that reached out to touch my hip was one I knew all too well.

"Priest." My body trembled with fear. I couldn't see him enough to know his intentions. "Please, let me go."

"Laney, I warned you, didn't I?" His voice wasn't his. It was, but the tone, the cockiness, that wasn't the big brother I knew and loved. "I told you not to run."

"Priest, something's not right. Please let me go!" I tugged on my arms and felt the knife on the other side dig into my palm. Hot tears slid down my face as I fell forward into the hedge wall, defeated. The pain was too much. I couldn't fight anymore. I closed my eyes and accepted my fate. I was to be one of them. A victim of the Vincent Hotel.

Priest's hands slid down my hips, cupping my ass through my skirt. My legs were pressed together and he pushed his knee through them and then kicked them apart, splaying me for him..

"What are you doing?" Instinctively, I pulled away and the person gripping my wrist yanked me back, stabbing me again, causing me to scream out. The knife went deep, hitting the bone. I bit down and tried to contain the screams as best as I could.

"You like to run and hide? I like to play games too, Laney." Priest bent over me, and I felt his cock against my ass. "Little sister isn't so little anymore, are you?"

"Priest," I sobbed. "I'm stuck." His hands lifted my skirt and yanked on my panties. They tore and fell to the snowy ground. His cold fingers probed my lips, sliding inside with ease.

"You must like this, do you, little Laney?" He slid over my clit and despite the pain radiating from everywhere, my core responded to him. I groaned. He pulled back, and there was a shift behind me. He brought his length to me. "I've never seen a slit this wet. Does it turn you on to know just how many men I've killed for you?"

"No!" I cried out as he pushed inside me. Poor Marco! Moth! I groaned as the fullness enveloped me. No! This was wrong. It was one thing when I couldn't recall everything when I was blissfully ignorant as to who was under the mask, but now there was no mask, nothing was blocking my memory. Priest and I were... were...

"Fucking you is the most depraved thing I've ever done, Laney. And that's saying something." He pulled out and then rammed back into me. A gasp escaped my chest. Priest reached around and tugged on my blouse, tearing the buttons, and ripping down the bra. My nipples hardened instantly to the cold exposure and he began kneading them as he thrust in and out of me.

I closed my eyes and gave in to the sensations overwhelming me. I was cold but hot. In pain but feeling pleasure. I was horrified, yet turned on. I'd always loved Priest, but now, that took on a whole new meaning for us.

Priest dropped one of his hands, and I heard shuffling from behind me. Something fell out of his pocket, and I looked down between my feet to see one of the paper roses from my room. I didn't have a chance to ask about it, because he was thrusting something between my legs. He clicked a button. I gasped, as my clit was deliciously attacked.

"I want you to drench my cock, little sister. Can you do that for me?" Priest growled into my ear. I could barely handle how intense the pleasure was. I didn't know where to focus. The rose toy was sucking on every nerve ending on my clit, while his cock pounded my G-spot inside me. I closed my eyes. "Answer me."

"Mhmm..."

"Mhmm what? That's not what you tell your big brother as he's fucking you, Laney."

"Yes, big brother. I'll come for you!" I shouted. "Please, please make me—" I lost my coherency as he pressed the toy deeper against me and then shoved himself so far inside I wasn't sure I could take any more of him.

"Now!" he demanded. As if waiting for his permission, my body exploded. This orgasm was inside and out, my body was filled with wave after wave of warmth and relief. Suddenly, it was incredibly slick between my legs. So much so it ran down my thighs. My knees buckled and Priest held me up. He waited until I came down to take control again, shoving so deep inside of me, in and out, until he filled me with his cum.

He pulled out of me and took the toy, running it down my slit. Our juices combined together, and he brought it to my face. I stared at the rose in awe, covered in... us. He urged me to take it between my lips. I did so, sucking it clean and then looking up to my big brother for guidance.

Did I do good?

He smiled, as if reading my thoughts, and nodded.

"Good girl."

"Let me go!"

The hands holding me to the maze wall suddenly dropped me. I stumbled back, falling into Priest's arms. He seized me and caught my wrists, holding them up to his eyes. Blood ran down my arms in thin lines across my exposed chest. I looked to the ground, where my tattered clothing lay bright in the snow beside the paper rose. I reached for the flower, and the blood from my hand dripped onto it. The red made for a beautiful contrast. I stared at it. How perfect it was, and now ruined with blood, a symbol of my stay here at the Vincent.

The beautiful story I'd wanted to create while here was ruined by the spilling of blood.

Priest lifted me up, naked, scared, and confused. I stared at his expression, trying to figure out what he was thinking. It was almost as if he was wrestling with something internal.

What we'd just done?

What we'd been doing?

A sob escaped my throat as I finally admitted to myself

how long I'd wanted to feel this way with Priest. Long before this week, long before Marco. No wonder I let him into my bed so fast that first night. Deep down, hidden by all the therapy, my dark desires for my brother lay dormant, but not gone. The moment he reappeared, so did my feelings for him.

"Priest!" I sobbed. "Let me go. We shouldn't have come here."

"Where? To the maze?" His voice wasn't his own. It was a blend of his and... something else, someone else. "Saw something you didn't like?"

"This hotel," I moaned. "There's a reason Mom and Dad split us up. They knew!" I tugged on my wrist, and he squeezed tighter, causing more blood to gush from my wound and spill onto the rose I was holding. I beat on his chest with my good fist as he took us through the maze and back inside. I screamed and begged for him to put me down, but we were in a dark tunnel, and no one could hear me. We reached a door with light peeking from the other side.

"I'm taking you to your room. If you scream, you'll regret it." Priest opened the door, taking me up to my room. He tossed me on the bed and went to lock the door.

I watched him carefully. While I could remember everything now, I was still confused. How had I gone from stuck-up virgin who couldn't write a good kissing scene to suddenly wanting and needing sex more than I wanted anything else? As Priest paced the floor, I pressed my thighs together, admiring how his muscles tightened and stretched. There was something very wrong with him, but I couldn't focus on anything but my carnal desire.

"Don't move," he warned and quickly left my room, heading into the living room.

The moment the door closed behind him, it was as if the air had been returned to the room and my sex-charged brain disappeared. Pain shot through my hand. I had to put some alcohol on it. I had no clue what exactly I'd been stabbed with. I scrambled, knowing my time was limited. Priest would be back any minute. I found a scarf and quickly wrapped it around my hand, but I wasn't fast enough. The door opened as I stood by the fireplace, still wrapping the scarf.

My head shot up to the door. Priest slammed it closed and glared at me. "What did I tell you?"

"I know, but my hand! It's an open wound and—" I stopped short when I saw what was in his hands. Handcuffs. His eyes went to the bed, and a slow, evil grin spread onto his face. I stepped back, stumbling on the small wood stack by the fireplace. I looked down and saw the hatchet beside it. Slowly, I bent down and picked it up, my hand shaking.

Priest laughed. "What are you planning on doing with that? I doubt it can even cut the wood it was sitting next to." He took a step forward, and I waved the hatchet wildly.

"Don't come near me," I warned, but even I knew my threats were nothing. I was smaller than him, injured, and the weapon I held was more decorative than deadly.

"Laney, you wouldn't hurt your big brother, would you?" As Priest moved toward me, my heart beat faster, beat louder, and I couldn't move, couldn't think until he was snatching the hatchet from me and tossing me onto the bed! I screamed as I used my hand to catch myself. The weight came down hard and tears burst from my eyes as white hot pain shot through my body.

Priest yanked my arms up and quickly handcuffed my wrists to the bedposts, stretching my arms as far as they could go. I kicked my legs but I could feel the heavy blanket of desire sliding over me as he ran his hands up my calves and to my thighs, pausing at the apex of my thighs. My body relaxed, but I continued to struggle against my restraints, knowing it was pointless to fight. Fight what exactly? I loved Priest. I wanted Priest.

I closed my eyes and remembered the feel of him not even an hour ago, his thick, rigid length sliding in and out of me. I needed that feeling again. I needed pleasure, I needed... him.

A groan escaped my lips and Priest chuckled as he loomed over me, resting between my thighs.

"Laney, baby, you have such a pretty pussy. You know that?" His pointer finger slid along my slit, teasing me. "And you're wet. Is this from before, or do you want more?"

"More." I arched my back. I wasn't sure where the words were coming from, but I knew them to be true. I needed more of Priest.

"More what?" His words were sharp, and I knew what he wanted me to say. I knew because I wanted to say them as well. The knowledge that what we were doing, how we felt, was forbidden only spurred our lust for each other. If telling him what he wanted to hear helped us both get to the finish line, I'd shout it for everyone at the hotel to hear.

"More, big brother. I want more of you!"

He removed his shirt. His muscles were sharp and beautiful, each line a testament to how long we'd both waited to be together in this way. He undid his belt. I let out a loud gasp as he slid his boxers down, revealing my name inked on his body, right at the V-line. It was real.

"I did that for you, Laney baby."

My body screamed as my longing became too much. It physically hurt to not have him touch me. Priest chuckled and trailed his finger across my inner thighs. I stared at his hard cock. My mouth watered at the thought of it in my mouth. I wanted to taste every part of him.

"I know what you want, and I'd love to give that to you Laney, but you didn't listen to me. I told you not to move, and you did."

I blinked rapidly as he moved away from me. My body screamed for him to come back. He returned a second later, holding up the hatchet. His beautiful green eyes shone with something... terrifying, and he turned back to me.

"Looks like I'm going to have to teach you how to listen."

RULE 52 - PRIEST
YOU CAN MAKE IT FIT.

"What do you mean?" Laney's voice shook as she eyed the hatchet in my hand. I lowered the weapon between her legs and whirled it around, resting the wooden handle against her folds. Her brown eyes widened and she shook her head. "Priest, please."

I grabbed her skirt, the only thing left from the maze, and tugged it down and off her completely. Laney was something to behold, naked and handcuffed. This was the second time I'd gotten her like this. It was a good look for her. Splayed out and at my mercy.

"Please what? Because all I asked you to do was not move, and you couldn't even do that. Now, you're not going to go anywhere until I say so."

I dropped the hatchet, letting it sit right at her entrance. I leaned forward, taking one of her tight, brown nipples into my mouth. I bit down hard enough to elicit a sharp gasp from her and then licked it, moving to the other breast to do the same. Her moans of pain turned to those of pleasure. "How long will it take for you to learn how to listen to your big brother, Laney?"

"I can listen," she said. "I promise."

"Mmm, I think you'll have to do better than that. Do you remember—" I ran my tongue down her chest to her navel. "How often Dad would beat me for doing something bad, but only scold you for doing the same thing?"

"That was years ago!"

I parted her pussy lips and flicked my tongue across her clit. "It used to piss me off so much. Why should you go unpunished? You were a spoiled little princess, and it only made me want to hurt you more. I knew, when I finally got my chance to make you mine, I was going to punish you the way you should have been punished then."

"You were my protector!" She cried out. "Don't you remember?"

I tried to silence her by running my tongue down her wet pussy. Our juices from before only turned me on further. By the time we left this hotel, I was going to make her pregnant.

Fool! You're never leaving this hotel!

The voices controlling me screamed into my thoughts. I blinked and tried to push back against them. I didn't want to do any of this. I didn't want to punish Laney. She was right. I was her protector, not her punisher. Where had that all come from?

"After the storm, remember? I was hiding in the closet and you found me."

I continued eating her pussy, causing her to moan and lose her train of thought.

Don't worry, she's under her own spell of The Vincent. Her desires are overtaking her thoughts. Keep going.

Laney cried, and I fought to return, but it was beginning to feel more and more like a useless battle. The more I fought, the stronger the spirit became, taking over more of my body and mind. My hand shook as it reached for the hatchet just under me.

"And with Marco. You saved me from him. I knew it was you. You took the mask upstairs to your room right before it happened. I knew it was you and I didn't tell anyone! It's because I love you, Priest! I love you!"

The Vincent and its dead inhabitants had a plan for us. She cried out with orgasm, and when she came down, I pressed the handle to her wet folds and slowly pushed it inside her.

She let out a sharp cry the instant she realized what was happening. She bucked her hips, but I held her steady. I sat up, watching her with excitement as I slowly, inch by inch, drove it deeper inside her. Tears slid down her face and she closed her eyes as I continued until I couldn't see the wood anymore.

"Your words mean nothing. I'm going to beat you and eat you and stretch you." I pulled the handle out, then thrust it back in. "Until you can behave and act like a good girl. Now moan for me, Laney."

Her mouth parted and the sound I'd demanded from her came from her throat. I pinched her nipple and continued to shove the tool in and out of her, sometimes pulling all the way out, other times only an inch or two, but the more I worked it, the looser her body became. Her eyes relaxed, her cries of pain turned into sharp gasps for breaths, and when I began to lick and suck on her breasts, her hips began to buck with need for more.

"Yes, take it, Laney. Take everything I have to give you. You've been bad, coming here, desiring another man. How many times did you come thinking it was Moth under the mask? Because that's how many times you'll be punished."

"None," she groaned. "I always knew it was you. I always wanted you."

I grinned. "Good girl, now come."

I drove the hatchet deeper into her, moving faster and harder. She let out a cry and her body arched as she came. I continued fucking her with the weapon as she screamed out in total ecstasy. She relaxed against her restraints, and I removed the hatchet. She tried to close her legs, but I pushed them back open.

"Aren't you done?" She sniffled. "Humiliating me? Hurting me?"

"Did it hurt? You seemed to be enjoying it." I crawled between her legs and fondled her swollen pussy. She was probably sore, but it only served to turn me on further. I wanted her to hurt.

No, I didn't.

They did.

"It's different in the moment." She sniffled. "Once it's over, you think differently."

"Who said it was over?" I positioned my cock at her widened entrance. I hadn't gone even a tick soft the entire time I'd been fucking her with the weapon. Watching her take it to its base only made me hornier. I pushed into her with ease and found her still wet, hot, and the sigh that released from her body told me she too, was still wanting. I thrust into her, our hips colliding in pleasure. "I told you. You're not going anywhere for a long time."

"Like hell," I said through gritted teeth. Finally, my own thoughts and words burst through the wall the spirits invading my body were trying to build inside my brain. There was no way me or Laney were staying here for eternity. In two days, Les would be here to save us. We just had to make it out of this hell-hole hotel. But it was hard when everything in my brain was screaming for me to stay instead.

Doesn't this feel good? Fucking your little sister. You can't do this anywhere else. The world will shame you.

I looked at Laney, still handcuffed, naked, and gloriously panting as I thrust my cock in and out of her soaked pussy. I couldn't remember how long we'd been doing this. Hours, days? It felt like every time I came, we'd rest only a moment before I found some other way to torture another orgasm out of her while I waited for my cock to rise again. This wasn't me. I was never this... cruel.

I spilled my seed inside her for the umpteenth time and slid off the bed, grabbing a discarded towel off the floor and cleaning myself up.

"Can you... clean me?" Laney said in a weak voice. It was taking everything in my power to push through the haze. I snickered and stepped to the foot of the bed, where her legs were splayed open. My cum spilled from her swollen pussy lips, and my cock stirred. I wasn't ready to go again, but the need to fill her pussy was strong.

"Why would I clean you up?" I asked. "I told you. You're not leaving this bed until I'm satisfied that not only have you learned how to behave, but you're also pregnant."

The idea of Laney's belly stretched round and breasts massive turned me on immensely. I'd wanted to put a baby inside of her long before this vacation, and now, I was going to make that happen.

"Can you imagine, going home, and having to tell Mom and Dad what you were up to during your retreat?" I walked around the bed, admiring her exhausted, weak but beautiful body. "Eventually you'll have to confess once you're pregnant and they're going to demand who the father is, and I'll get to sit back and smile, knowing that it was me who did that to you."

"You're a bastard!" Laney cried.

"Do you want me to stop?" I crawled onto the bed. My hands started at her toes and slid up her smooth legs. "Because I thought you liked what I do to you." I continued upward, reaching her breasts, and twisting her nipples. She winced, but her lips twitched at the corners. She liked me hurting her.

"We can't have a baby, Priest. They'll find out!"

"And then what?" I slid my body on top of hers, licking and tasting her nipples, sucking on one until she whimpered in pain, and then switching to the other. "While they may not like it, it's not like we share blood. Our baby will be perfectly healthy. Hell, we won't even have to fight over the last name, as we already share the same one."

My hand reached between her thighs and I spread her lips.

She'd already taken the hatchet and myself, but something inside of me, something dark, something not quite myself... wanted more.

"I don't want to tell them." Laney shook her head, forcing my attention back to her face. "They'll hate us. Hate me. We'll embarrass them. We can't. Priest, please don't do this. I'm sore. My arms and..." Her legs trembled. "... it hurts."

My hand drifted back up, lavishing in how warm and soft her skin was, and settled on her throat. I was sick and tired of her crying. I didn't care what our parents or their friends or anyone else thought of us. I gripped her neck and squeezed.

Laney's eyes widened, but there was more than fear in them. Despite her protests, she liked this. I squeezed and let off, allowing her to breathe, and then squeezed again. I pulled a nipple into my mouth as I continued to squeeze, on and off, until finally I'd had enough. I sat up, looked her directly in the eyes, and choked until her eyes rolled into the back of her head and her body went slack.

Good girl, go to sleep.

I unlocked her arms. She begged me to stop, but I couldn't. I wouldn't. But I could give her pussy a break. I rolled her over onto her front and raised her arms again.

She began to rouse as I was handcuffing her again to the bedposts, only this time she faced the mattress.

"Wha..." she said groggily and lifted herself to her knees. I left the room and proceeded to shove pants on and walk out of the suite, leaving Laney handcuffed, naked, with her ass in the air.

The kitchen will have something to help. Back in my day, we used olive oil.

My own thoughts were pushed to the back and when I came to again, I was back in the room, a small jar of coconut oil in one hand and the belt I'd discarded earlier in the other.

"Why did you leave me?" Laney cried. "It's dark in here!"

I ignored her and tossed the jar onto the bed. It rolled under her, but she couldn't reach for it to see what it was. I cracked the belt and went to her. I ran my hand over her perfect, smooth ass, sliding a finger down the center. She tensed immediately, and I pulled my hand away. I raised the belt and swung it down on her curvy, soft skin. She screamed and lurched forward. The belt left a thin red line across her ass. It was beautiful. I crawled onto the bed and rested my knees on the back of her thighs, keeping her down.

I raised the belt again and spanked her one, two, three times. Each time, her skin welted, and her screams grew louder. My cock strained against my jeans as I gazed at her reddened ass. I spanked her again, three times, and then finally eased off of her, pushing between her legs.

My dick was hard and ready to go. I reached under her, pulling the jar of coconut oil out. I opened it and dipped my hand in, scooping out a good-sized amount. My hand went to her sore ass and slid between her cheeks, finding the tight little puckered hole.

"No!" she gasped, but I ignored her, rubbing the oil all around it until it was off my hand. I pulled her up and then unzipped my pants, pulling them completely off.

I pushed my cock between her cheeks. She whimpered, but didn't beg me not to as I reached for more oil, and rubbed it on my cock, and then her asshole again. My finger, now completely lathered in it, tested the entrance first. Laney cried out as I pushed through the first ring of muscle, and then slowly went deeper, until my finger was completely hidden inside. Her sobs fueled the darkness inside me, urging me to continue. I massaged her, slowly thrusting in and out with my finger until her body began to relax.

"See, I knew you were a good girl," I purred into her ear as I lathered my middle finger to slide inside as well. She sobbed, but nodded, and as I continued using my fingers inside her ass, I found her thrusting back. Then, I decided it was time for the real thing.

RULE 54 - DELANEY
LEARN TO TAKE ORDERS.

P riest had tortured me to orgasm so many times my body was exhausted, but yet, with each earth-shattering explosion, it only caused me to want more, to crave more, and as much as I wanted him to stop and let me rest, I couldn't bring myself to say it with any real passion.

Everything around me felt foggy, as if on a sweet-smelling pink cloud. I knew that he had shoved the handle of a small axe inside me, that it should have hurt, and it was meant to degrade me, but... I liked it.

I was fully aware that I'd been choked to the point of unconsciousness and woken up in a different position, but it was okay. I was safe with Priest. And as he spanked me with his belt so hard I thought it'd bleed, I tried to clamp my mouth shut, because I knew I'd be rewarded.

My big brother promised.

His fingers were exploring a painful, yet incredibly interesting piece of my body I had never given any thought to as far as pleasure went. Priest wanted my little tight hole, and I wanted him to take it. It hurt at first. Tears streamed down my face as his fingers moved inside me, but Priest's words from before echoed in my brain, and I began to relax. There was nothing wrong with this, us. He was right. No blood, no DNA, no genetics that would hurt our future. We could have a baby, a real family, and a life together once we left The Vincent.

Why leave? It's so nice here. Don't you like being able to be free with Priest?

A voice I wasn't familiar with drifted into my mind. What was that?

You wouldn't have to tell anyone, you could just stay here.

Hmm... maybe that wasn't so bad. Maybe for a little longer. At least until we knew I was pregnant. Flashes of Priest ran through my mind. Him raised above me, his face perfectly relaxed and glowing as he spilled inside me made my pussy wetter, and I began to truly enjoy the feeling of what he was doing behind me.

"It's time," he said.

"But we can't make a baby this way."

"There's time for that." He removed his fingers from my backside and I instantly felt it return to its natural state. Oh, no. Had he given my body enough time to be ready? I tensed, and in a flash was feeling the sting of Priest's slap on my ass cheek. He directed his cock between them and pressed against my hole.

"Relax, Laney," he warned. "Or this is going to hurt more than it should."

I grit my teeth as he began to push inside me, stretching me to unfathomable size. I wanted to scream, I wanted to cry, but I also wanted to please him. I wanted what he wanted, and he wanted this. I trusted him.

Priest scooped up more oil and rubbed it around my ring as he continued pushing inside. It helped, but only so much. It hurt, and tears kept coming, despite trying hard to be strong. Finally, when it felt like I couldn't take even a millimeter more, he stopped. I gasped with relief, but then he pulled me up, shifting under me quickly, and shoved me down onto his lap, pulling hard on my restrained arms.

A scream escaped my lips as soring white pain shot through my vision. His full cock was inside me, and it was too much. Priest held on to my breasts, cupping them gently, massaging them.

"Get used to it, Laney. Get used to that full feeling and then we'll keep going."

I nodded and closed my eyes. Priest chuckled and began to tease my nipples. "When you're ready, I want you to bounce."

"Bounce?"

I cocked my head to the side in question, but he didn't clarify. He continued to play with my nipples and slowly slid down to my clit, strumming it leisurely, rousing me. He planted hot kisses on my neck, running his tongue down my shoulder, and as he played with my body, the muscles strangling his cock began to relax.

"Good girl," he purred. He must have been able to feel it. "Good girls get rewarded." He reached for something. His hand returned to my clit, placing something cold on it. It was made of rubber and felt familiar, and then... Oh!

Priest pushed the button and the rose toy whirred to life, sucking on my clit.

I lifted myself slightly, Priest's cock slid out of my ass just a smidge, and then I sat back down. It hurt! Priest kept the rose on my clit and urged me to move again. I did, and with each time, it hurt less and less. I moved up and down, bouncing on the balls of my feet, letting myself enjoy the feeling of his cock filling my ass. As I bounced, Priest muttered words of praise in my ear.

"You listen so well, Laney. I'm so proud of you, taking my full dick to the base. I knew you could do it. Perfect." His words and his touch spurred me on. Each time I lifted and sat back down the easier and more pleasurable it became. He was hitting a button inside of me that I desperately needed pushed.

"Are you ready, little sister?" he asked, sliding two fingers inside my pussy. I gasped at how full I truly felt and nodded eagerly. "I want you to come now. Can you do that for me? Can you be my good girl?"

Climaxing, I felt dizzy with ecstasy as I rode my finale. When I came down, my body slumped over. Priest held me to him, grinding and thrusting up into me, his cock still hard and needy.

I wanted him to use me. To take me as long as he wanted and where he wanted. If he wanted my ass or my pussy or my mouth, I didn't care, so long as he continued to give me pleasure along with him. Eventually, I began to bounce again and a low, guttural growl escaped his throat as he thrust hard into me and his cock exploded, filling my greedy ass with his cum.

He removed himself from my tight hole, and I felt a twinge of sadness and emptiness. I didn't want our love-making to end. I wanted to keep going forever. I wanted to take him in all my holes until my body couldn't take it anymore. I wanted him to fill my body with his seed and make my belly round with his beautiful, green-eyed, black-haired perfect baby. We were meant for each other, soulmates, thrust together by our parents, unknowingly.

Priest finally cleaned us both, and then much to my surprise and dismay, uncuffed me. My arms were sore, but my body was too enthralled by the warm feeling of multiple orgasms to care. I'd waited far too long to return to Priest. I could have had this all along, in our house, in our bedrooms. If only our parents hadn't forced us apart. And if we returned home, they'd do it again. Baby or not, they'd find a way to keep us away from each other.

Maybe the voice calling to me was right.

Staying here at the Vincent wouldn't be terrible, would it?

"I'm going to let you sleep now. Don't leave this room until I come get you." Priest slid out of the bed and began picking up his clothes. "Understand?"

"Yes."

"Good." He stormed out of the room, and no sooner had the door closed I was slammed with a wall of pain. A scream slid from my lips as I fell back onto the bed in horrible, agonizing pain. The dreamy, pleasurable spell I'd been under was gone, and I was experiencing reality. The hand that had been stabbed in the maze felt like it was on fire. Both places Priest had inserted himself into were bruised.

With shaky arms and hands, I brought my hand into view. The profuse bleeding had stopped, but my skin was hanging on both sides, exposing red muscle. I had to get this taken care of. How could I write like this? Swallowing my fears, I stood from the bed and looked for something to bandage my hand. I turned toward the door. Did I dare risk Priest's wrath to go to the bathroom to clean myself? I didn't have a chance to decide, because he came back in, holding some towels and what appeared to be an ace bandage.

"Let me see your hand."

He cleaned me and wrapped it tight. The entire time his face was hard and cold. His eyes had an almost lifeless look to them as he worked. When he was done, he helped me to bed, putting the covers over me and repeating his initial order for me to stay put.

While my body still hurt, my hand felt better with the compression, and I fell asleep.

The next morning, I was awoken by Priest coming into my room, with wet hair and only a towel around his hips. Knowing what was under the towel sent my heart and body ablaze.

My name and nothing else.

"I want you to shower, then we're going downstairs."

I did so quickly, and when I came back to my room, he redressed my bandage. We left the suite and went down to the dining hall. The room was deathly silent as we came in. Only Annie and Juniper were at the table. They didn't look up when we came in.

"What's going on?" I asked. "Where's Tristan?"

Annie and Juniper's heads shot up together. Annie glared at me and Juniper began to cry. I furrowed my brow in confusion. What had I missed?

"Tristan is dead," Annie snapped. "You were too busy getting railed by your model boyfriend to come down last night."

I shook my head. "Dead? No. How?"

Juniper sniffled and used a napkin to wipe her tears. "We're not sure exactly. Annie was walking across the lobby when he fell from one of the upper floors. The impact was so hard it..."

"It splattered his insides all over me!" Annie screamed and stood. "Something isn't right. Tristan is the one leading this all. He's not supposed to die. What are we going to do?"

Juniper stood up and went to a hysterical Annie. She put

her arms around her and tried to soothe her. "It's fine. We're going to figure it out."

"No, we're not!" Annie shoved Juniper off of her. "Everything is fucked up. Half of the guests didn't show. The virgin isn't a virgin anymore. And now Tristan's dead!" She stepped away from the table toward the door. "We're all gonna die now. And it's your fault, Delaney!" She pointed at me as Juniper shoved her out the door.

I turned to Priest, who made himself a bowl of cereal and was digging into it as if it were a normal day.

"Did you know Tristan was dead?" I asked, my chin trembling. He didn't respond, so I asked again. "Priest."

"Yes, he knew. He was there when it happened." Moth's ghost appeared, sitting across from us. "Care to share the story?"

Priest continued eating. I looked to Moth for answers.

"I'm so confused. How is any of this my fault?"

"Did you know that at one time my ancestors lived here?" I jumped when Tristan walked into the room. He looked just as he had when he was alive. If I hadn't just been told otherwise, I wouldn't know the difference.

"I didn't."

"Yes. My great-grandfather helped build the Vincent. He worked right with Mr. Vincent to create and make this place just as grand as his vision was. But with perfection comes a price."

"A price?"

Tristan sat beside Moth. They exchanged a look and turned back to me.

"Mr. Vincent was willing to do anything to have his dreams come true, even mess with the dark arts. When he called upon the spirits that inhibited this place, one answered. An evil being, who agreed to give him success and wealth and the perfect hotel, so long as he kept the walls red."

I remembered... someone saying that. "What does that mean?"

"It means that the next morning Mr. Vincent woke up, took an axe off the wall, went up to my great-grandfather's room, and proceeded to swing down, painting the suite walls with blood."

I gasped.

"Yes. Mr. Vincent brutally murdered someone to ensure that the Vincent could be all it was meant to be. Mr. Vincent thought he'd done his end of the deal. A full year went by and the hotel was completed, people stopped getting hurt, and guests were aplenty. Everything was perfect until suddenly it wasn't again. The demon wanted more. And if it didn't get more, then the bloodlines of every person who worked on the hotel would be snuffed out one by one."

"That's why you're here."

"Yeah. Mine and Annie's families are the only ones left of the original crew that worked on the Vincent. My family has been diligent in coming every year to make the sacrifice, but I was going to hand the torch off to Annie this year. You'll have to forgive her outburst. She's just scared."

"I don't understand."

Moth tossed his head back in frustration. "He was going to sacrifice you, you—" He snapped his mouth shut. "But then you fucked it up."

"Did you know about this?" I asked Moth.

"Not the full details, but to an extent," Tristan answered for him. "Yes, I realize now that I should have planned better. I should have told everyone exactly what was at stake. And probably shouldn't have picked a hot girl as our sacrifice."

"But why does it have to be a virgin? Your grandfather obviously wasn't."

"My grandfather wasn't the one Mr. Vincent murdered.

My great-grandfather's fiancé was in the bed, not him. She was a virgin."

My breath left my lungs. How horrible! She had no idea.

"So what's going to happen then? If the hotel doesn't get what it wants?" I shivered and looked around. Tristan stood and leaned over the table.

"Who knows? It's not really my problem anymore, is it?"

"Well, it's not mine either." I stood as well. "My family isn't tied to the hotel. We'll just leave."

"You can try. The Vincent isn't going to let you though." Moth snickered.

"Why not?"

"Because it's already taken over your boyfriend. Or brother. Whatever."

I looked at Priest, who was staring straight ahead, his eyes glossed over again.

"What do you mean?" I asked cautiously.

"We mean," Tristan said. "That Priest isn't in there anymore. He's been possessed. And whatever spirit has him isn't letting him go. It's not going to let you go either. Face it, sweetie, you're as good as dead."

RULE 56 - PRIEST
MOVE FAST. DON'T BOTHER WITH CLEAN UP.

I was losing time. The longer I stayed here, the stronger the spirit possessing me became. I wasn't sure how I got where I was, and I was only coming in and out of consciousness for small pieces of time.

"What do you want?" Annie's voice pulled me from the darkness. I looked around and found myself in a library. Annie was behind a desk with a dozen books opened. "You can get the fuck out. I'm trying to fix everything you screwed up."

I didn't understand what she meant, but I couldn't walk away.

"You know, your line should have been the first. I'd always hated Gwendolyn." The loudest spirit spoke through me. He had almost taken over me completely.

Annie's face paled. "That's not your voice. How do you know that name?"

I clicked my tongue. "Annie, Annie, Annie. Do you think I can't recognize the bloodline? You look like her. The hair, the eyes, the attitude. For a cook, your great-grandmother's meals were shit."

"Who are you?" Her eyes widened with fear as I stepped toward the desk.

"What are you going to do now that your precious little virgin's been taken? You know we won't accept anything but pure blood."

"I know that." She stumbled back, hitting the wall. "I'm working on it. I might try to go down the hill. We can find someone in the town below."

"You think we're going to just let you leave?" I laughed.

"You have to give me a chance," she pleaded. "I'll be fast. There's a snowmobile in the garage. Me and Juniper will go down in the morning and be back in the evening, right in time for the ritual."

I shook my head and grinned. "See, you're lying. You know how I know?"

"I'm not!"

I stepped up to her and pressed my chest to her soft, shaking frame. She whimpered as I whispered to her.

"How are you going to get the sacrifice back, if there's only two seats?"

Annie stopped breathing. There was a long moment, and then she ducked and flew out of the room. I spun around and looked for something to take with me on my chase. Where was my axe when I needed it? I stormed after her, empty-handed.

"Juniper! Gloriana!"

I followed Annie's shrill, panicked screams. She was giving herself away. I stalked her through the hotel. She was taking corridors that were uncommon and dark, but I recognized where she was going.

I'd built this place.

She was trying to leave. I caught up with her in the garage, as she was frantically pulling out drawers in a cabinet. I slammed the door at the exact moment she squealed with glee and raised a key up into the air.

"Nice try, Annie. You're not leaving the Vincent."

She spun around and dropped the key onto the concrete. She dropped to the ground to look for it. "Please. Just let me go. I'll find someone. I can get the walls painted. You just need to let me go down the hill."

"That's not happening. You know that. I know that. I don't know why we're playing this game."

"This isn't a game, Priest! I don't know who you are, or how you're tied to this place, but you've got everything wrong. I'm trying to save everyone!"

"By killing my stepsister?" My own words came through. My anger rose to the surface. The spirit of Mr. Vincent receded and let me have my body and mind back. "You invited her here, knowing nothing about her, just to brutally murder her for your own gain?"

"It's not about me. Between our families, her life would save a hundred. Now my family is screwed."

"Sounds like a you problem. Actually, it sounds like you've all had this coming. How many people have you killed to keep this going? A hundred for a hundred? Seems fair."

"Who the fuck do you think you are?" Her eyes lowered to slits. "There's something wrong with you. Moth tried to warn us, but we were all too blinded by your hotness to pay atten- tion. Where is he? Did you kill him?"

"Why do you think he's dead?" I laughed.

"I'm not stupid. I know who's alive and who isn't here. I've already seen Moth's ghost. Tristan's will come around before long to see me. But I'll be damned if you make me one." She lunged her arm forward and I gasped as something pierced my stomach. I looked down to see her holding an icepick.

"You little bitch." I shoved her back. She fell against a tarp and cried out as her back hit whatever was under it. I steeled myself and reached for the icepick still in my gut. Clenching my teeth, I pulled it out and dropped it to the ground. Blood poured from the wound, and I stumbled. I should have just left it in.

I'll take care of that. You just take care of her.

The pain began to tighten and recede as the wound healed up. I lifted my shirt to see, and Annie and I both stared in wonder at my unblemished skin.

"What the hell are you?" she gasped and scurried out of the garage. She was going straight back to the hotel when suddenly she made a sharp right turn and disappeared. What the hell?

I paused right where she'd turned and saw the wall she'd hidden behind. It was so covered in snow I couldn't see it from a distance. I reached out and grabbed her, squeezing the breath she had out of her.

"Stop, Priest! I'll do anything. Do you want me? My body? You can have me!" She tugged on my hands, trying to bring them to her breasts. When I didn't budge, she tried the other direction, urging me to touch between her legs. "I've been wet for you since I saw you at the airport. Just let me go and I'll let you have any hole you want. I bet I'm better than that little virgin you've been rooming with."

Laney. She'd wanted to kill Laney.

I snapped. I was tired of the games. I let her go and pushed her to the ground. Annie grinned and lifted her shirt, exposing her bra. "I knew you wanted me. Come on, I bet we can melt the snow with all this heat we're putting off."

I crouched over her and smiled. Her eyes reflected amusement. Did she really think I was that fucking stupid? A man controlled solely by his sexual urges? She thought she had me, that I'd forget all she'd done just to wet my cock. I didn't forget anything.

I smiled and reached for her head, petting her hair. She relaxed, and then my hand went down, circling her throat, and squeezed. Annie's eyes shifted to panic in an instant when I brought my other hand down, cutting off her airway completely. She tried to roll and swat me as her face turned red and then purple, but I held firm, watching the life slowly leave her eyes until she fell limp.

I counted to thirteen, then lifted my hands from her body, certain that she was gone. I flinched as snow flew up and hit my face. I looked up to see Annie glaring down at me and her dead body.

"Thanks a lot, asshole. Now what?"

The relief I'd felt when the spirit possessing me receded was short-lived. I could feel the pressure of Mr. Vincent's spirit returning. It had used its energy to heal me, but it was coming to again. Annie's ghost was glaring at me, but I didn't have time to argue with her. I needed to get back to my room. I spun around and started back to the hotel.

"You can't just leave me like that!" Annie followed me.

I rolled my eyes. What was she going to do? She was dead.

"You know, if you'd just let me go down the hill, I could have figured out a way to save our asses."

"Fat chance." I smirked. "If anyone is going down that hill, it's Laney and I."

"You think the spirits are going to let you leave? They've already gotten inside of you. I can feel it. I knew something was wrong!" She waved her finger and followed me back to the hotel. "Your eyes changed. They get glazed and... evil-looking. But now, now I can feel it." She shivered.

"What do you mean, feel it?" I paused at the doors and

turned to the spirit. She looked up at the building and raised her hands slowly.

"I'm part of the Vincent now. It's a hive mind. I can feel the darkness, the hatred, and the jealousy. It's a tingling." She turned her head to me and her eyes went white. "You don't have much time before he returns. I suggest you go find that mask, Priest."

I left her on the stairs and ran inside. Voices called to me in the lobby. Annie was right. I could feel Mr. Vincent's spirit returning. My chest burned as he tried to rise up inside me. I turned up to the stairs and was stopped by a strong hand on my arm pulling me back down. I turned to see Juniper glaring at me.

"We need to talk."

"Tristan's already dead. I'm not trying to be the next one. Laney and I are leaving."

"You can try, but unless we give the hotel what it wants, it won't let you leave."

I swallowed, my mind flashing back to Annie's corpse in the snow. Have I not given the hotel enough blood?

"You don't have much time, do you?" She reached out and put a cold hand on my chest. "He's coming back. What are you going to do?"

I brushed her away. "If I can get that mask back on, he won't be able to control me. Now excuse me, you're right. I'm running out of time." I reached the suite and began tossing my things around, looking for that stupid rubber mask. It was the only thing keeping me from losing my body and mind completely. When Vincent came back, I was done for. Had someone taken it from my room? Where the hell was it?

"What are you doing?"

I spun around to face Laney. Her eyes were red and her cheeks were swollen from crying. "I'm looking for something. What's wrong?"

"Priest?" Her face crumpled. "Is that really you?"

I hurried to her, putting my arms around her and pulling her close. "Yes, it's me. I don't have much time. I need to find that Michael Myers mask."

"Why? So you can kill more people?" She shoved me away from her. "I know about Moth and Tristan and Marco. You can't keep doing this Priest!"

"Laney, I need to hurry."

"How convenient."

"It's true! Laney, I made a deal with the spirits here and they want to take over my body and I don't have much time."

She crossed her arms. "I know. Moth and Tristan told me. But I want to know the truth. Was it you or were you possessed when you killed them?"

"Why does it matter? They're dead regardless." I ducked under my bed.

"Priest, I need to know. Did you kill them or was it..."

I popped my head up and then stood. "The spirit that's slowly consuming my soul? What do you want to hear exactly, Laney? Why does it matter?"

"It matters because I can't tell the difference!"

I sat with her words for a moment. "You want to know if it was me or not who you slept with."

She closed her eyes. "Yes."

I crossed the room and pinched her chin. "And what if it wasn't? What if it was some spirit fucking you? Would that be more palatable than your brother?" I slid my other arm around her waist, pulling her to me. "Or do you like it more when it's me?"

"Priest." Laney cleared her throat. "I don't know what to think. I'm scared. Do you have feelings for me more than just..."

"Brotherly love?" I leaned down and planted a firm kiss on her soft lips. "I do. I love you, and I want to have a life with you outside of this god-forsaken place. So I need to find that mask, because without it... I can't think straight."

"So, it is true. Without the mask, you're someone else. It wasn't you who handcuffed me. Or you in the maze..."

How could I explain that it wasn't... but was? That while my body and mind were taken over by Vincent, deep down, I wanted to do those things to her. It turned me on to see her scream and writhe in pain, while also moaning and pleading for more.

"It's complicated."

"I don't see how. Did you do those things to me or was it someone else?"

I spotted something behind the bedside table. Hair. I shoved the table aside and sighed with relief as I pulled out the mask. I turned to Laney.

"It wasn't me, but it can be. You want me to shove you down, choke you, and then fuck you 'til you cry? I can make that happen, just let me put the mask on."

I shoved the mask over my head. The spirit attempting to inhabit my body left and I took a deep breath. It was hot underneath the mask, but the freedom over my body was worth it. I lifted my heavy tongue and huffed. This was it. Until I could get us out of the hotel and down the hill, I wouldn't take the mask off. Laney let out a small squeak and my attention returned to her. She hadn't said a word about what I'd offered just a moment before, but her eyes said more than her mouth ever would.

I took a step forward, and she flew back, hitting the wall and then spinning out of the room.

Oh? She wanted a chase? I could do that.

I locked the door of my room. My heart was beating furiously. Why had I goaded him like that? Why did he look so hot in that mask? This wasn't the time for games. We needed to figure out how to get out of this place before the hotel trapped us in.

A loud pounding came from the other side. I jumped away from it as the door rattled. My eyes shot to the door handle. It shook, but Priest abandoned it in favor of pounding on the door.

"Priest! I didn't mean any of that. Don't!" We only had a few more hours. In three hours, it would be Valentine's Day, and if we weren't gone by morning...

Another thump came, along with the sound of wood splintering. I screamed, and suddenly the door exploded in the center. Priest dipped his head in, still in the mask. I couldn't see his mouth, but his eyes were wild with excitement.

He was going to do exactly what he'd said before. Shove me down, choke me, and fuck me until I cried. But I didn't want that. That was sick. Things I'd enjoyed just the night before were morally so wrong. Nothing like what we'd done could ever be in one of my romance books. I was so fucked up.

I backed away from the door. Priest put his arm in, unlocking it. I flew to the door to the hall and ran out. I looked both ways and went to the left.

My door opened and slammed and I turned around to see Priest in the mask, holding the hatchet from before. The very one he'd put... I gulped. He saw me and started stalking toward me. He was so cocky; he didn't care to run. But I wasn't going to let him catch me. This was all so wrong! Tears filled my eyes as my world came crashing down on me. What had I done?

This entire week I'd spent every night in bed with my step-brother. The things I let him do to me were... How could I? I reached the end of the hall and froze. My only choices were to go into the elevator or use the rickety ladder to go up to the third floor. What had I been thinking? I should have gone to the right. With Priest gaining on me, I turned to the elevator and ripped the metal door closed.

It squeaked in protest. I pushed the buttons furiously. They were lighting up, but nothing was moving. Panic shot through me, and I peered over, trying to see just how far Priest was from me. I let out a scream as he jumped out and yanked the door open.

I fell to the floor and crawled back. Priest came in and the elevator groaned and jolted as it moved upward. It made it halfway to the next floor before it stopped abruptly. Fear slid up my spine as I stared at the concrete between the floors, trap-ping us in. The elevator jostled slightly, and I nearly peed myself. I could not die in a broken elevator. I closed my eyes and said a silent prayer. Please, don't let the cables break.

Priest's hand reached out and I leapt back. He tilted my head up. I shifted to sit on my knees and looked up at him.

He dropped the hatchet, and with his free hand, he undid his belt and popped his pants open. Priest's hand on my chin slid down, curling around my throat, and lifting me up. He pulled his pants down further, unsheathing his cock, hard and ready. I reached for it tentatively. He nodded, and with his hand shifted to the back of my head, I rose and brought my mouth to him.

My tongue explored the rigid length. I wanted to be praised and told I was a good girl.

A good little sister.

Was it wrong to like it so much when he called me that? I took his cock further into my mouth, circling it and then sucking on it completely. A low grunt came from Priest's throat but nothing else. Was that good? As I sucked and licked and explored the lines of Priest's length, I thought about our timeline. All the times we'd teased each other or the stolen glances and touches. How at some point his tickles turned into bullying, and I should have known then, that something was different between us. That this was more than just siblings not liking each other.

He'd been fighting his attraction to me the only way he knew how. By pushing me away.

Priest pushed my head deeper into him and I began to choke. I relaxed my throat to allow more of him into my mouth and soon, arousal pooled between my legs. I opened my eyes and looked up. I swirled my tongue around him and then looked back down, finding his tattoo for me just off to the side.

Laney.

Priest dripped precum, and I licked the tip, savoring the salty taste. I wanted that between my legs. I let out a groan, and suddenly he pulled out of my mouth. I was about to object when I was hit with a warm spurt once, twice, three times.

"Did I do good?" I asked meekly, his cum splattered across my face. Priest nodded slowly, and then the elevator jolted back to life, taking us up to the next floor.

RULE 59 - DELANEY
ALWAYS BE PREPARED FOR SURPRISES.

As we stepped off the elevator, I tried to wipe away the cum from my face but Priest put his hand up and forced mine back down. He glared at me through the mask, and I nodded.

Okay, big brother.

While I thoroughly enjoyed tasting Priest's cock, I'd been given no release and my body was screaming in protest.

Someone came from the shadows and I reached for Priest's hand. He squeezed and pulled us forward. It was Arden. He didn't seem to see us. He looked around suspiciously and then pulled out a key and opened a door, hurrying inside.

"He looked odd, right?" I asked Priest. He nodded. "Do you think he's in on everything? We should go ask." I tugged Priest forward, hurrying to the door the caretaker had gone through. I tried the knob, but it was locked. My stomach tightened as nervously, I brought my hand up and knocked. There were footsteps, and a moment later, the door swung open and Gloriana stood there, wearing a robe and glaring at us.

"Yes?"

"I-I'm sorry." I stepped back, embarrassed. Not only had I rudely knocked on someone's room at night, but I had cum on my face still.

"Come in, if you must." She huffed and opened the door wider. I looked to Priest, and cautiously we went inside.

"Something is going on with the hotel," I started. Gloriana shut the door behind us and I heard the click of her locking the door. I looked around for an exit. That was the only one.

"Yes, this happens every year. Tristan will figure it out." Gloriana waved away my concern. "I see you two are no longer keeping secrets." She motioned to my face. Embarrassment flooded me again and despite Priest's warnings earlier, I lifted my top and wiped myself clean. "It's okay, play your little kinky games. We don't mind, do we?" She looked past me, and I turned.

I jumped with surprise at Arden stepping from the shadows in just his boxers.

"Aren't you two..." I pointed between them. Gloriana went to him and dramatically disrobed, revealing a matching red lingerie set.

"Aren't you?" She raised an eyebrow. "There's no need to shame one another here. Isn't that why you came to the Vincent? To be free?"

I glanced at Priest, whose eyes had hardened under the mask. "We're not blood-related. You two are," I accused.

"That's only a concern if children are involved, yes? Arden and I choose not to reproduce. We have enough fun together." She moved in front of him and crouched down, tugging on his boxers. His cock sprang free, and I darted my eyes. I couldn't turn my ears off though, and I heard the telltale slurping sounds of a blow job.

"Please," I pleaded. "We came here for help. We need out of here. Tell us what to do."

I opened one eye. Gloriana stood and pushed Arden to the bed.

"You want help leaving? Good luck. If the hotel wants you, you stay."

"There's got to be something," I argued. "Please, we'll do anything."

"Anything?" She looked at her brother and they chuckled. I didn't like the look on their faces. Gloriana walked across the room and lifted a lanyard off a shelf, waving it to us. "This is the key to the van. You want it, you earn it."

"How?"

"You look at us with disgust, but you are just the same." Gloriana shook her head. "You are ashamed to show your love outside these doors, but not here. You want the key? Show us what makes you so different."

"I don't understand." I reached for Priest, who put his arm around me. Gloriana strode over to me, sliding her hand down my arm.

"We want to watch," she whispered. My body went still as I took in her words. I looked up at Arden, who lazily stroked himself while watching us. Could we do this? Let them watch us to earn our escape? I looked up at Priest, and it was as if I could read his mind.

You take the lead.

I took a step forward and turned back, reaching for him with shaky hands. I looked to Gloriana, who crossed her arms smugly.

"Okay," I said and went to the bed. I sat on the edge and closed my eyes, breathing in and out. We could do this. If we pretended we were alone, it was nothing. Just making love. I reached for Priest and ran my hands down his chest. He lifted his shirt, keeping the mask on. I pulled on his pants. Would he be able to perform so soon after... yes. He was already hard again. Did he like this idea? Priest removed his pants and underwear, revealing himself completely to the eager siblings.

Arden took the chair and Gloriana sat on his lap, watching us with lust.

Priest reached for me, making me stand. He tugged on my clothes, teasing my nipples the moment they were exposed. With one hand on my breast, his other went between my thighs, parting my lips and swirling my arousal around. I groaned into his chest.

Turning, I pushed Priest onto the bed. He moved to rest his head on the pillows, and I straddled him. We didn't have time to play these games. We needed to leave this hotel, but I couldn't think straight until I had my release. Grinning, I sunk down onto Priest's cock.

I cried out as he penetrated me. Oh, how I needed this! I ground my hips into his and Priest thumbed my nipples, pinching them.

Priest couldn't say anything, but his eyes were expressive enough. I shifted and rotated my hips, gasping and moaning as pleasure filled my body. He bucked underneath me, sending his cock deeper inside me, and soon we gained a rhythm. I needed release. I thought back to the elevator, and how I wanted desperately for him to fill my pussy with his seed. That tipped me over the edge.

I opened my eyes mid-scream and saw Moth standing off to the side, his arms crossed and watching us.

As soon as I came down, Priest rolled me over. Tristan appeared beside Moth as Priest began pummeling my pussy with his cock. My eyes rolled into the back of my head as I enjoyed the knowledge of all these people watching Priest send me right into another orgasm. My pussy pulsed so hard that in moments he was coming, spilling himself inside of me. The feeling was incredible, and I prayed that we had just made a baby.

We collapsed into each other. I glanced around and only saw Gloriana and Arden, still in the throes of their own passion. I was too far gone with pleasure to care about what we'd just done. It was worth it.

We reached for our clothes and began looking for the key. Priest found it and raised it in the air. I hurried to him, and together we fled the room, leaving the couple panting and moving together. We shut the door and started down the hallway.

I found myself wanting to be disgusted with their actions, but Gloriana was right to an extent. There were no risks for her and her brother. And while Priest and I were safe to have children, if we came out publicly to our family and their friends, we'd be shamed. No wonder those two stayed here, away from prying eyes. They could be exactly who they wanted to be.

I paused at the elevator.

Should we stay?

RULE 60 - PRIEST
ALWAYS BE PREPARED TO CHASE SOMEONE.

The elevator doors squealed open, and we took one step out and were instantly met with resistance.

"Where do you think you're going?" Juniper stepped out from the shadows. I squeezed Laney's hand tighter and brushed past the woman in our path. Mask on, I couldn't do much other than glare.

"Juniper, I'm sorry, we can't stay here," Laney explained as I dragged her along.

"You can do anything you want, Laney. You don't have to do what Priest tells you to do. Make your own decisions."

I stopped short and turned back. Was she really pulling this card? Juniper smiled and stepped closer.

"Why exactly do you want to leave? What's waiting for you on the outside?"

I glanced at Laney. Her resolve was crumbling. She wore her feelings on her face. I saw everything she was thinking. Shame, guilt, disownment. Probably. All of those were likely waiting for us. Before I'd been shipped off to Cunningham's, Dad had said just as much. And when they discovered that I'd found Laney after my escape, they'd turn me back in. I wouldn't be allowed back at a mental health facility. This time, they'd send me to prison.

I wasn't leaving Laney's side. Now that I've had a taste, I couldn't.

"What if we stayed, Priest?" Laney whispered what I was thinking. "We could be free here. No one would ever have to know."

There were so many things I wanted to say. While the idea of staying in a place where we could be free to love each other sounded like... paradise, it was no way to truly live. I shook my head.

How would she ever publish a book? How would she ever explore the world like she wanted? And what about our future? We'd never get married in a ceremony surrounded by people we loved. Any children we had would be raised here. The rest of our lives, surrounded by ghosts. Laney would have to watch guests come and go while she was trapped here for the rest of her life. I couldn't do that to her. We had to leave.

She sniffled, and her eyes grew shiny. "Okay." She looked back to Juniper. "I'm sorry. We have to go. Come with us."

"You don't get it. We can't. The hotel isn't going to let you go. Jesus Christ." Juniper tossed her hands up. "When Tristan told me who he'd picked to be the sacrifice, I knew you had to be stupid, but this is bad, even for him. How dense are you?" She stormed over to Laney and put her hands on her shoulders, shaking her violently. "You can't get out!"

Her screams echoed across the empty lobby. A loud chime of a clock startled us all. Juniper laughed and spun around with her hands in the air. One by one, all the curtains on the windows rolled down, and the doors around the room slammed shut and locked. Spirits appeared, lining the exits and walls.

I recognized many of them from the upper floors. The naked, rotting woman in our bathroom, the male leather twins, Moth, Annie, Tristan, and finally, Carson, my child-hood friend.

My blood ran cold. Could we fight them off? The room grew deathly silent, and suddenly, the click of shoes on the marble floor caused us all to turn. A man I didn't recognize came forward, but when he spoke, I knew who he was. Mr. Vincent himself. The spirit that had been inside me.

"They can leave. We just want what's due. We need a sacri-fice, Juniper."

Juniper's face went pale. She began to back away. It dawned on me then. She could see the spirits, which meant... they were expecting her to die. And she knew this.

"Tristan said you needed a virgin," Laney said. "We don't have one. Is there any alternative?"

"We have one." Tristan came forward. "We always brought a backup, just in case."

The three of us stared at each other, trying to understand, and then it dawned on us. *Juniper.*

"You think you're going to kill me? Fat chance. I've lied, Tristan." Juniper turned to her old friend. "I've lied every day since we've met. I only used you because I wanted to come here. I wanted to see the ghosts. I tricked you!" She shook her head and laughed. "Did you really think I'd be so stupid as to leave myself open to being murdered?"

"Yes." Annie stepped forward. "You told me you were a lesbian, but you're not." She turned to Tristan. "She's lying now. She is a virgin."

"Why?" Juniper scoffed. "Just because I turned you down? Newsflash, bitch , just because someone's not interested in you doesn't mean they don't like women."

"No, but you left your computer open during one of our writing sprints and then left the room. I saw the book you're writing about ace people living sexless, happy lives."

Juniper's lips trembled. "Ace doesn't mean I can't have

sex." Her words wavered. "You sound so fucking ignorant right now."

"You're right," Annie agreed. "I'm not saying that. I read the first chapter."

"You bitch." Juniper's expression turned from irritation to rage.

"The first chapter is all about how you've lived a happy life never having had sex, nor needing it. Tristan, you can't believe her."

"So what is it?" Juniper tripped on her long skirt as she continued to step back. "I'm lying then or I'm lying now?"

In my eyes, there was only one way to see. The room stirred with conversation between all the spirits, and eventually, they all settled on the same opinion as me. Juniper felt the energy in the room and swore.

"Fuck all of you. I'm not dying for this place. I came, I saw what I needed to see, I'm out."

"That's not how that works, Juniper. You know that." Tristan clicked his tongue. "You know, my mother always said you'd end up being my eternal companion, and I used to brush it off, but who knew she'd be right?"

"Tristan, you can't." A tear slid from her eye. "Please, let me live."

"If you give us what is due, your bloodlines will live another year," Mr. Vincent said.

Juniper crumpled to her knees and began to cry.

"I've never seen you cry." Tristan crouched and reached for her. "I'm sorry, friend. Surely, you knew this might happen. We brought you along every year knowing you might have to be the sacrifice."

"Yes, but it wasn't supposed to!" She sniffled and glared back at Laney and me. "But you just had to invite a hot one. You always thought with your dick, Tristan. Fuck you."

"Is there anything else we can do?" Laney asked the room. She had begun to cry silently. "She doesn't want to die."

"Who wants to die?" Mr. Vincent asked. "It's interesting that you have sympathy for a woman who wanted you dead."

"You know what? If you're going to take me, I'm not going alone." All eyes swung back to Juniper. She raised her skirt and slid a kitchen knife from her tall, black boot. She lunged forward, sprinting toward Laney. I leapt in front of her and Juniper's knife dug deep into my thigh. I fell to the floor, and Laney screamed. My mouth opened, but nothing came out. Bracing myself, I tugged the knife out and looked up to find Juniper. She was halfway across the lobby, pushing through ghosts to go upstairs.

With strenuous effort, I got up, stretched, and started toward the stairs, knife in hand.

Fuck, this was getting old.

Run.

My muscle was on fire and my jeans were damp from the blood pouring from my wound. I probably shouldn't have pulled the knife out, but fuck, it hurt. I paused on the stairs and ripped off my shirt, tying it around the hole in my leg.

"Your stupid, slow stalking doesn't scare me, Michael Myers," Juniper mocked from the top of the stairs. "I'll kill you too before I let myself go down."

Yeah, that's not what was happening tonight. I only had a few more hours to escape; I wasn't going to fuck it up now. Laney and I were getting out of here alive. I finished the tourniquet and stood up, wincing under my mask. Testing my leg, I found it bearable and continued my trek up, slow, but on a mission.

Juniper waited until I was feet away before taking off down the hall. She was taunting me. She wanted to wear me out, but I wasn't going to let that happen. I'd done too much to get here. With each laborious step, I reminded myself of everything I'd done.

I killed Marco, the predator.

I agreed to go to a mental hospital to avoid jail. Knowing that it could be worse, and in many ways it was.

I had to pretend I wasn't in love with Laney. Each therapy session, I had to deny my obsession and my love for her. It hurt so badly; I tattooed her name on me in my room one night. It was that or murder my therapist.

Juniper slid the elevator door shut when she saw me coming and pushed the buttons to go up, leaving me to take the stairs. I knew the elevator wasn't coming back down. I clenched my jaw and kept moving.

I escaped Cunningham's, making myself a wanted man. I was on lists that had big money attached to turning me in. But I lost all self-preservation the moment Laney came home.

I'd do it again.

All of it, I realized, as I continued up to the next floor. I'd smash Moth's head in with the axe, I'd let Tristan hang himself, and I'd choke Annie to death over and over so long as I could keep having Laney. I'd awakened something in both of us that we couldn't just forget. She'd turned from the shy, virgin into a sex-fiend goddess. I had done that to her, and we needed to further develop this. I'd opened Pandora's box, there was no closing it now.

Juniper had her back to me, and I came upon her silently, shoving the knife deep into her shoulder blade. She screamed and fell to the ground. I held onto the simple kitchen knife and leaned over her.

"Please, don't do this," she begged.

If I could speak, I'd laugh. Downstairs, she was hellbent on killing both Laney and me, and now, she wanted mercy. I shook my head as she crawled away.

Juniper stopped, and I looked up to the end of the hall at what had frightened her so. The twins from before were standing at the end of the hall. They'd been the ones to hold Laney in that dark room and the same ones to hold her in the maze while Mr. Vincent overtook my mind. They were deviants. In sync, they tilted their heads to the left.

"We were sure it was Delaney that would be playing with us. It looks like you, sweet Juniper, will be taking her place. Come." They raised their hands and motioned for her.

Juniper struggled to her feet and backed right into me.

"No. Not you two." Her voice was filled with fear. She spun around and clung to me. "Please, don't let them take me."

I shoved her away and the twins moved forward, each taking an arm, and dragging her down the hall and into a room. I stood, waiting to hear a scream, but no wails of torture came. Instead, a loud bang and what sounded like a wet explosion came an instant later. My stomach tightened at the image that came to my mind of what happened, but I didn't have time to think about it. I had to get back downstairs.

The wound in my thigh was making it harder and harder to move. I took the elevator down, pausing at the second floor. I knew I had to get out, but I couldn't leave without going to our suite one last time. I found Laney's laptop and shoved it into a backpack, along with mine. I grabbed our coats and hurried down to the lobby. I stumbled out and found Laney where I left her, shaking with fear.

She slid on her coat and backpack, and I took her hand. The spirits of the Vincent, all but the twins, stood in the lobby silently. They bowed or nodded their heads as we left. Almost as if giving us permission to leave.

We ran to the garage, running right past Annie's body. Laney screamed, but I pushed her forward. I pulled the key Gloriana had given us and threw Laney into the van. I turned the key and it clicked once, twice, three times and nothing happened. I swore inwardly. Those assholes knew the van was dead.

I scrounged the floor for the key Annie had lost while we were out here, finding it finally. It took all of my remaining strength to get the snowmobile out of the garage. Laney was forced to help me push it out. I gave her the helmet and directed her to sit behind me. I started to take off my mask, but Mr. Vincent's spirit began to return, and I slid it back down. We were still too close to the hotel.

Turning the key, the snowmobile roared to life and we started our trek down the snowy hill. While I hated the mask, it helped shield my face from the sting of the snow coming at us. Laney held tight to me and rested her head on my back, and finally, just as the sun was coming up, I saw Les's car waiting for us at the bottom of the hill.

Relief flooded through me as Les got out and waved. I stopped feet away and helped Laney off the snowmobile and urged her inside the warm car. I ripped off the Michael Myer's mask and threw my arms around Les.

"Thank fucking god you came."

He laughed. "Of course, man. I owe you my freedom. Let's get you two somewhere safe. You look like you've been through hell."

I joined Laney in the back. "We'll get a hotel and figure things out from there. We just need out of here."

"You're ready for another hotel?" Laney looked up at me with her beautiful doe eyes.

I chuckled. "As long as it's not trying to kill us, sure." I looked up at Les. "Maybe just a chain place, a Holiday Inn, or something."

"You want this? It's giving me the creeps." Les lifted the mask I'd tossed in the front seat. I began to shake my head, but then Laney reached for it and gave me a raised eyebrow.

"Maybe we just hold on to it for a little bit?" She blushed, and I could almost hear her thoughts.

Laney, you dirty girl. I nodded and stuffed the mask in my jacket. For her, I'd wear it for eternity if she asked me to.

"So long as you like seeing my regular face from time to time." I kissed the top of her head tenderly and relaxed into the seat. "Consider it a Valentine's Day thing."

"Oh! I forgot that was today!"

"Happy Valentine's, Laney baby." I kissed her deeply.

"Oh, Priest, I wish we hadn't lost all this time."

"We're not going to look back at that, okay? We're only moving forward, understand?"

She tilted her head to look at me, and I leaned down to give her another kiss. We were free from everything now.

"Okay, big brother."

Epilogue - Laney

One Year Later:

The shrill cry I'd been expecting for some time came from inside. I started to stand, but Priest put his hand out. "I'll go get her. You sit."

Priest hurried into the house, returning back to the veranda with Crystal, our daughter. I slid down the sleeve of my dress, exposing my swollen breast to the chill air. Priest set the baby in my arms and I helped her latch to my nipple.

"I could stare at you two forever," he said, sliding back into his chair across from us. His emerald eyes shone with utter joy.

"You're not bored with us yet?" I teased. We'd hardly seen anyone since we left the horrors we'd experienced at the Vincent. Instead, we chose a quiet life, in a house away from prying eyes, in New Jersey. Far away from Cunningham's mental facility and from the electroshock therapy doctors I'd experienced in Shelley Vale. Here, we were safe and happy.

"How could I be? I dreamed of this every day for years. You're beautiful, pregnant, and a mother."

I blushed. This entire last year had been a dream, one large, erotic fantasy. We'd escaped the Vincent and returned to our childhood home, just long enough for Priest to get the money he'd been storing, and then we left. Priest found us a home, we married in a quiet ceremony, and then, soon after, we found out we were going to be parents.

Every day, Priest doted on me, letting me write and helping me edit and get my manuscript into shape to self-publish, and at night, he worshipped me in bed, giving me more than enough inspiration to write a whole series of spicy romance novels.

"So, have you given any thought to what I'd suggested?" Priest asked as Crystal suckled herself back into a food coma.

"I have. I think I could give it a shot. It'll take some research, but I have a feeling you're up to the challenge." I raised an eyebrow, baiting him.

"I am if you are. You could really make a career out of dark romance, Laney. I think you'd be spectacular at it." He slipped out of his seat and dropped to his knees. Taking my hand, he began to kiss up my arm, finally reaching my lips.

"Fine. Let's do it. Where should we start?"

Priest reached for Crystal.

"Let's start with taking her to her crib, and then I'll come back and take you to bed. Can you be a good girl and wait for me?" He winked, knowing I was his good girl.

"Can we bring out the mask?"

The mask we'd taken from the Vincent was a regular item in the bedroom. He loved indulging in my fantasies, and I loved doing the same for him. "It is Valentine's Day."

It was odd to think that all of our troubles started on this day, but now, we were finally able to celebrate it for what it was meant to be. A happy day for lovers. I'd never been happier as Priest's wife, mother to his child, and—

"Oh right, happy Valentine's Day, little sister."

The End

One last thing before
you go

Thank you for reading Slay Less. If you enjoyed it, please consider leaving a rating or review. Reviews are extremely important to authors and helps us continue to create books.

Did you figure out the easter egg for what movie book 3 will be inspired by? I talk about it in at least 2 different flashback chapters. My clues aren't very obvious, so you may have to think outside the box. If you did, totally post about it and tag me. I want to see who gets it.

I'll give you one hint, since I'm breaking my formula for book 3: There's only one movie franchise I'm pulling from this time.

About the Author

After watching *Heathers* and listening to My Chemical Romance one too many times in her teens, Chicana author, Tylor Paige, was drawn to the darkness where the villains remain villains, but deserve love stories too.

Shifting her focus to Horror Romance, Tylor writes snarky, psycho vampires, troubled but beautiful Goblin Kings, and slashers so sexy you'll be begging your partner to buy a mask.

When she's not writing about women railing the villains, she enjoys watching horror films, sewing, comic books, and participating in her local community theatre, the Three Rivers Community Players. At the time of this update Tylor has now written and published twelve full length novels.

Oh, and feel free to call her Ty. She prefers it.

Acknowledgments

Wow, I'm actually kind of excited about this one. Where do I start? I guess, the Whorror Babies.

So, wow. Lol.

It's hard to really explain how speechless I am about your guys's reactions to my Final Girls series. Considering the first eleven books were met with no real fanfare, I wasn't sure what to expect. But holy fucking, shit man.

When I started writing Slash or Pass, you guys came out in droves for me. Sure, we lost some, (a lot) along the way. Readers who signed up and became super angry that my horror romance listed as a slasher with lots of triggers was dark, but that is to be expected lol. But with as many of them that left, the ones that came and stayed doubled.

You guys were (still are, let's be honest lol) in my instagram inbox daily telling me to ignore the haters and keep on writing. You've sent candy, stickers, books, socks, and even a peacock! (Who is now my couch peacock, he never leaves the couch. I call him Prescott.)

But it's not about the gifts. It's about the words. Sometimes, when I'm feeling nervous that I was just a one hit wonder, or that I'm failing, you guys pop in to ask questions, send memes, or on occasion, call me an asshole. I love all of it so much, and 100%, I would not continue to write the Final Girl Series if you all didn't love it so much. Thank you.

Next.

Sadie, Connie, Lee-Anna, Amber, Chelsea. My original Street team members. About a week before Slash or Pass was set to release, each of you came to me privately to check in on me and see how I was doing. It was very weird, and almost felt planned, but also, not. It was like, you guys could see what was coming, and wanted me to be prepared. You guys had the insider scoop, some of you were alphas for it, and knew that I had something. That Slash or Pass was about to blow up, and I had no clue. No clue! But I still think about how kind you all were to message me and give me that pep talk like the sports people do before the game of my life. Thank you.

Next, my author friends. Aiden Pierce. I never got the stepbrother thing, so I had to read Stepdevil, your novella, to understand what was going on with that trope. I got it. I hope my book is as good as yours is.

Leesa Mason, Alby Blazo, Alyssa Alexander, Meika Usher, Liz Zerkel, Lyssa Kay Adams, Christina Mitchell, and Erin King. The Sisterhood of the traveling cocks. I love freaking you guys out every day with my unhinged bullshit. I also love being able to come to you guys when I'm having a panic attack, or have questions about if something is legal or not. You guys are so supportive, and I love that we all write in different genres and welcome each other just the same.

My publishing team. Zainab, my editor. I know you don't like these books. They spook you, and you don't entirely get the whole slasher horror thing as a romance, but I love that I can send you anything and you're like, sure, okay, let's do this. You're so fun, kind, and I love talking with you about non writing stuff too.

Victoria! My cover artist and graphic designer for most things. Holy shit man. Who fucking knew. WHO KNEW? I love our friendship so much, and that you get me. Not only do you continue to make awesome covers and graphics, but your TikTok game?

My alpha readers! Chelsea, Lee-Anna, Dezi, Amber, and Lilly. This time around I picked up some new faces, and holy shit am I so happy to have brought you onto my team. You guys are so supportive, yet make sure my shit is good. You have no problem being like, nah, you need to go look at this, and that's what I need in a good alpha team. Thank you guys.

And one last time for the ones in the back. Thank you Whorror Babies. Thank you.

ALSO BY TYLOR PAIGE

Final Girl Series:

Slash or Pass

Slay Less

Knife Comment Share

Final Girls 4

Final Girls 5

Final Girl Featurettes: (100 page novellas!)

Like Father Like Slaughter

Little Deaths: a Vampire Mafia series

Seven Little Deaths

Lay Your Body Down

Bury Me in Blood

Little Taste of Death (FREE VALENTINES SHORT!)

Standalones:

Surrender to Forever- a Goblin King reimagining

Want More?

I have a few deleted scenes for Slay Less, and I put one out into the world for you if you want to join my mailing list. This particular chapter has Laney and Priest's parents interrogating Laney after Marco's murder. Enjoy.

https://dl.bookfunnel.com/bc21epe6jc

FINAL GIRLS INFO

Did you enjoy Slay Less and want to be an arc reader for the next books? Check out these sign up forms!

Book 3 arc sign up:

https://forms.gle/6eKcUHgjSJeAvtL69

Final Girls Featurettes ARC sign up:

https://forms.gle/GFHJMGnaP7yywzUc6

Find Me!

Www.Tylorpaige.com
   https://linktr.ee/Tylorpaige
   Facebook.com/Tylorpaigeauthor
   Instagram: @Tylorpaige
   TikTok: @authortylorpaige
   Join Tylor Paige's Whorror Babies group on Facebook!
   https://www.facebook.com/groups/376190999768893/?
ref=share

www.ingramcontent.com/pod-product-compliance
Lightning Source LLC
Chambersburg PA
CBHW020247010826
48973CB00006B/1686